DRIFT

DRIFT

STORIES

Victoria Patterson

A Mariner Original • *Mariner Books*

Houghton Mifflin Harcourt

BOSTON NEW YORK 2009

For information about permission to reproduce selections
from this book, write to Permissions, Houghton Mifflin
Harcourt Publishing Company, 215 Park Avenue South,
New York, New York 10003.

www.hmhbooks.com

Library of Congress Cataloging-in-Publication Data
Patterson, Victoria.
    Drift : stories / Victoria Patterson.
        p. cm.
    ISBN 978-0-547-05494-0
    1. Newport Beach (Calif.) — Fiction. I. Title.
    PS3616.A886D75 2009
    813'.6 — dc22   2008036768

Printed in the United States of America

DOC 10 9 8 7 6 5 4 3 2 1

The following stories have been previously published in slightly
different form: "The First and Second Time" in *Freight Stories,*
Spring 2009; "Winter Formal: A Night of Magic" (originally
titled "Winter Formal") in the *Southern Review,* Winter 2009;
"Joe/Christina" in *Snake Nation Review,* issue 22, 2007. "The
Locket" won the Abraham Polonsky Award in Fiction.

for Chris

7/09

To be out of harmony with one's surroundings is of course a misfortune, but it is not always a misfortune to be avoided at all costs. Where the environment is stupid or prejudiced or cruel it is a sign of merit to be out of harmony with it.

—*Bertrand Russell*

In 1870, Captain S. S. Dunnells guided a ship called the *Vaquero* into an unnamed harbor. Captain Dunnells, feeling distinctly uncreative, decided to call the harbor "Newport."

—*From the 2005 Wikipedia listing, since
revised for historical accuracy*

Contents

DRIFT

Remoras

I MET ANNETTE when Jim hired us to work at Shark Island. The sun was setting and a golden light engulfed the restaurant, making everything look soft. I sat in the waiting area, an extended plush red bench near the front wood doors, with four other applicants — three women and one man. The women had a manufactured attractiveness: blond hair, blue eyes, tanned and toned bodies. The advertisement from the *Orange County Register* was crumpled in my pocket: "Hostess and Server wanted for fine dining establishment with excellent reputation - in Newport Beach. Experience a must. Ask for Jim."

My chances of getting the server position were good: I was better looking than the other man; he saw it and was slumped over, sighing. We were quiet but the restaurant was bustling, including a table of businessmen talking loudly, trying to impress the surrounding customers. A woman with the savage face of a plastic surgery client chattered piercingly into her cell phone.

Separated only by an archway from the bar was the Shark Island Emporium, selling resort sportswear, cashmere sweaters, watches, leather jackets, belts, sunglasses, scented candles, even a cologne and a perfume; the polo shirts were embossed above the left breast with a half-inch-sized sleek black shark. All the merchandise had the logo planted somewhere: it announced membership in an exclusive club that, upon further consideration, wasn't that select — most everyone in Newport Beach adorned themselves with Shark Island paraphernalia.

Jim sat in a darkly lit booth near the back of the restaurant, making us wait. Behind his booth, a large tank posed as a wall, casting multiple wavy shadows over Jim, small sharks gliding through the water like black darts. Our résumés were stacked on his table, and every now and then, with an odd mocking smile, he looked at us from across the restaurant. I toyed with the idea of leaving: Fuck the interview; fuck Shark Island; and a final fuck you, Jim, for making me wait.

Two men in light blue jumpsuits made last touches on an elaborate flower arrangement near the front doors — plucking a flower here, reinserting one there — and another man swept up debris, causing particles of dust to hang in the air like flecks of gold. Annette came through the wood doors and the dust looked like confetti celebrating her entrance. She glanced around nervously before she made an attempt to find Jim. I asked her if she needed help.

"I am looking for a job," she said softly. She had an accent that we later found out was Armenian. "It is so beautiful here, maybe I do not belong."

I mumbled something about how it was only an interview and not to worry. I told her that we were waiting for Jim and offered her my seat. Jim looked up from his paperwork, and he beckoned with his hand — *you two, now.*

"The rest of you can leave," he called out. "You're not hired." A few customers laughed, and the cell phone woman said,

"Oh Jim, you're so bad!" The wood doors creaked as the three women and the man exited.

Jim watched us approach his booth and it was as if he was planning something. He was handsome, with wavy dark hair, but he reminded me of a ferret, like no matter how well he dressed or groomed himself, at any given second he might scurry under the table. Annette looked like she'd never seen the inside of a gym and that was fine by me. Her hair was silky and black and her dark eyes looked sad. I touched her elbow to direct her. She had this way of walking — both timid and seductive — her hips shifting, as if off balance, and it made me want to protect her. She wore a modest dress, fringed with lace, but her figure wanted to announce itself: here are my breasts, here are my hips, look at my legs; this is what a woman should look like.

She smelled good. Jim liked her fragrance as well, asking what kind of perfume she was wearing.

"Alleu," she said.

"What?"

"Alleu," she repeated.

"Like hallelujah?" he asked.

"No, alleu." This went on until he had her write it down.

"She's trying to say Allure," he said, smiling. "It's Chanel."

Right then — because Jim knew the brand — I decided that he was gay and began to wonder if that was the cause of my hostility. I was used to battling other people's assumptions that I was gay. Past girlfriends respected my sensitivity, sex went well enough, but while I valued a beautiful woman, I also appreciated a good-looking man. In my efforts to mollify suspicions, I'd manufactured an interest in sports for the better part of my life: tennis, baseball, basketball, and water polo. In my deepest, secret, most hidden self, I believed I was a *little bit gay*.

The closest I'd come to testing my theory was in my fantasy life, and in my sex dreams, there was no stopping the vast ocean of my subconscious from tossing in man, woman, tree, animal, and on one particularly distressing occasion, albeit during the peak of puberty, my grandmother. My zealous attraction to Annette might have been overcompensation, but as usual, when it came to my sexuality, I couldn't quite work it out.

"You're hired," Jim said, before Annette had a chance to sit. "In fact, you're both hired."

Annette looked at me quizzically, wanting to believe him. She sat in the booth next to Jim and her body relaxed. "But what do I do?" she asked.

"What you're already doing," Jim said, touching her hair. "Look beautiful and innocent and be our hostess."

"Don't confuse her," I said.

Jim set his hands in the air in mock horror.

"No," she said, "I understand."

Jim spread his arms along the back of the booth and turned his gaze toward the front of the restaurant. A man carrying a bucket and a long pole was walking toward us with an air of importance.

"Oh good," Jim said, scooting over from the booth and standing. "Here comes Dale to fix my poor shark."

Dale had a weathered tan, and his severe facial features made him appear serious, even when he smiled for our introductions.

"See," Jim said, peering into the tank. He pointed — "There, there!"

Dale stood back and we watched the shark; a long fish was attached to its underbelly, the space around where it was attached a dark, painful pink.

"What's happened," Dale said, sober with authority, "is that your beautiful white-spotted bamboo shark is trying to scrape the remora off by rubbing"—he nodded to a bar extending across the tank for support—"against that steel rod. The remora swims under the rod and reattaches itself in the same position, and your bamboo shark is rubbing itself raw."

"I bought the remora to clean the tank," Jim said, "not to kill my shark."

"Why does it stick to the fish?" Annette asked, a hand at her cheek.

Dale prepped his pole; there was a metal nooselike device on the end of the pole, and what looked like a trigger to make it cinch around the fish and trap it. "Remoras have sucking disks"—he moved a planter and climbed onto a platform, his gaze steadfast on the shark and remora—"they're smart; they don't do much, except latch on to sharks and feed off their scraps." His pole swept the pink crushed coral at the bottom of the tank and sand danced like specks of glitter.

As the shark swam over the steel rod, the remora slipped into the noose and Dale pulled the trigger; the metal clasp clanked against the glass as he swung the pole from the water. The remora flicked its slick body and I caught a glimpse of its marble eye, cold and steady.

"I want it gone," Jim said, looking like he was about to sneeze.

Dale released the remora into the bucket of water—a curl of black, its lower jaw projecting beyond the upper, armed with small pointed teeth. The sucking disk was an oval pad on the top of its head with a double row of movable flanges like venetian blinds.

After Dale left, carrying his bucket and pole, we sat in the booth on either side of Jim. I imagined the remora curled inside the bucket, a skinny alien. Annette's face had gone pale.

"So," Jim said, changing the subject, clapping his hands. "Two years out of USC. Business major. Why would you want to work here?" His fingers drummed along the table—one, two, three, four, one, two, three, four—waiting for my response. Annette looked interested.

"Service is a noble profession," I lied. "I'm interested in fine cuisines and wines."

"Liar, liar, pants on fire," Jim said.

Later, lying in bed, I came up with a more honest response: I could've told him the truth. I was being primed to work with my dad (he'd invented a new form of drywall and had made a fortune), but my parents' recent divorce and its aftermath made me reconsider. I'd a nagging suspicion that my dad's arrogance and sense of entitlement were morally wrong, and his leaving Mom for his younger secretary congealed my suspicions into a hard and bitter defiance. I lived with Mom, helped her lick her wounds; although she'd been Dad's business partner, she was shut out, now working as a receptionist in a doctor's office. Dad tried to buy me a Porsche to pay me off, but I drove an old rusted 1973 Chevy Impala instead. My ex-girlfriend complained that I'd never grow up, that I was afraid of success, and that it was a downright tragedy that a man of my intelligence would squander his days. She married a stockbroker soon after our breakup. Last week, I saw her big with her first baby in the parking lot of the post office, and I hid behind a Land Rover. Mine was a voluntary exile, an angry soul search. I had no real goals.

In other words: I was all fucked up.

The following afternoon, Jim was training me, going over wines, when a woman came in who looked familiar. She began walking over to us, even though she didn't appear to want to. Jim pretended not to notice her, so she stood right in front of him until he had to acknowledge her.

"Meet your replacement," he said, putting a hand on my shoulder.

"Hello, replacement," the woman said. Her expression hardened back to Jim, but she was very nervous, it was clear.

"I want my check," she said.

"It's in the mail," he said, turning his back to her, faking interest in a bottle of wine. He walked away, leaving her. And then it came to me.

"Rosie," I said, and she looked at me: if anything, she didn't seem so nervous anymore. "Rosie. From Newport Beach High School—you were on the tennis team, right? I was a sophomore when you were a senior."

She didn't remember, but she covered, reciting a mindless cheer that the cheerleaders used to chant when we played inland teams, her voice flat: "It's all right, it's okay. You're going to work for us someday."

I wasn't sure what to do, whether to tell her my name, spark a memory. Most likely she wouldn't have remembered me anyway. She was one of those seniors who was never there, but had mythical weight to people like me, probably for that same reason.

Finally, I said, "Go Sea Kings," my voice equally flat, holding her gaze.

And then she smiled a real smile, even if it was sad. Her eyes lingered on mine, a silent exchange: warning me about Jim. And I thanked her, let her know with my eyes that, yes, Jim was an asshole, but that I'd be okay. When I saw her walking out of the restaurant only a few minutes later, she had an envelope, and I was glad because it appeared that she'd gotten her paycheck. She must have known where to look for it, but I liked to imagine she confronted Jim and demanded it.

That same afternoon, Jim took Annette shopping and picked out her clothes, paying for everything, explaining, "You're my investment." She wore skirts and heels, the skirts so tight I could make out her panty line. After a few weeks, I was able to interpret her body language and signals: she'd roll her shoulder back if a customer was a jerk; she'd tap her finger against the hostess podium if the customer tipped well, giving me a heads-up. Video cameras watched us, their glass eyes tucked in the corners. Jim said their purpose was to identify thieves. At the side entrance, there was no video camera, and Jim had a secret meeting place within the restaurant. That first week, on a Friday night after we'd closed, Jim took off his jacket, loosened his tie, and climbed through a partition of fake foliage. Annette and I followed, along with two dishwashers — a straight shot between the tables, between the cameras, where no one could see. You could light a fire, no one would know.

Jim uncorked two bottles of wine, slipped one of his CDs into the CD player, and asked Alfredo to show us some salsa moves. Because Alfredo was a dishwasher, my usual interaction was with the back of his head, but Annette danced with him, whipping her hips this way and that, and my heart beat fast. We were Jim's favorites, and we got to drink the best wines in Newport Beach. Jim had taken a shine to me even though I'd assured him that I was neither gay nor interested in experimentation. He said he was a patient man and he could wait. He said that it was nice to have someone around who could compete with him intellectually.

We'd known Annette about a month when she told us she was a virgin. We'd climbed through the artificial foliage — a regular Friday night occurrence—and sat enjoying a Merlot while listening to Jim's Julio Iglesias CD. Annette wore a skirt with a long slit up the front, sitting with one leg crossed over the other, making the skirt fall open. She'd taken her heels off and her toenails were painted a dark red. Her smoky eye shadow and black eyeliner made her look exotic and experienced.

"I'm waiting for my wedding night," she said, and she sighed, looking toward the floor, her eyelashes long and curled.

"You've got to be kidding," Jim said, and Annette looked up, her face serious. She appeared a little bit hurt but I could tell she was also amused.

"How will you know if you're sexually compatible?" Jim asked, resting his feet on the chair. Annette's sexy black sweater was unbuttoned enough so that I could see a beauty mark on her breast, close to where her breasts squeezed together in a kiss.

"What do you mean?" she asked. "What do you mean by this 'sexually compastible?'"

Jim shook his head.

She smiled.

"Honey, honey, honey," he said, and he delicately fingered her hair. "Honey, don't you see it? They've got you right where they want you. Don't let them do that to you."

"It's our customs," she said. "It's my family."

"Yeah, they've got you right where they want you. That's what religion does." He swung his feet from the chair and set his hands on his knees.

"I'm not religious," she said, fiddling with the material of her sweater. "What's the biggy deal? Does it really hurt?"

"The only advice I have for you, baby," he said, "is that men can, you know, come really quickly. You make sure Bill takes his time with you. You say to him, 'Bill, don't come until I'm ready.'"

Annette was engaged to Bill, an Armenian who worked in a men's retail store that his uncle owned in Fashion Island. She said Bill was part owner, but I was suspicious. Bill's real name was too difficult for customers to pronounce, some Armenian name, so everyone called him Bill.

Jim poured more wine into her glass and asked, "What do you and Bill do? I mean, do you give him head?"

"What does this mean, to 'give head'?" she asked, wide-eyed.

"It means," he said, with enthusiastic exasperation, lifting his wineglass so that the wine sloshed, "do you go down on him? Do you put his dick in your mouth? Do you give him something, at least?"

"Do women like that? Do *you* like that?" she asked, her face pinched.

"Of course," he said, shrugging. He took a sip of his wine and contemplated. "Sometimes, I really like it. What I like even more though, I'll tell you, is when a man goes down on me."

She gasped.

"That's right," he said, scanning the room as if the video cameras could move. "Trust me: it's the closest you'll come — in this lifetime, at least — to heaven."

Jim nicknamed me Nice Boy. The others thought it was because I was a nice person, but in private, Jim said that it was because I was bad on the inside but nice to look at on the outside. The other waiters were jealous: he was giving me the best shifts, letting me go home early, and saving wine for me. Another month went by — Christmas came and went — and then came the New Year's party, an annual event where Jim sucked up to his customers and gave them a thank-you, only the cream of the A-list was invited. The A-list had tabs at Shark Island and liked to party, like Whitey Smith. His Mercedes dealership lights up the sky like an airport — the cost of the wattage alone could pay off the debt of a third-world country. Whitey Smith was in Europe, but his son came in his place.

Tables were pulled together and spread with candles, plates, roses, fruit — like a feast for a king. Someone (I suspected a disgruntled waiter) had stolen the baby Jesus from the nativity scene, and Jim had swaddled a child's doll and set it in Jesus' place — twice as big as Mary and Joseph, its eyes at half-mast. Customers dropped generous tips in a drunken stupor, the glow of Christmas a lingering impetus. Jim spent most of the night doing lines in the bathroom with Whitey Smith's son and the son's girlfriend.

We brought trays of asparagus, toasted almond and Gruyère strudels, coconut shrimp, and filet of beef and red pepper skewers, but the customers were too drunk to really eat. What a waste, I thought, but later the dishwashers and busboys ransacked the leftovers. I stood back with a fat bottle of Veuve Clicquot champagne and filled and refilled glasses. The owner's wife, a French woman that we were afraid of, stared irritably. Rumor had it that she was the one with all the money and that the owner lived off her; he hated to work, and that was why Jim ran the restaurant. He made bad use of his lack of hair with a weak ponytail, was loud and brash, and smacked his knife against his champagne glass, toasting customers over and over to much hollering and laughter.

By the time midnight came and went, I'd been dropped a couple of hundred-dollar tips, and Jim came over to remind me with his boozy breath that we needed to pool our tips. I nodded in agreement, knowing he'd be too high to enforce it: there was no way I was parting with my cash. I fingered the hundreds in my pocket—they weren't going anywhere. I decided to use the bathroom to count my money in the privacy of a stall.

Hanging on the wall between the women's and men's bathrooms—among the displayed restaurant reviews and culinary awards—was a framed newspaper clipping, and since no one was there to bother me, I leaned up against the wall and read it for the first time. It explained that in the late 1800s, before canals were dredged, when the land was still considered uninhabitable, camps of entrepreneurial fishermen (Mexicans and outcasts mostly) went to sea in small boats and caught sharks by harpooning or shooting them as they rose to the surface to swallow bait, and then towed them to shore, where their carcasses were used in the business of manufacturing oil. Along with a malodorous and uncanny atmosphere, the shark remains lying on the sand in various states of rot—from mildly decayed to skeletal—gave Newport Beach the unofficial nickname of Shark Island.

When I left the bathroom, Annette was leaning on the bar with her hips shifted just enough to make men swoon, a white scarf draped on her shoulders. I stood next to her and breathed in her Allure.

Jim came over, his flamingo legs wobbling, teeth clenched from all the cocaine.

"Are you okay?" Annette asked.

"I'm going to get him," he said, villainous in the dark candlelight, eyes sparkly and deceitful.

I didn't know what he meant until I followed the direction of his gaze. He was talking about Whitey Smith's son, sitting at the table with his girlfriend. She would hate my Chevy Impala, I thought, and I laughed. Jim and Annette believed I was laughing at Jim. Annette looked at me disapprovingly, and I felt a pang of hurt that she would protect him. She put her hand on his shoulder and kissed his cheek, leaving her kiss print, and I was jealous.

"Come with us," he said, smacking his hand on the bar. "He invited me to his dad's house. When his girlfriend passes out, pretend to pass out. I'll prove it. You don't think I can. Let me prove it."

Annette gave him an uneasy look, and he stuck his tongue out at her like a child. He waved at a matronly woman who'd set him up with her gay hairdresser. "I'd better say hi to that old bag," he said, and he skipped away.

"I won't go," Annette said, peevish. "I want you to go and make sure he is okay."

"Jim can take care of himself."

"Do it for me," she said, fixing my tie. "You're a good man," she said.

I sat in the back seat of Whitey Smith's son's Mercedes with his girlfriend. She wore a black halter-top cropped below her breasts, black leather pants, and a ring with a diamond the size of a dime, although not on her ring finger. When she got out of the car, I made out the beginnings of a sun tattoo on her lower back reaching down, I imagined, to her ass.

The dad's house was modern and ugly, at the end of Narcissus along the ocean on the crest of a cliff, all metal and glass. The son buzzed a series of alarms, fingers tapping at the numbers of the final alarm, but it kept buzzing us out. Too high to remember the code, he pulled out his soft leather wallet — God, it was beautiful — and all the cards, scraps of paper, and money fluttered to the sidewalk. He found the piece of paper with his alarm code, and his girlfriend gave me a look like — What an ass, but do you see his house? That was the most she acknowledged me all night.

He was still working on getting us inside the house when a whooshing noise swept past us, and a chill ran up the back of my neck, tingling at my scalp, like it was a ghost or something. But it was only a skateboarder, crouched low, shirtless, his long hair flapping behind him; I wasn't the only one he'd frightened because Whitey Smith's son completely overreacted, yelling, "Watch it, fucking cunt!" But the skateboarder didn't even flinch, like he was deaf or didn't care, and we all watched him until he disappeared into the night.

We went for a Jacuzzi — the thing heated up fast, extended over the cliff like it was floating in the middle of the sky. Everyone stripped, but I kept my boxers on, the water bubbling through the material. I felt weightless looking up at the stars, waves crashing below. My toes moved against the domed surface of a light at the bottom of the Jacuzzi. And then Jim said, "Nice Boy's hiding his cock because it's so big it would blow us all away." The truth: I didn't want Jim to see me naked, as if my body would reveal my sexual ambivalence — I didn't care about the others.

The girlfriend was getting bleary, her head knocking to one shoulder then bobbing up again only to knock to the other side. "I need to lie down," she confessed, slurring, and we helped her inside, dripping water all over the floors since no one had thought to bring towels. I got a good look at her sun tattoo. Also, below her hipbones she had double cherry tattoos, as if between the cherries was a jackpot.

I found a bathroom, slapping my hand around the wall until I hit a light switch. It lit up a bank of mirrors, reminding me of a salon or a gym. I dried myself with a towel, leaving my wet boxers draped along the bathtub, and I gave myself the best smile I could summon, until I couldn't stand it, which didn't take long; then I wrapped a towel around my hips and took a stack of towels just in case the others needed them.

The girlfriend was passed out on a white leather couch. The only illumination came from a fire in the gas fireplace, flames throwing light on her body, one breast stacked upon the other since she lay on her side. I saw for certain what I had guessed: fakes, more like bricks in this position. One leg crossed the other at her ankle, and I saw the V of her vagina, her pubic hairs shaped like the number 1 — a trimmed strip. I put a towel over her body, careful not to make noise; I was close enough to see goose bumps around her erect pink nipples, and I suppressed the urge to press her nipple like a doorbell.

Jim was sitting cross-legged on the white shag rug, his penis semi-erect in a coil of pubic hair, and his hand was on the son's knee; the son was leaned on his calves, almost like he was praying, his voice soft and solemn. Jim looked over the son's shoulder and passed me a signal. I lay down behind the couch, gas flames making shadowy patterns along the wall, and the girlfriend snored, loud and steady. I closed my eyes, imagining red moths flying across my eyelids.

There were sucking noises and wet noises. And I kept my eyes closed because it could have been me.

The next night at work, Jim snapped orders at me, nervous and sulky. "What's your problem?" I finally asked.

"You're my problem," he said, giving my shoulder a little shove. "Don't ever talk to me like that again."

Annette brought him a glass of wine; he took it and skulked off. "What's going on between you two?" she asked me.

"Why do you *like* him?" I countered.

She looked right at me, her expression defiant, lips the color of a bruise. "Jim taught me to dress nice and he gives me a job," she said, her voice loud and protective. "He is a brave man."

"He hired you so that men could look at you and feel good," I said.

She looked at the floor and her dark hair swung down so that I couldn't see her sad eyes. "I know why you are Nice Boy," she said, lifting her head and meeting my gaze straight on. "It's because you have a nice life. You don't know what it's like to be poor. You just get born with it." She paused, as if trying to decide whether to say more.

"You don't even know who you are," she said, flipping hair over her shoulder with a hand. "You only know how to be Nice Boy."

After our shifts, Annette and I walked to our cars parked in a nearby residential neighborhood. Jim didn't let us park in the Shark Island parking lot, and the homeowners complained when we parked near their homes, our beat-up cars sullying their streets: it was a tricky thing, parking our cars.

The sky was dripping with stars. We were both a little high, having sampled a chi-chi, a lime rickey, and a vodka gimlet, gifted by our bartender and presented in coffee mugs, so we wouldn't get caught. Annette reached for my hand, and I could smell her perfume. She'd pulled her hair into a loose ponytail, the angle of her collarbone exposed, and she swung our hands together like a happy little kid; I wondered if she was making up for the way she'd spoken to me earlier, but I didn't care, just as long as she was with me.

On impulse, I pulled her body to mine, pressed my mouth on her mouth. Her lipstick felt like lotion and she tasted like vodka. Her tongue soft and pliant, she opened her mouth wider, and it surprised me so much, I opened my eyes. I saw the side of her face, the dark slope of her neck. I wanted to put my hands there, but she pulled away, her chest rising and falling.

For a moment, we just stared at each other, her eyes angry and unsettled—but I got the impression she wasn't mad at me. She rubbed her hand along her arm as if she was cold, and I could make out the outline of her bra beneath her lace top. She leaned on one leg, jutting out her hip.

"Be my girlfriend," I said.

She laughed. It was an uninhibited laugh, maybe a little bit cold. I had not heard it before. She looked more beautiful than ever.

"You do not have the spirit," she said, her voice almost a whisper, "to be with me."

Annette started taking pulls off Jim's cigarettes; she believed it was a nasty habit, but her craving was stronger than her decorum, and she took to it quickly, smoking like a seasoned veteran: blowing rings, tapping ash with her forefinger, and mastering other mannerisms. Her wedding was two weeks away, and I didn't understand her urgency to marry. But she said she couldn't explain it, that for her, in her culture, a wedding and marriage meant everything. She said I might not understand, but she was marrying up in caste and her parents were pleased.

We'd been hanging out after work, and I'd gone shopping with her, helped her pick out a nightgown for her honeymoon. She'd tried on at least ten, sneaking me into her dressing room, slipping nightgowns over her slip, until we found a silky one that we both agreed on. She sat next to me — wearing that nightgown — on the bench in the dressing room, and when her knee touched mine, she tapped it there three times. "I like you," she said. When we walked out of the dressing room, she was at least a foot behind me, but it was as if her body was pressed right against mine: there was a definite sexual charge, but I didn't act on it. After all, she was getting married, and I needed to protect myself. And maybe I was a little bit scared of her, of what might happen. When I was with her, time passed quickly, and we laughed at stupid things — everything was funny and easy and pleasant.

"You are like a woman," she said, "because you care all about clothes and movies and all the names of cheeses."

"Thanks a lot," I said. But I could tell she thought she had complimented me.

Then, with such conviction and sincerity, she said, "A man is not supposed to wear the pink, but then when he wears the pink, he is more a man than all the men that say to him, 'Do not wear the pink!'"

Her wedding invitations were in Armenian and Arabic, with a slip of paper typed in English to translate for the likes of people like me. On the front of the invite was a picture of Annette and Bill in matching white sweaters, a piece of gauze over it to impart a dreamlike quality.

A bouquet of red roses was delivered to her two days before her wedding, and she said that they weren't from Bill. "Who are they from then?" I asked. And when she told me the flowers were from her uncle, I didn't believe her and said so.

"You are Nice Boy with your nice easy life," she said. "What do you know?" She'd been drinking Cuba libres (more rum than Coke), and I knew she was a bit drunk. "Boo hoo," she said. "Nice Boy works to serve people food and make his money. He doesn't like his rich daddy. He drives an old Chevrolet car that has rusty. Boo hoo hoo."

I was so flooded with anger that I thought I might yell at her, but I didn't say anything. "Boo hoo hoo," she said, twisting her hands up and pretending to rub them against her eyes. And then she looked sorry and angry and unhappy all at once. When she went to the bathroom, she left the tiny card near the light on her hostess podium, and I opened it. The penmanship was slanted to the left, letters leaning on each other, as if for support, reminding me of the signature of a doctor or a psychiatrist, intentionally difficult. The signature was indecipherable, and the only part I could read: Opened like a flower to the sun, your heart — something-something — forever. I tucked the card back in its envelope, and when she returned from the bathroom, she placed the card in her black purse, and I wondered if she'd purposefully left it on the podium for me to read, a concession of sorts.

After we closed, I was still angry, but I decided to climb through the foliage anyway. She wobbled unsteadily as she passed through the leaves, and I put my hands at her waist to steady her. When she turned her head and smiled back at me, all of the sudden I wasn't mad anymore. We heard Jim uncorking champagne, his Frank Sinatra CD playing in the background.

He poured us glasses, and Annette licked the bubbles before they slid down her flute. "We're celebrating Annette's wedding of convenience!" Jim said, raising his glass in a toast.

Annette held my hand. Her makeup was smeared but it only made her more attractive. We lifted our flutes and clinked them. She didn't let go of my hand, leaning into me and whispering, "Will you be my husband in secret?"

I didn't like Jim watching.

"That's not funny," I said. Half the time I wondered if she was teasing me, but could find no proof.

"No," she said in a sincere voice, looking down at her hand in mine. "It isn't funny. I must marry Bill. There is no choice, that is the way it must be. But you are my very best friend in the whole world."

"Look at the lovebirds," Jim said. "Don't worry" — he ran his fingers along his mouth like he was zipping it shut.

I decided not to go to the wedding. Annette said she understood, and she promised to think of me during her vows. I watched four Hitchcock movies and tried to forget about her. I regretted having agreed to be her secret husband.

At 2:47 A.M., Annette called. She told me right off she was drunk. At first, she wasn't making sense, alternating between self-righteous indignation and self-pity.

"It is not right," she said. "I am a good, good girl." She started crying.

"Where are you?" I rubbed my eyes.

"I'm at the pay phone in the lobby. There was no blood. All this waiting and no blood. They will send me home."

I got scared when she mentioned blood.

I tried to make my voice steady and calm. "What blood?"

"The parents give me a special cloth and I lay on it. They get to see it to prove that I am virtue." She paused, taking a long breath. "I am good. I am a good, good girl. I was not lying when I say I have virtue."

I kept my voice down so as not to wake my mom. "Let me get this straight: Your parents and his parents get to look at this cloth that you lay on when you had sex and it's supposed to prove that you're a virgin? Your hymen is pure?"

She cried so hard that her body made hiccup sounds.

"Where's Bill?"

"He won't wake up. He drinks lots of that alcohol his uncle gave."

She blew her nose. I wondered if she wore her nightgown — the one we'd picked out. When she spoke again, her voice was serious.

"It is no one's business. These things I have to do. That is why you are my husband in secret. You do not make me choose." She breathed heavily into the phone. "I have a plan but I am scared and drunk."

It didn't take long to get to Palm Springs since there wasn't traffic. I kept the radio off the whole drive and considered my life: Was I in love with Annette? When she moved her hips just a little, like she was bumping into an imaginary line, I wanted to laugh and shake her at the same time. Annette, Annette, I said her name when I jacked off, and I could hear her taunting, Nice Boy, Nice Boy. Jim slipped into my mind — his noises from when I lay behind the couch, but I quickly extinguished the memory.

Before I got to her hotel, I stopped at a Ralphs supermarket. She had explained her plan over the phone. It was five in the morning and the people working looked tired, probably coming off their night shifts. I went to the meat department and selected an especially raw and bloody piece of top sirloin. The checkout woman pointed out in good faith that the expiration day was today, but I assured her that it didn't matter.

Annette waited in the hotel lobby, barefoot, a toe ring on the middle toe of her right foot, not wearing her nightgown as I'd imagined, but a yellow sundress. The only signs of her distress were her unruly hair and her puffy eyes. She was relieved when she saw me, like a lost kid who suddenly found her mom at the mall, and she ran to me and hugged me.

"We don't have much time," she whispered, smelling of cigarettes and Allure. "Bill will wake soon."

The coffee in the lobby was percolating and the management had set out a pink box of doughnuts. She motioned for me to follow, and then led me by my hand inside a darkened women's restroom, locking the door behind us. We were so close — her breast against my arm and her mouth near my ear. She passed her lips over mine, tasting of alcohol and cigarettes. I wanted her then, and I pulled her against me, knowing she felt my hard-on against her thigh. She stayed like that for a couple of seconds before she pushed away, turning on the light switch.

"Let us take care of business," she said, her eyes passing over mine. It was a knowing look, reminding me of the way she smoked cigarettes.

She lifted a piece of cloth from beneath the paper towels and wadded toilet paper in a trash can, handing it to me like a baby. The cloth was as soft as the nightgown we'd picked out, and like the pansy I feared myself to be, I set it against my cheek.

"I wish I'd made you bleed," I said, lowering the cloth from my cheek and balling it in my fist.

She looked confused.

"You think I'm like Jim," I said, my throat tightening.

She stared at me for a long moment, as if willingly abandoning her own troubles. She opened her mouth to speak, reconsidered. She shook her head, eyes firmly on me. "I think," she said slowly, pausing with deliberation between each word, "that you are you."

A rush of gratitude spread through me and I felt like crying, but instead I took the top sirloin from the paper bag. I opened a corner of the wrap where the blood had pooled, letting it dribble on the cloth.

"Some girls get sewn up down there," she said dreamily.

"Tell me when," I said, like I was delivering pepper to a salad.

"Stop!"

"Are you sure that's enough?"—a Rorschach-like smear.

"Yes, yes. I don't want to be too much good."

Bill's parents had given her a wooden box—the size of a birdhouse—to put the cloth in, and she folded it and set it inside. I dropped the top sirloin in the bathroom trash can and it made a loud slap and clank.

We said our goodbyes in the hotel lobby. The sun was already bright and I was sure she would have a good time in the desert. The mountains looked so near it was like you could touch them. I imagined Bill and Annette would lie by the pool all day.

It would be a long night at Shark Island without her. And I knew she planned on quitting soon since Bill didn't want her to work. The drive home I kept the radio off. I thought about how customers saw Jim as refined and clever, but how I knew him to be unhappy and cynical. Jim and I were meant to suffer, I decided. We both knew it, but I'd been blaming him. We were similar but I would quit my job. If I didn't, I might end up a professional scavenger, in limbo between the haves and have-nots, pretending to adore the haves while hating them, a fate that killed me even in the imagining.

Annette was a whole other thing: the more I thought about her, the less I understood, and the harder I tried to understand, the more tightly I held on, the less I could appreciate. The wind picked up and the Impala shook. Out the car window, the freeway shrubs trembled. And I thought about her last words to me. "Thank you for helping me, Jonathon Harold Pearl the third," she'd said, swiping hair from her sad eyes. It had surprised me that she knew my full name, and it continued to whirl inside me, lit up with her accent, declaring itself a person — complex and unmoored — and hopeful for the first time in a long while.

Holloway's: Part Two

ROSIE STUDIES HER REFLECTION in the veined mirror behind the cappuccino machine. She stands near the bar of Holloway's. An hour before closing. Yawns: pale and flat-faced,
mouth agape, eyes squinting. She wears a white cap, puffy skirt
with a small lacy apron, thick red stockings, and black clogs: a
peasant woman serving royalty. In profile, her nose angles sat-
isfactorily and she appreciates the way her dark eyes are soul-
ful in contrast to her pale skin, but her reflection serves as
shameful confirmation. A voice nags at her. You fucked so
many men, the voice says. Trying to get attention and love.
You're disgusting, filthy. Your family hates you. You can't ever
tell them who you really are.

No, no, no way: she can't ever tell. Most times, she came
to in a sickened bafflement. Who is this man? Where am I?
And then there was her dad's golf friend: she recognized him
at a bar, they were both drunk, he was in the middle of a
divorce; they went to his apartment near Fashion Island, he
talked about his son; and then they were on his couch, kissing,
kissing; that was fine, but then her hair was in his fist, and she

was encouraging him, taunting him; it ended with him horrified and embarrassed, practically weeping, even when she told him that it was her fault, that she would never tell anyone. His friendship with her dad obliterated, no more golf. But that got her to quit drinking, seventeen days sober, as shaky and vulnerable as a newly hatched chick; she's not sure about this life-without-drinking thing. Less than three months to her twenty-first birthday.

She turns to face the dining area. Fourteen tables surrounded by pale flesh-colored walls, large gilt-framed mirrors, mounted animal heads, and a chandelier made entirely of crisscrossing antlers. Holloway's has recently been redecorated, and along with the renovation came "fresh and flirty" uniforms. Near the deer head is an unflattering portrait of Bacchus, god of wine and pleasure, but the waitresses joke that it's a portrait of Julie Anne, boss and manager, a woman in her midsixties with rolling fat on her thighs and a double chin. There used to be another portrait in its place, but Rosie never saw it.

The customers are mostly men: cavalier, entitled, flirtatious. But the tips are fat, the men trying to impress one another. Julie Anne oversees the French Provençal kitchen, claiming to be the inspired chef, but anyone who works for her knows that the real genius is a cantankerous, hard-working Guatemalan who, hunkered in the small kitchen and sweating over the stove, rarely sees the light of day. One table is occupied in the corner, two men engaged in a quiet conversation, probably about real estate. She tried to pour the large one with the argyle socks more ice water so she could get a glimpse at the tip (seven dollars), and he set his thick hand over his water glass without looking at her.

She turns back to the dining area, runs her hand along the marble countertop of the bar, fingers grazing glass salt and pepper shakers that need to be refilled before her shift ends. The hard texture of the objects makes her feel vaguely connected to a larger definable reality.

Kat gave her the go-ahead to clear the tables even if Holloway's doesn't technically close until five. The ice machine behind a large bookcase obscures Kat from customers, but Rosie stands at such an angle that she can see her leaning against it. The bookcase is filled with leather-bound classics and books with French titles. Fakes: when opened, the pages are blank. Is she the only one who has tried to read them? Julie Anne has taped the specials of the day and other notes of interest on the ice machine. One is a reminder to employees — No Laughing. It Disturbs the Customers. The other is an advertisement for the new exclusive Porsche. Julie Anne highlighted the amount, and, in a striking display of passive aggressiveness, scribbled in pen — Start Saving Your Tips!

Kat has seniority and consequently lighter side-work. Somewhere in her late thirties, she's by far the oldest waitress; she used to man the snack bar along the ninth green of the nearby golf course, but she can make more money as a waitress, and Julie Anne is giving her a chance. Even in repose, she looks alert, in case she needs to simulate productivity. She eats from the dirty dishes stacked in a tray — all the waitresses eat from the leftovers — and she uses her fingers to lift a pork chop, nibbling close to its bone. Her peasant server costume looks disobedient, breasts jiggling from the top, slightly askew, as if she wears pajamas rather than a uniform. She looks at Rosie as she eats, but her eyes are impenetrable.

Julie Anne is waiting for a legitimate reason to fire Kat, not only to appease the other waitresses who dislike her, but because Julie Anne doesn't like her either. Maybe they're afraid they'll end up like Kat, hustling for money beyond their twenties, or maybe it's that Kat doesn't even try to be cheerful. Her smiles are sullen and quick to pass and two prominent customers have complained that she's morose. Dark eyeliner outlines her brown eyes, and Julie Anne tells her to soften her look, but even when she softens her look, she looks hard.

Kat doesn't chatter the way they do, and she never asks Rosie questions, prying in the way the others do. Kat doesn't care, and Rosie likes that she doesn't care. Whenever she walks with Kat to their parked cars after work, Kat pulls on the jacket she wears after every shift: dark blue with a hood. She says a sudden, quiet bye — turns and she's gone — walking with down-turned shoulders, to her dull red Volvo station wagon.

"I'm back!" Jennifer returns from her break, the kitchen doors flap behind her. She's twenty-one, has worked at Holloway's since her late teens, and she likes to talk about herself. Tall and thin, her blue eyes carry a perpetual look of astonishment, as if to say, *Can you believe it?* Pleasantly and purposefully naïve and Julie Anne's favorite, she's finishing her degrees in sports medicine and psychology. She's made good decisions and her path is clear and direct. Standing next to Rosie, her eyes surreptitiously watch herself in the veined mirror as she talks.

Rosie tilts her head back and gazes upwards for a long second, but it makes her dizzy, the ceiling uncommonly high with an ornate mural of naked cherubs playing flutes and harps, their ambiguous genitals veiled by wisps of ribbons and clouds. She wishes she could stuff cotton in her ears, anything to mute Jennifer and the repeating soundtrack of Enya, opera, and Edith Piaf.

Jennifer discusses her life situation: whether to marry a man she's not sure she's in love with. She loves him, don't get her wrong, but sometimes she can't stand him. She's worried about her sudden loss of sexual appetite after a prolonged weekend where she was a bridesmaid to her best friend and she had to manage the demands of her boyfriend as well. He's an engineer and makes over one hundred thousand dollars a year. She loves him, don't get her wrong.

Rosie often worries that she will go insane, and she thinks about it now. This fear is mixed with her anxiety about death, which feeds into an ever-present and hyper-sensory awareness concerning her body's nuances, down to the tumorlike knob in her left breast where the underwire in her bra lies; the bump waxes and wanes according to her menstrual cycle. Taking a "temporary hiatus" from college and financially independent from her family (to some extent by choice), she pays for car insurance, health insurance that does her no good unless she's struck with a terminal illness or involved in a catastrophic accident, and car repairs when she doesn't give a shit about her car: she took the bus to work this morning because it wouldn't start again. She consumes money and makes money, consumes it and makes it and makes it and consumes it. What kind of life is that? Money is confusing, especially now that she doesn't have as much of it.

She wonders how she will function this day, the next, and all the days that follow. When she can't sleep, she sits in the closet in her small musty room that is a converted garage that she rents. She cries and thinks about cutting her arm with her nail file, even with her own fingernails, or drinking the bottle of Smirnoff the landlady stores in the freezer, but she just sits and cries for a long time until the urges pass.

She moves her gaze so that the Bacchus portrait is hidden then released, hidden then released, behind the bookcase of wordless books. A crown of thorny flowers wraps around Bacchus's thick, curly hair, his bowlegged stance reckless. A mix between an infant and an old man, his expression is belligerent, his loincloth more like a soiled, baggy diaper.

"Mr. Vanderkemp is coming for lunch tomorrow," Jennifer says, as if she's giving a warning, and she makes an expression like she smells something foul. "He's really old and he reeks like a fart. Julie Anne brings him to lunch once a year on his birthday because he's loaded. You know, *The Vanderkemps.* Don't tell Julie Anne I told you, but he owns this restaurant. She's been trying to get him to sign it over. He had a stroke or something. He's a total perv."

"Hey, Rosie," Kat says from the ice machine, interrupting. "Last night I dreamed about you." She holds the L of her pork chop. A pause. The ice machine rattles and drops ice. Her eyes look bold and shy at the same time and she sets the pork chop gently amongst the other remains in the tray. "In my dream you said, 'He used me like toilet paper to wipe his ass. And then he flushed me.' You were so hurt. Then I thought about it —dreamed about it—more. Whoever it was fucked you more than once. You're no one-night stand."

Kat has never spoken this extensively. Rosie feels heat in her cheeks, but there's a smile playing at her lips. Someone has finally said something real, challenged her. Kat gratifies her in a beguiling and direct way.

"That's horrible," Jennifer says, mouth parted.

Rosie doesn't say anything, but she wants to talk to Kat privately, ask her questions, the first one being, How did you know?

The kitchen doors swing with a flap and it's Julie Anne. She rarely works, but when she's at the restaurant, she sneaks up on the waitresses, tries to catch them eating or talking. Rosie turns to clean the cappuccino machine, body tense and alert, and from the corner of her eye she sees Kat wiping the ice machine with a rag. *Tap tap tap.* Julie Anne's high heels hit the marble floor and come closer.

"I just got off break," Jennifer says, cleared from culpability.

Julie Anne's fingers squeeze Rosie's shoulder. "What's this?" Her mouth is a blur of red and she wears a shiny blond wig. Her eyes narrow in the direction of the glass salt and pepper shakers and the ceramic sugar decanters. She's always putting her hands on the customers and waitresses — touching, patting, squeezing — going from table to table. Her blouse and skirt are maroon-colored silk, the blouse sheer enough to reveal a lacy camisole beneath, and she wears high-heeled leather boots. She's perpetually dieting — losing and gaining the same ten pounds.

"I feel like a babysitter," she says. "Why have the tables been cleared when it's only" — she looks at the face of her diamond-studded Rolex — "four-thirteen?"

Little fingers of nervousness play at Rosie's throat. Kat's fault. Kat will be fired. Julie Anne smells like lilacs and pepper — new perfume? — and it makes the place behind her eyes and nose tickle. "It was slow," she says, glancing at Kat wiping the ice machine, skirt swishing.

"Why are you looking at her?" Julie Anne asks.

"I wanted to save you money by having us clock out early," she says, making sure not to look at Kat. "It's my fault."

Julie Anne lets out an aggrieved sigh and her mouth stays open. The men from the corner table look over. She fidgets with her diamond clip-on earring. Takes it off, rubs her ear-lobe. "You should know better," she says.

"I'm sorry; it won't happen again." She once heard that if you look at a person's forehead, it seems like you're looking them in the eyes. She makes her expression apologetic, but there's a fist of defiance in her stomach.

"Our customers expect the best," Julie Anne says, tucking wig hair behind her ear, "which means, we have to give our best."

Kat has turned and her eyes meet Rosie's with an acknowledgment. Julie Anne notices. "Ladies," she says, "ladies, ladies. Such pretty girls." She repositions her earring. "I'm curious, Kat," she says. "Do you like your job? Or do you want to go back to your hot dog stand?"

Kat holds the rag with both hands in front of her lap.

"Unlike Rosie and Jennifer, you're too old," Julie Anne says, "to perform lap dances."

"I want to keep my job," Kat says.

"I saw on a TV show," Julie Anne says, putting sweeteners into a ceramic sugar decanter, "that prostitutes and exotic dancers get their names by combining their first pet's name and a remembered childhood street name." She pauses for effect, sets the decanter down. A smile. "That makes me Mandy Vista Real." She laughs — it sounds like ho, ho, ho. Rosie feels herself smiling, and Jennifer is laughing, but Kat is quiet.

"I'm Fuzzy Marguerite," Jennifer says, excited.

"Perfect," Julie Anne says. She stares at Rosie in a bright-eyed way. "A dear friend of mine is dining with me tomorrow, a party of five," she says. "Rosie will be our waitress. Jennifer, you may leave."

Jennifer looks unsure, as if her good fortune might dissipate, but she grabs her purse from under the bar and makes it all the way out the door.

"Tomorrow's lunch," Julie Anne says, "is very important. I

want you at your best. My friend is old, he's a difficult man and sometimes says things he shouldn't."

Rosie hears Kat spraying cleaner on the ice machine. When Julie Anne moves away, she can still smell her perfume. Julie Anne rests her hand on the shoulder of the larger argyle socks man and her voice rises and falls in a singsong. The men appear bored by her attention.

Rosie and Kat finish their side work in silence, and later, when they walk out together, Kat pulls on the dark blue jacket with the hood. "Where's your car?" Kat asks, her jacket making a nylon brush sound with the movement of her arms.

"Wouldn't start," she says, and her palms itch. She wants Kat to drive her home, not so much for the convenience, but so she can sit in Kat's car and ask her questions.

"Come on," Kat says, head down.

Hanging from Kat's rearview window are prayer beads with a crucifix, Jesus Christ's palms facing up on the cross, fingers cupped. "My daughter found it in a bush," Kat says, fingers brushing Jesus' feet. "Right outside my bank. Maybe someone got mad and threw it."

"Julie Anne's a bitch," Rosie says, wanting to remind her of their newfound allegiance.

"She hired you because you're pretty," Kat says, "and she can't get a man." Kat has set Jesus in motion; he swings slightly. She leans over and the nylon from her jacket swishes on her red tights. "Started smoking again," she says, fumbling with a pack of Marlboros from her purse, "after two years." The car lighter ejects. "My daughter knows, she can tell."

When she lights her cigarette, her face draws in on itself, and she watches Rosie, as if testing her reaction. She approves —smoke exhaling. She drags on her cigarette. Exhales. Drags. Exhales. She cracks the window and flicks it with her middle finger. Gray specks of ash float and drop. "Hey," she says, "it was really nice the way you covered for me. No one's been nice to me like that in a long time."

"Let's quit," Rosie says, and they both laugh.

"Yeah," Kat says, "but I'm too old to be a prostitute."

A comfortable silence gathers between them. The sky is dusky, day ending. Out the window, Rosie watches a squirrel scurrying up the trunk of a palm tree. The squirrel pauses, stares back.

"Why'd you say that," she asks, looking back at Kat, "about the dream?"

"It's true," Kat says. "I did dream it." She stares at Rosie long and hard, the cigarette burning close to her fingertips.

"What does it mean?"

"It means, it means," Kat says—"God, I don't know. It means a man used me because I let him; I still wear his jacket. That you probably let men use you, even if you dress it up different; that maybe I should've followed my gyno's advice when he told me to keep my skirt down." She stubs the cigarette out in the ashtray. "The whole point," she says, "is to find some dignity."

"Your gynecologist told you to keep your skirt down?"

Kat turns the key and warms the engine. "I was thirteen," she says. "That was right after he stuck his hand inside me."

"My grandma says I need to be smart about men and booze, that I take it too far, but I don't know how to be smart. My family hates me."

"They probably don't know you," Kat says.

"When I imagine being with a man," Rosie says, a piercing in her chest, "maybe having a boyfriend or something, I can't ever imagine us doing normal things: going to a movie, eating dinner, or even just talking."

Kat considers. "If that's what you want," she says, shifting into gear, "you'll have it."

The next day, the door opens and Julie Anne and her party arrive. Mr. Vanderkemp walks with a cane, dragging his left foot at an odd angle. Rosie sees one side of his face, his mouth tweaked in a frown, and his eyelid droopy, giving his eyeball a sliver to see through. There are five people in the party, Julie Anne directing, and they arrange themselves at a table. Julie Anne is at the end of the table, directly under the deer head. Rosie senses her orders, body tense and alert. She remembers to smile: "You're a Holloway's girl now and you need a Holloway's smile."

Mr. Vanderkemp sits at the other end of the table. On one side of his face is a bulbous, red mass, like a birthmark but worse. She doesn't know which side of his face is more grotesque. His face sags on the other side, the cheek slack and a pale purplish color like granite. His breathing is deep and slick with saliva. He wants to talk, but Julie Anne orders for him. He smiles and appears genuinely happy, at least more than Julie Anne and the others.

When Rosie sets his plate of steaming spaghetti down, he motions for her to come closer so that he can tell her something. The others at the table are watching, and there's an edge of danger, as if they're also waiting for something bad to happen. His breath is warm and gurgled and she worries that he'll smell like a fart, but she can't smell anything except spaghetti.

She expects the worst: that he'll say he wants to put his dick in her mouth or lick her cunt, remembering how Jennifer called him a perv. He puts his hand on hers and it's dry and light. She puts her ear closer to his mouth and he says, "I love you," very serious. "I love you. I love you."

She raises her body and looks at him. His eyes are filmy, the left flecked with a cataract. She knows the others are watching and she faces them. Julie Anne — water glass lifted — stares, her eyes shimmery and bereft of commands.

Rosie avoids Mr. Vanderkemp's side of the table the rest of the meal, but whenever she looks at him, his expression is earnest and his eyes are on her, the napkin tucked under his chin speckled with spaghetti sauce. After their meals have been cleared, she sets down a flourless chocolate gâteau, garnished with three strawberries and a green striped candle, flame dancing. Her arm brushes his back, and she sees white and gray hairs curling on his neck and a yellow-streaked sweat stain at his collar. She wants to sing "Happy Birthday" but singing is prohibited.

He stares at the cake and candle, a hand gripping the table, and the woman sitting closest to him leans over and blows the flame out. Rosie is aware of Julie Anne's hard stare and she knows that she'll get in trouble later, but she can't think of what she's done wrong. Above Julie Anne's head, a spider web is caught in the deer's mouth, laced across its red tongue. Another web is wrapped in the eyelashes rimming one of the deer's eyeballs.

When the party is done with coffee and dessert, they leave without paying, no tip. Mr. Vanderkemp leans on his cane, the side of his face raised and deformed, the color of raspberries. Julie Anne opens the wood door, says something to a woman, and the woman nods, taking him by the arm and guiding him. The door shuts, but Julie Anne hasn't left. There's heat on Rosie's face and neck as Julie Anne's gaze finds her.

Tap tap tap — Julie Anne's heels hit the floor. Jennifer moves closer, standing with her back to Rosie, as if cleaning the bar. Julie Anne notices, leans in, holding Rosie by the elbow, making sure no one can hear. Her breath is warm, smelling of coffee and garlic. "What'd he say?" Outside the window, she watches two people getting into the back seat of a Mercedes, Mr. Vanderkemp collapsed in the passenger seat, the woman holding his cane at the curb.

"Nothing." She shifts her gaze to Bacchus, forlorn and belligerent; she imagines Julie Anne as a child.

"You're lying."

No answer. Her elbow is released.

"Why aren't you clearing the table?" Julie Anne says, loud enough for Jennifer, and for Kat — shoulders slumped, uncorking a bottle of wine at table two — to hear. "Always clear the tables immediately. How many times do I have to tell you?"

Jennifer repositions her body so that Rosie can get a silver tray from under the bar. When she turns around with her tray, Julie Anne is still watching, and she's confronted directly by her unhappiness. Behind Julie Anne is the table, and she sees that the plates have been cleared by the busboy already, only a few glasses left. Julie Anne's heels tap against the floor, out the wood door. When she gets into the driver's seat, none of the passengers acknowledge her, as if wary of upsetting her further. Mr. Vanderkemp's head is down, and the Mercedes moves out of sight.

As Rosie clears glasses onto her silver tray, Jennifer comes toward the table with another tray at her side to help; but she knows what Jennifer really wants is information.

"What the fuck happened?" Jennifer says, an excited ring in her voice. She sidles closer so that their arms touch conspiratorially. Her eyes glitter as she stacks glasses.

"Nothing," she says.

"Come on," Jennifer says, anger darkening her expression. "I'm not stupid. Julie Anne looked so weird."

Jennifer is persistent, but she doesn't tell her.

"Nothing," she says. "Nothing, nothing."

A dull but loud voice comes from behind the bookshelf: "For fuck's sake. Leave her alone." The flat confidence reinforces Rosie's resolve, makes her smile.

"What's your problem," Jennifer says, bumping against the table so that the glasses rattle on her tray. She speaks to the bookcase. "It's none of your business, so why don't you go back to your hot dog cart and shut the fuck up."

The voice says nothing. Rosie imagines Kat leaning against the ice machine, savoring the leftover flourless chocolate gâteau behind the bookshelf. Rosie slows her breathing, holds it in and then lets it out through her nose. Mr. Vanderkemp's words spin inside her, cracked with dignity, an imperfect offering. And she can feel herself fingering possibilities, not in spite of who she is and what she has lost, but because of it. She will tell no one what he said, except for Kat. She doesn't want anyone to make fun of him.

Castaways

MICHAEL RULE, TWENTY-SEVEN YEARS old and officially separated from his wife for four days, woke Friday morning at nine-thirty to the buzzing of a digital alarm. The clock was on the floor, and for a frightening second, he didn't know what the shrill *hee hee hee* sound was, only that the noise emanated from the faded olive green carpet of an unfurnished and unfamiliar apartment.

As Michael leaned over and turned off the alarm, an awareness moved through him like warm jelly pulsing through his veins: today he needed to pick up his five-year-old son, feign control and manliness while explaining the separation and impending divorce, and answer Anthony's questions, of which he knew there were typically a multitude. He imagined Anthony's face — trusting, earnest, worshipful — and he felt helpless.

Michael went over the facts: four days ago his wife, Penny, had confirmed that she was in love with Donald — wealthy, established, his father-in-law's contemporary and business equal — and she wanted a divorce. (Ever since: rage, jealousy, bitterness, a reassessment of his masculinity and worth, and the bone-crushing dead weight of sorrow.) Thus far father-in-law, William Deader, hadn't fired him from Deader Industrial LLC.

The apartment was a former office overlooking Newport Car Wash, at the periphery of the Newport Beach shopping mecca Fashion Island. Deader Industrial LLC owned the property; Deader Industrial LLC owned Newport Car Wash. The apartment was a concession, Michael believed, for Penny's infidelity. But how long would Mr. and Mrs. Deader's pity last, now that he hadn't shown up to work and was ignoring Mr. Deader's — Bill's, Dad's — phone calls?

The last four days Michael had been going to bed (two mattresses stacked on the floor) at three, four in the morning, sleeping fitfully, and waking in the hazy sunlight near noon. He lay there for hours, listening to the sounds of the car wash below, aware that he had to persevere through another day, but unwilling to begin: held back by a keen disbelief and a profound hurt at the power of circumstances to develop against his will.

Once he got out of bed, he sat with his back against the wall and studied the activity below, how the customers assembled, their backsides to him, on a cement bench and waited for the men to flag them with towels. Customers slipped cash (mostly dollar bills) into the men's hands, and the men nodded, but rarely spoke, except to one another.

Michael had discovered that the men had a system to alert one another of the periodic visitations of their manager, a white man with a mustache. Upon spotting the manager descending three cement steps, the employee at the head of the car wash snapped his towel, and the men successively snapped their towels down the line, until the last person got the signal.

Naked, walking to the bathroom, hands cupping his groin as he passed the window, he caught a glimpse of the tan-uniformed men toweling the shiny blacks, blues, and reds of Porsches and Mercedes. He was beginning to recognize the men, noting who was more animated, who came to work hung over, and he imagined their whispered conversations.

Everything was new in the apartment, cheaply assembled, transformed from an office, and a fine dust coated the sink and toilet from their harried, half-assed construction. He imagined the office's hasty conversion had been for his convenient elimination from Penny's life. Lifting the toilet seat to pee, he concluded that after a nearly six-year determined hiatus from alcohol, instigated by Penny's pregnancy with Anthony and their mutual decision to "live healthy," he might very likely get very drunk very soon.

The hot spray from the shower hit him directly in the face with an irregular hissing noise, thumping little pellets against his eyelids, nose, and lips, as if the showerhead had never been used and was trying to sort out its purpose. It was his first shower in four days. Unlike the removable and multiple-choice showerhead in his bathroom at his home in Newport Shores — Penny's home — he discovered the apartment showerhead had one spray option: Unrelenting Beady Squirt.

Never before had life hurled him in such loathsome directions, reminding him of how it was to struggle under the foamy tow of a wave, his body pushed and pulled. As a boy and teenager, he believed he wasn't manly because he didn't care about the things his own father revered — business, football, politics — and what sweet revenge when he succeeded beyond his father's middle class aspirations anyhow. Penny fell in love with him because he was different. A novelty, she said. They met at UCLA, both philosophy majors, English minors, and married soon after graduation. Affluence and a generous position at Deader Industrial were added benefits to marrying

Penny, and he learned to ignore any qualms about working for a large corporation. Over the years, he'd grown accustomed to the advantageous lifestyle.

Penny's main reason for falling out of love, Michael believed, was that his success was connected to her family, that he'd claimed their affluence as his own, as if he'd disappointed and betrayed her, even though they'd decided together that he should work for Deader Industrial. And in his mind, she was irretrievably connected to her family's prosperity, therefore connecting him — it was complicated. On further analysis, he conceded that besides working for Deader Industrial and living in the three-story home in Newport Shores — a wedding gift care of Mr. and Mrs. Deader — he'd conveniently overlooked any prior ambition to write novels and teach. What had happened to him?

Michael put on his socks, pants, and shirt. His clothes fit loosely, he fastened his belt to the last hole, but his pants sagged. Since about a year ago, when he'd first suspected Penny of infidelity, he'd begun losing weight, mostly muscle tone. In the corner of the small kitchen stood an Arrowhead water dispenser, beside it three blue plastic containers of water, leftovers, no doubt, from the apartment's time as an office. No one had noticed him since he rarely left the apartment, and he wondered if the other offices had been warned that he lived among them, since they worked for Deader, too. The container made a gulp as he poured a cup. He drank, his hair damp from an unenthusiastic towel dry, rivulets along his ears collecting at his earlobes, and then crumpled the paper cup in his fist.

When the phone rang, he knew it was his younger sister even before he answered. The phone was on the floor, and he sat with his back against the wall, letting it ring, his palm against the receiver, feeling its vibrations. Lisa, divorced, mother of two sons, and remarried at twenty-five, called daily. Normally they only talked on holidays and birthdays, and although he was grateful to her for being worried, he was reluctant to talk.

"Hello, Lisa," he said, answering by speakerphone.

"I thought I'd have to wake you," she said, her voice echoing. At seventeen Lisa had moved to San Francisco where she continued to live. She chose men that bullied her, reminding Michael in the worst ways of their father. Although a respected church member and community leader, their father's form of discipline had been a backhanded slap when least expected. "Take me off speaker," she said.

He held the receiver and switched over.

Her voice became cheery. "Good for you — you're already up."

He didn't answer.

"Today you see Anthony." It was a statement.

He nodded, and then realized she couldn't see.

"Have you talked to Mom?"

"Not yet," he said. Submissive and unadventurous before widowhood, their mother was on an extended vacation in Central America; timely, since if she were around, he imagined long, heartfelt discussions loaded with her disappointment and self-blame.

"Listen to this," she said. He heard the rustling of a newspaper. "Sagittarius. June sixth. Life changes inevitable. Time to return to true nature, true self." She paused, as if waiting for him to say something.

"Here comes the best part," she said. She cleared her throat.

"Take opportunity in next few days" — she paused again, as if preparing him — "to make decision regarding loved one. Trust instincts!"

He said nothing.

"Did you sleep?"

"Yes; no."

"Can you take something?"

"I'm planning on it," he said, thinking again about getting drunk.

"Have you called your lawyer?" she said. When he didn't answer, she continued, "You need to protect your rights with Anthony. Deader Industrial is big, big, big."

He heard her light a cigarette, take a drag. His greatest fear was that Penny would take Anthony from him, as she'd threatened in their worst argument, a tightness in his chest every time the subject was brought up; he'd been careful and pragmatic with Penny ever since, unwilling to jeopardize his chances. In the background, clothes rumbled in a dryer. He knew Lisa called from her laundry room, where she had the most privacy.

"I'm only saying," she said.

"I know," he said.

"Did you shave?" she asked.

He didn't answer.

"Did you shave, Mikey?"

"Not yet," he said, fingertips against the coarse hairs on his cheek.

"It gets better, Mikey," she said. She hadn't called him Mikey in years, but these last four days, she did so every time they talked. "Remember what I told you," she said.

From where he sat, he saw the detritus from the All-Occasion Basket he'd bought at Harry & David in Fashion Island. He'd been feeding off pears, apples, cheddar cheese, honey-roasted nuts, and smoked sausage, and had subsequently suffered mild constipation, in four days discharging three firm marble-sized shits. Now all that remained was half a jar of Wild 'n Rare Strawberry Preserves and Moose Munch Popcorn.

"Sure it does," he said, and he wanted to hold her through the telephone, drag her with him through his pain. Tears were in his eyes, and one slid down his cheek before he rubbed it away.

"I'm unraveling," he said.

"That's okay," she said tenderly. "Sometimes you have to; sometimes it's necessary."

"Tell me something," he said. "Was I an asshole? I mean, what happened to me?"

"You became a Republican," she said, deadpan.

"I mean it," he said. "Did I act like a rich prick?"

Her dryer buzzed and the rattling stopped. She seemed to be considering his question, and he didn't want to press, hoping she would be honest. She sighed theatrically.

"Answer," he said.

"Water under the bridge, Mikey," she said, confirming his suspicion. "Water under the bridge."

Walking to the front door of the house he had lived in just four days ago, Michael was aware that the past was dominating the present, every detail loaded with memory. Before he rang the doorbell, the front door opened and he realized Anthony had been waiting, watching from a chair positioned to allow him to look out a small window carved near the top of the door. Anthony smiled sadly, bravely, a gap in his mouth from a lost tooth, as if acknowledging the seriousness of the visit but trying to make Michael less nervous. His hair had recently been cut short so that his ears appeared vulnerable, fleshy. Michael hadn't seen him in four days, and the haircut startled him. Anthony looked older, holding his Ninja Turtle backpack, unzipped, filled with toys, and it never failed to astonish him how much they looked alike, even though genetically this made sense. "Daddy," Anthony said, his face crumbling all at once. He let go of the backpack. "Daddy, Daddy."

"Anthony," Michael said, lifting him, hugging him tightly to his chest. He swayed Anthony back and forth — Anthony's fingers clutched the hairs near the back of his neck, and it hurt, but he didn't ask him to stop. Anthony was a sensitive boy, thin for his age, particular about food, with dark eyes and a naturally down-turned mouth. He cried with frequency and like most children, he was partial to physical contact, wanting to touch, kiss, and hold hands. The sharp angles of his shoulder blades, the definition of his ribs, and the slimness of his arms and legs filled Michael with a stinging, protective devotion.

Certain that Anthony was done crying, he set him down, and there was a wet splotch on his shirt, below his chin, from Anthony's damp face. He knew Penny was inside somewhere, and he hoped she'd witnessed the emotional exchange, thinking, See what you've done. When he looked past the door, he saw only the ticking clock on the mantel, a light from the kitchen, the antique Persian rug, and he shut the front door. He had agreed to have Anthony back by four.

Anthony's small hand in his filled him with a longing to reestablish his dignity, and as they walked the front walkway to his BMW — Deader Industrial's BMW — he vowed to be strong. With a flash of irritation, he saw from the dry soil that his roses — his Rugosas and Albas and his climbing Don Juans — hadn't been watered. Despite Penny's protestations, he'd shunned the idea of a gardener, taking on the responsibility, not submitting to the homeowner association's pressure to hire a community gardener for "aesthetic uniformity." He'd planted the roses on the southeast side of the house so that at four o'clock each afternoon, they'd get a couple of hours of shade. The hose was coiled perfectly, unused.

Castaways Park was a large piece of land with a winding dirt path located on a bluff that overlooked all of Newport. He'd taken Anthony to the park many times, so he thought it might be a comforting locale for the separation/divorce discussion. He carried the backpack, and as he put one leg in front of the other, it was as if he were outside his body witnessing a Father and Son walking together. The fingers of Anthony's left hand clutched at his shirt and he saw the roof of Penny's house. Beyond was Fashion Island, the apartment tucked somewhere among the glittery buildings. The sun made everything look bright and polished; even the ocean had a glistening surface, reminding him of the slick exteriors of the cars the men washed.

When they arrived at their favorite spot, a slight hill with a wooden bench and a view of Newport Bay, he handed Anthony his backpack. Anthony carried it with him to the grass. "Mom says I have to go to Italy for vacation," he said offhandedly, releasing and shaking out toys, not looking at Michael. "When she marries Donald."

The sound of the other man's name in his son's voice, associated with marriage and Italy, made his stomach rise, hit the top of his throat, and drop. The agreement had been that he would explain to Anthony, but after the shock subsided, there was some relief that Penny had told Anthony, even if it included her plans to marry another man.

"You don't need to worry about that," he said, a hint of belligerence in his voice. He walked over to Anthony, ran his fingertips through his hair. Like running my hand through light, he thought.

Anthony moved his head from his father's touch. "Donald is nice," he said, facing away. Michael did his best to hold back the hurt from his expression in case Anthony looked at him. "He took me to the Peninsula and I went on the bumper cars, but not the Ferris wheel."

Michael didn't say anything.

"He gave me cotton candy," Anthony said quietly, looking at his toys as if trying to decide which to play with. The last time Michael had taken Anthony to the Peninsula, he hadn't bought him cotton candy, despite Anthony's steady pleading, and he knew Anthony was reminding him of this fact.

They didn't speak for some time. Anthony dug in the dirt with his plastic shovel, forming a shallow hole. *Scrape, scrape, scrape.* He ignored Michael, acting strangely detached, even callous.

"I'm sorry about all of this," Michael told him. "You probably blame me, but I want you to know I'll always be your dad."

Anthony paused from his shoveling and looked at him. "That a beard?" he asked, narrowing his eyes, as if questioning his genetic linkage.

"This," Michael said, thinking that he would shave and call a lawyer, "is what is called a vagabond look."

Anthony nodded, unconvinced. "No matter what," he said, businesslike, "I don't have to call Donald 'Daddy.' Unless I change my mind someday."

"That's right," he said, stifling a catch in his throat, and suppressing his anger. "Don't you even worry about that. Ever." He believed that enough hadn't been said on the subject. "Ever," he said again.

Angry, distraught, and regurgitating the conversation — the words "marry," "Donald," "Italy," and "Daddy" throbbing in his mind — he watched as Anthony played indifferently with his bucket, shovel, and trucks.

It was in this frame of mind that he witnessed three plump men holding hands and wearing yellow and orange nylon vests, walking along the path. The vests reminded him of what community service workers wore when they picked up trash at the sides of the freeway. He was drawn to the scene by its rarity, and even from a distance, he saw that they weren't normal by their disorganized and clumsy gaits, despite a man — probably their counselor — trying to keep them ordered, touching their shoulders and directing. The word "retarded" came to mind, and he wondered if it was no longer an acceptable term.

The group milled around another bench, ten feet away. One of them, the shortest, noticed him watching and waved frantically, as if they knew each other. His earlier conversation with Anthony had made anger coil in his chest like a snake, and if he wasn't careful, he knew it might strike. The man kept waving and he didn't respond. But the man wouldn't give up, and he began walking quickly in their direction, hands swinging at his sides with a determined purpose.

"Who is he?" Anthony asked.

"I have no idea," Michael said.

The man's hair was in a lopsided bowl cut and he moved rapidly. His pale and hairy stomach showed through where his shirt had ridden up and the latches on his orange vest had come undone. When he stopped, he stood directly in front of Michael, and before Michael knew what was happening, the man hugged him tightly, arms thick and fleshy wrapped around him. Despite being short, the man was able to lift him from the ground. The swiftness of the event prevented him from responding logically, and he panicked, especially when his feet left the ground. The man smelled like sweat mixed with pancakes. Michael noticed Anthony staring, mouth open. He was set down, his feet settling in the soft grass.

"What the" — he put his hand on the man's shoulder and pushed — "hell are you doing?"

The man took a step back and regained his balance. He looked crestfallen, his bottom lip jutting out like he might cry.

"Daddy," Anthony said, standing, "he's being friends."

The man's shoulders were pulled forward, and his tongue seemed too big for his mouth, pouched between his lips. But he smiled.

A bewildering empathy came over Michael, softening his anger. The man's eyes slanted upward and he tucked hair behind one ear with two blocky fingers. The ear appeared unusually small and folded over at the top.

"Kenneth," the counselor said, reaching them, out of breath. "No, no." He pulled Kenneth by the arm, but Kenneth shrugged the counselor away.

"Sorry about that," the counselor said, putting his hands on Kenneth's shoulders, his fingernails painted a deep purple. "Down syndrome," he said. He wore nickel-sized earrings in both ears, causing his lobes to distend, and he had a weary look, as if his efforts to control his wards exhausted him.

Kenneth's body appeared doughy and soft — there was a bleariness to him, as if his joints were loose; his head moved down, up to his left, down, up to his right, as if responding to imaginary music.

"Kenneth seems to have a special connection with you," the counselor said.

The sun was hot on Michael's neck and shoulders and sweat had collected on his forehead. "Glad to meet you," he said, extending his hand for Kenneth to shake.

A surge of affection radiated from Kenneth, and Michael knew what was going to happen even before it did: Kenneth came at him for another hug and this time he submitted. His body slackened and he shut his eyes. Kenneth made sounds, not words — a soft humming noise.

In the seconds of darkness, Michael imagined Anthony's face watching, and the ocean breeze moved through his hair. When he was set down on the grass again, he opened his eyes, and Kenneth's mouth and tongue were coming closer. Before he could move, Kenneth kissed the side of his face, settling there, lips hot and cheek sweaty. Kenneth needed to shave, the same as him.

There was wetness on Michael's hair and the side of his face, but he didn't wipe with his palm. Kenneth walked back toward the others, and the counselor followed, shooting them a glance over his shoulder, pale and alarmed. When they were a safe distance, the counselor turned and called out, "I'm so sorry," painted fingernails in the air, as if to suggest defeat. Kenneth's back was to them, his pants sagging at his rear.

Michael didn't call back. Feeling as if he'd been smashed and dragged across the park, he wondered what his face must look like — as if he'd shattered into nothing. "Strange," he heard himself say, and his voice brought him back, like a magnet attracting loose bits of metal. He imagined Kenneth collecting tickets at a movie theater, more useful to the world than he was. Then he saw that Anthony was staring at him, shocked, like he'd never really seen him before.

"Don't worry," he said, wanting to reassure Anthony from

whatever it was he was thinking. "I'm okay. Everything's going to be okay."

"I don't want to go to Italy," Anthony said, eyes big, his son again, through and through. Anthony's head dropped, and he began shaking it determinedly. "I don't like spaghetti. I don't like tomato sauce. No planes. I don't like planes. They smell bad and I don't like Italy."

When Anthony looked up, Michael saw that he was about to cry, and that he would need to be held.

Michael found it far more palatable thinking of Anthony, his future outside Deader Industrial LLC, and Penny's engagement with a few slugs of Wild Turkey inside him. He sat in his apartment with a paper cup from the Arrowhead water dispenser between his legs, the bottle of whiskey within reach, his back against the wall, staring at the heads of the men and women who waited for their cars.

It was dusk, close to closing time, only four customers left. After delivering Anthony to Penny, having a perfunctory conversation with her on the doorstep regarding Anthony's diet, thinking as he spoke that it was amazing Anthony had once been in his custody, that he'd taken this fact for granted, that he hated Penny for betraying him, and that he would never be allowed to live with Anthony again—"We ate at the Food Court. He had two chicken nuggets and a small fries"—he had stopped at High Time Liquor. Six years had markedly decreased his tolerance, and within two pulls from the bottle in the parking lot on an empty stomach, warmth spreading through his chest down to his groin, he was drunk.

The window was open and he could hear one of the car wash employees whistling. The mustached manager had arrived, and Michael had witnessed the men snapping their towels as an alarm. Thinking about how they looked out for one another made him want to weep.

Instead, he attempted to light a cigarette from a pack of Marlboro Reds he'd bought at the same time he'd purchased his Wild Turkey. After repeatedly trying to strike a match from the packet the clerk had given him, it finally sparked, but the match had bent to a ninety-degree angle, confusing the cigarette-lighting process.

Because Penny's love had been finite, he wondered if she'd ever truly loved him; he was a fool because he loved her, a part of his bones, impossible to extricate. Had he not changed, if he'd proved himself outside the Deader kingdom, like her precious Donald, would she have continued to love him? Would time allow perspective? A gust of fear passed through him, speculating whether Anthony's love was made of the same ineffably limited substance. But this fear slid from him quickly.

Watching the little fire burn all the way to his fingertips, he decided he didn't like cigarettes anyway, and he let the cigarette drop from his mouth as he waved the flame away. The desire to smoke had only been to further destroy his and Penny's "health plan," which along with abstinence from alcohol, tobacco, and caffeine had included a large vitamin regimen.

He thought about how he'd been disgusted, even frightened by Kenneth, as if Down syndrome might rub off, but in his limited interaction, Kenneth had been more open and alive than anyone he'd interacted with in years. Then he remembered Lisa saying that it was okay to fall apart, that it was necessary, and he wondered if that was what was happening now. If he fell apart, would he come back together as the same man that had married Penny, with the same goals and ideals, or had the Deader influence changed him? He'd grown fond of golf, even the country club — the lifestyle; it had made him feel important, as if his dad could never hurt him again, which didn't make sense, since his dad was dead. Then he pictured the Deader family like an octopus, tentacles gripped around Anthony.

He finished the whiskey in his paper cup and poured some more. As he drank slowly, he thought of how he'd held Anthony, cradling him in his lap while he cried, and he began to cry a little himself, tears sliding down his cheeks and collecting at his chin.

The phone rang, and he knew it was Lisa calling to find out how his visit with Anthony went. He fumbled with the phone, making sure not to answer by speakerphone.

"This afternoon," he said, "I got blessed by a retard at the park."

"How's Anthony?" she asked, pretending not to hear.

"She's not watering my roses," he said, wiping his chin with his shirt. He let out a strange soblike laugh. His fingers felt good on his forehead. "They're dying," he said.

"Shit, Mikey," she said. "You're drunk?"

"You have to bear in mind," he said, "factors such as temperature, light, humidity, rainfall, soil fertility."

"Mikey," she said.

"Shade," he said, "needs to be taken into consideration."

"Mikey," she said. "God."

"I used to imagine Dad had a timer on his shoulder," he said. "I had sixty seconds to say what I wanted before I lost his attention. I could almost hear it buzzing."

"What an asshole," she said, seemingly forgetting her worries because of her dislike for their father. "Weed out the weak, all that bullshit." She became impatient. "Why are you thinking about him now? It's useless."

"Dad would've hated Kenneth," he said.

"Who's Kenneth?"

"I love you," he said. "I'm afraid."

"Shit, Mikey," she said gently. "I love you, too."

"You're snapping your towel," he said.

"What are you talking about?" she said. "What towel?"

"I didn't for you," he said, fingers on his forehead. "I didn't look out for you, and that's why you left." He felt himself shaking his head. "I've got to for Anthony." He stood, the phone cord stretching and the phone clattering beside him — but he held on tightly to the receiver. The floor rolled under his feet, as if he stood on the deck of a rocking ship, and he steadied himself against a wall. "I've got to snap my towel because Deader Industrial is coming to take him away. Listen; I've got to go now, but I'll call you back later."

Leaning against the sink, Michael watched in the mirror as foam expanded in his mouth while he brushed his teeth. Brushing his tongue, something he'd never tried before, seemed like a good idea in order to camouflage his breath. When he was done, he spit forcefully and foam splintered across the mirror. He wiped his mouth with his arm.

The building was vacant, all the offices deserted for the night. He walked unsteadily to the Newport Marriott, two blocks away, where he knew taxicabs waited at the front entrance for the tourists. He saw a young man with long hair sitting on a bench, a skateboard at his feet, who appeared to be contemplating a water fountain outside the hotel. He approached him, with a sense of unity, and when he sat beside him on the bench, the young man smiled at him.

Tenderness came over Michael, a general sense of goodwill;

he was impelled to sing an instantly made-up song: "Deader, Dad-der, Deader, do-der; Donald is a fucker; Deader, Deader, Deader —"

The young man was silent; his eyes were calm and steady, and his bare feet were perched on his skateboard.

Michael hummed the song some more, and when he got bored with it, he stopped. He knew he was staring, and he leaned even closer. "I should leave," he said. "But I don't know where to go. I don't know what to do." Then, "Does your hair get tangled?" When the skateboarder didn't reply, he repeated the question, "Your hair — does it get tangled?"

"Sometimes," the skateboarder said.

"How old are you?" He looked like he was in his late teens, maybe his early twenties.

"Sixty-five," the skateboarder said.

Michael laughed, a good hard inebriated laugh, and although his new friend didn't laugh, he appeared to enjoy his joke. Michael kept laughing, it came out and out and out, as if there was boundless noise inside him, but when the doorman shot him a warning stare, he raised his hand in acknowledgment and quieted down.

They listened to the fountain, a gurgling flow in the center, water hissing at the base and along the edges, and then spurting back toward the center at a range of levels, as if someone hidden somewhere were controlling it. Michael had a desire to stay on the bench and be with the skateboarder — he felt a peaceful and drowsy alliance — but when a cab pulled up, he remembered his purpose.

"You take care now," he said, because he couldn't think of anything else to say, and the young man gave him a little wave. He slipped at the curb, getting in the back seat, but the cabdriver pretended not to notice.

Peeling a twenty from his wallet, he thanked the cabdriver, and stepped out of the cab, again stumbling at the curb. Lights were on in Penny's home, and a surge of shock passed through him at the sudden thought that Donald might be inside, ruining his plans to reason with Penny. If he couldn't have her back, at least she could witness his pain, and he'd make her promise not to fight when he asked for joint custody. That's all I want, he'd tell her. Joint custody. The taxi moved along the street, stopping at the corner, and disappeared.

Seeing the coiled hose next to a planter sidetracked him, and his body swayed as he focused on the path to get to his roses. Sweat tickled his forehead and dampened his underarms, and he told himself he must not fall, must not make noise. Before beginning his task, he unzipped his pants and pulled them, along with his boxers, down to his knees. He urinated in the planter, pressure releasing in his bladder; his stream arched wonderfully, a dark-golden hue in the moonlight. A flicker at the curtain of Penny's bedroom window worried him, but he decided he'd imagined it, and he pulled his boxers and pants back up.

The familiarity of hosing his roses, the weight of the hose in his fist, the spray soothing his Rugosas, Albas, and Don Juans, calmed him. A small, chilly wind passed over him, and he leaned his head back to stare at the dark sky. He sat on the grass and contemplated the night, letting the hose leak into the grass, spreading wetness on his pants. He lay down beside an enlarging puddle, hearing the flow of water near his ear, and from this angle, the misshapen rosebushes seemed to have eyes. He floated, not a part of anything, completely lost. He was afraid of falling apart, but it was already happening, and in the end, although he wasn't a confirmed believer in God, he decided that it was beyond his control anyway.

He closed his eyes, the darkness of his lids a blurred black-purple. The dampness of the grass and the soothing trickle of the hose encouraged slumber, and he let his body fall into the earth, release. His breathing slowed, succumbing to the large weight of something deep and heavy.

"Michael," said a voice that sounded very much like his father-in-law. "Son." He opened his eyes, and Mr. Deader stood over him, wearing a dark robe, sleeves folded at his elbows. "Time to go," Mr. Deader said, reaching out a pale hand.

He grabbed hold of Mr. Deader's hairy forearm. "That's right," Mr. Deader said encouragingly, lifting him to a stand. "Come on, come on." He noticed Mr. Deader's leather slippers, the kind he imagined an old writer might wear. Tiny lakes of gleams and shadows had formed in the grass from the hose.

"I'll drive," Mr. Deader said, staring at him without any apparent judgment. Michael estimated his intoxication level: he'd sobered up like lightning.

Mr. Deader sidestepped the wet grass and puddles, and when he leaned over to turn off the hose, his rear appeared soft and pillowy. The curtain at the window above Mr. Deader flickered, and that's when he understood that Penny had witnessed him peeing in the planter, and she'd called her father, who lived just three blocks away, requesting that he dispose of him.

Inside Mr. Deader's copious Rolls-Royce, warm air blew at Michael from the heater, while Mr. Deader drove him back to the apartment, explaining his and Mrs. Deader's position regarding the situation: "Donald's three years older than my wife," he said. "You think I'm happy?" His pale hand released from the steering wheel and lightly squeezed Michael's knee.

"We think of you as our son," he said. "We're heartbroken. But you've got to pull it together. Understand?"

Michael stared at the lit-up dashboard, the muscles in his arms and chest and legs tightening. "I want joint custody," he said. "That's all."

"Of course, of course," Mr. Deader said, nodding. He looked old and tired.

They were quiet, and Michael stared out his window. They passed rows of palm trees, the moon appearing and disappearing from the fronds. Michael looked back at Mr. Deader, who seemed to be considering unpleasant matters. His unwieldy and bulky body shape reminded Michael of Kenneth, and he wanted to tell Mr. Deader about how he'd been kissed by a man for no apparent reason.

Mr. Deader turned the knob for the heater and the warm air lessened. "You can't work for me," he said, as if they'd been discussing Michael's employment all along. "Penny, you know, she won't stand for it."

"I'm not much help anyway," Michael said.

Mr. Deader chuckled, kindly, and he heard himself laughing as well. He realized this was the most intimate he'd ever been with his father-in-law. Mr. Deader passed him a look, as if letting him know they weren't supposed to be enjoying each other, and they were serious and quiet for the rest of the trip.

"You're good at other things," Mr. Deader said, as Michael stepped out of the Rolls-Royce. "You'll find your way."

Michael came around to Mr. Deader's side of the Rolls-Royce, and Mr. Deader opened his door. He swung his legs around, leather slippers at the gutter, pale yellow pajama bottoms showing from a part in his robe. "Okay, Son," he said.

Pain ballooned inside Michael's chest. He shivered, standing in damp clothes before Mr. Deader, the breeze cool on his neck. He wanted to say "Goodbye, Dad," and was sure that Mr. Deader wanted to hear it—was waiting to hear it—but he couldn't: he'd always been Mr. Deader of Deader Industrial LLC. And he was now. "I don't know what happened," he said instead, shaking his head.

Mr. Deader grimaced, as if in pain.

"It's like I became someone different, and Penny saw me change, and she had enough."

"Disappointments," Mr. Deader said in a defeated way, "shape us."

"It's my fault," he said, wanting Mr. Deader to understand the full extent of his regret. "For not doing something to stop it."

"No more urinating in my daughter's roses," Mr. Deader said, unsmiling.

It was a planter, Michael thought. I peed in the planter.

"Find a job, get another place to live, pull it together," Mr. Deader said, looking hard at him, staring into his eyes, as if making sure his point had been taken. He positioned his legs back in the Rolls-Royce. "Get your joint custody," he said, turning his key and starting the engine. He shut his heavy door.

Listening to the motor fade as Mr. Deader drove down the street, the skin on his arms and the back of his neck prickled. His situation wasn't as bad as he'd imagined; he couldn't wait to call Lisa in the morning and tell her he had the favor and faith of Mr. Deader.

His stomach weakened as he poured the remains of Wild Turkey into the slick steel kitchen sink; and as he flushed the smell with tap water, he thought of how he might live up to Mr. Deader's expectations, believing, for the first time in four days, that he might have a chance at joint custody.

And it was Anthony's face he imagined as he lay on the mattresses, crying again. This time it was a soothing release, not self-pity, the tears running down the sides of his face into his hair, dampening his pillow.

He imagined swinging Anthony in the air, and he thought of how Kenneth had raised him temporarily from the earth, as if stirring his helplessness, reminding him that everyone was feeble. Power, he decided, was a tricky, capricious thing. He saw Anthony watching as he let himself be lifted, and he could smell the ocean, feel its breeze in his hair.

Tijuana Burro Man

ON A DRIZZLY WET-CEMENT Thursday, Rosie's second week of eighth grade, her English teacher turned off the lights and made the class look at a slide of Vincent van Gogh's painting *Starry Night* while Don McLean's song (inspired by the artist) "Vincent" played on a tape player. Then they were to look at the slide for ten more minutes, in silence. Miss Deleo said their assignment was "to feel." When the lights came back on, they were to write whatever came to mind. Miss Deleo called it "stream of consciousness."

Rosie wanted to be cool and hate the assignment like the other students — groans and eye rolls. She wanted to be like Heather, sitting at the back of the classroom, green eyes so light they looked translucent, elbow at her desk, chin in palm, staring indifferently at the screen. Heather (every other girl was a Heather, so Rosie preferred to think of her as the green-eyed girl) was beautiful. They'd just come from a school rally. The frequent rallies were supposed to foster school spirit and were a permissible opportunity to ogle: cheerleaders skipping, jumping, cart-wheeling to the middle of the gym floor

—whooping and hollering—ponytails swinging, skirts lifting to reveal blue panties, backsides embellished with the school logo: a white-bearded and bare-chested Sea King emerging victorious from the foam of a wave, wielding a trident. Cheerleaders, Rosie believed, proclaimed the requirements of her sex, an exaggerated example, an ideal. But say—just say—in her imagination, she'd been gifted with the looks, confidence, and agility to fling and contort her body before the entire student and teacher population—she could never fake that sort of enthusiasm, *ever*. The green-eyed girl was too cool to be a cheerleader: she always looked bored and this made her superior. Her family was hugely wealthy, exemplified by her wardrobe, and the combination of money and looks put Miss Deleo at a disadvantage: the green-eyed girl didn't really have to give a damn; she simply crossed her legs and the guys wanted her, the girls wanted to be her.

Last year in seventh grade, Rosie had a bad perm. As if that wasn't horrific enough, a photograph in her school yearbook (place the yearbook on a table, let it fall open, and it would land on the picture) had humiliated her. Newport Beach High School encompassed grades seven through twelve, ensuring her disgrace from peers as well as from the five grades above her. In a classroom full of students, it appeared as if the cameraman had yelled, Hey, Rosie!, hers the only face turned to the camera, startled, a *whooshed* fan of kinky hair, a glimmer of metal from the hardwire of her braces. She was pale, but appeared ghostlike because of the flash. The caption under the photograph: What planet are you from?

She'd make sure nothing like that ever happened again, and already had racked up hours naked and supine in the ultraviolet lights of a coffinlike tanning booth at NewportTan, smelling of sweat and chemicals, trying not to tip her protective goggles, ignoring claustrophobic sensations. She never got tan, was perpetually red hued, but it was a start—and her braces had been removed, her perm had died an unmourned slow death; and with the aid of Sun-In and lemon juice, her hair was streaked a dirty blond, coarse and weathered like the surfer girls.

Girls at her high school were so thin their legs resembled arms. Some came back from summer break transformed by breast augmentations and nose jobs. This past summer, in a great panic, Rosie had even persuaded her mother, B, to take her to a plastic surgeon. Her right breast was slightly larger than its mate and she was sure this was a deformity. B had no way of calming her, but the doctor had convinced her that she need not go under the knife and that the incongruity might modify naturally with time.

It wasn't as if Rosie wasn't used to adapting: she'd moved plenty as a child, traveling because of her father's job (Latin Coast representative for Namco Powder Metals Inc.), living in Argentina, Brazil, Colombia. Despite her shyness, her introspective and sensitive nature (Grandma Dot called her The Big Feeling), she was a scrappy survivor, even somewhat of a leader.

When Rosie was in third grade, her father started working for B's father, so that they could settle once and for all near Rosie's grandparents in Southern California. The divorce, three years later, was nasty and scandalous. B asked her father to fire her ex-husband as a show of solidarity, but Grandpa refused, whether out of continued loyalty or as a favorable business decision, Rosie wasn't sure, though knowing Grandpa, she suspected the latter.

There'd been rumors of B's longtime affair with Rosie's

new stepfather, Will, a gynecologist and obstetrician, twenty-three years B's senior. And a confirmation, a drunken phone call from Will's ex-wife, answered by Rosie three weeks after moving into their new home in Newport Beach, two days before she was to start the seventh grade. "Look at your birth certificate," Will's ex-wife had said, after expounding on the number of years she'd been married to Will (thirty-four), and her children's (Stanford graduates — two surgeons, one lawyer) shared hatred for B, and (even though she hadn't stated it), by association, Rosie. There was a hint of shame in her slurring voice, "Can you find your birth certificate? I want you to look at it." And then, as if sensing that Rosie was about to hang up in self-preservation, she hung up first — but not before coolly adding, "Your mom's a slut."

Rosie did find her birth certificate, fishing in the avocado-colored file cabinet next to B's dresser in the walk-in closet. The attending physician's signature was Will's, confirming her suspicion: A pregnant B had met Will when she'd traveled solo (not counting Rosie, in utero) to California (from Colombia, Argentina, Brazil?), to deliver Rosie — troublemaker by birth — in a state-of-the-art hospital. It was a large, complicated, indigestible piece of information that she'd been attempting to digest in secret ever since, considering B, Will, Dad, Grandma Dot, and Grandpa weren't keen on heavy discussions, particularly anything having to do with the communal pain of the divorce. All B had told her was that she'd flown to California in her final trimester of pregnancy because she was experiencing "difficulties" (further questioning, futile); that Grandpa had driven her to the hospital and stayed in the waiting area; and that before they'd left for the hospital, she'd taken a shower and shaved her legs (she didn't want to have stubble-haired legs). But Rosie wasn't so sure she wanted to talk about it either, a blossoming of shame — in her fertile imagination, an undeniable responsibility.

Tell the green-eyed girl that her birth had been the catalyst for her mother to meet her lover, subsequently instigating the dissolution of her parents' marriage (not to mention the marriage of the spiteful woman with the slurring sad voice), and she would've been nonplussed. What would it be like to be someone like that? Did she even think about death? She didn't worry. She wasn't sensitive. She looked good. It never occurred to her to ask questions. But Rosie could tell she was dumb. Last week, after being called on by Miss Deleo, the green-eyed girl had earnestly tried to answer a question about the difference between a first person and a third person point of view: "A third person is someone who has heard something through someone else . . ." She'd played it off, but not before giving Rosie a secret look. The look said, Yeah, I might be pretty but I'm really stupid. What am I going to do with my life? It was gone in a flash and then she returned to her normal bored and superior posture, and Rosie was relieved: it wasn't natural to be worried for the green-eyed girl.

The slide projector was propped on a stack of books. Rosie's desk was toward the side of the classroom so that she could see the slightest ripples of the screen, a fist-sized rock tied to the end of a cord keeping it weighted down. The song finished, the projector hummed, tittering laughter swept through the classroom. "Shh," Miss Deleo pressed a scrunched index finger to her lips — then quickly withdrew her hand, placing it behind her back. "Ten more minutes. Silence."

B was pretty in the same casual and confident manner as the green-eyed girl. Rosie was doing her best to develop in that direction, but she had a brooding intensity. Grandma Dot said it was like the cloud of dust that circled Pigpen from the *Peanuts* comic strip. And unlike B, who thrived in her new cherry red Mercedes convertible, wealth hadn't lessened Rosie's anxiety. She envied people who found comfort in material possessions: shallow, naïve, carefree, happy. (Although she did appreciate the "emergency bankcard" Will gave her: stick it in the bank machine and it magically spat out twenties.) She was subject to depressions, insomnia, melancholy, increased by the nagging guilt that she *should* be happy: she could've been born an Untouchable in India, for instance. She'd just read about them in World History. Talk about a shitty fate. She pitied the stupid-wealthy, hated them for their ease, and she certainly didn't want to end up like them. She'd never be able to live under the illusion that owning a Mercedes would make her a worthwhile individual — although she did believe that having perky breasts and a cute little figure might help.

Grandma Dot saw through people across the financial spectrum with a vocal judgment akin to a searing laser beam, often sharing her insights. She usually left Rosie out of her judgments, thank God, because Rosie didn't want to cry. When Rosie had asked Grandma Dot what she would change, if she could change just one thing about her life, Grandma Dot had said: "I wish I'd been more beautiful." "But you are beautiful," Rosie had said, because it was true. And the pictures when she was younger! "Pah," said Grandma Dot, lighting up a cigarette. "Phooey."

Her parents' divorce, in collision with puberty, had amplified a desperate hunger: *love me, love me, love me* — even if I hate you — *love me,* and fulfillment appeared (to a large degree) to be contingent on her physical appeal. When she'd fantasized about becoming a writer, she'd written a story about an ugly librarian who had developed a pen pal relationship with a handsome widower that eventually evolved into a deep love.

The man begged the ugly librarian to let him meet her. He wanted to marry her. The ugly librarian worried that the man would take one look at her and run. The ending of the story eluded Rosie: Did love prevail? Or did the widower's love dissolve? Hard as she tried, she couldn't compose a satisfactory ending and had decided not to be a writer (too hard!) soon after.

Miss Deleo stood near the corner, bluish in the light, leaned up against the wall, hands behind her back. Something was wrong with her hands—deformed—fingers scrunched together; she hid them behind her back or in her pockets, made the students write on the chalkboard. She reminded Rosie of a hummingbird, frantic and excited. She probably shopped at JCPenney. Her dress had a bold flower print; her wide belt had stars studded across it. It was her first year of teaching and she had ideas. Was she aware that the students called her Miss Dildo? Her big brown eyes looked on the verge of tears and Rosie wanted to learn for her sake, just so she wouldn't cry. Besides, no one had ever turned off the lights and instructed her to feel.

Rosie rested her head on her arms against the cool of the desk and tried to drop into the Van Gogh painting. She rubbed her fingers against a tiny sentence carved into her desktop, FUCK YOU AND YOUR MAMA, appreciating the crude frank message and the meditative feel of the grooves. She could hear B's voice, "La di da di da—we live and we die and that's it." It bothered her that her stepfather made his living by exploring women's vaginas. After the phone call from Will's ex-wife, she'd come across his medical books, stacked in his office— slick photographs of vaginal disorders, close-up and inside: pink and red and sores and ooze. He wasn't the type of man she expected to steal B's heart: spindly and freckled legs scattered with bruises and burst capillaries, like beads puckered beneath the skin of his calves. A gut. Reddish gray hair, thinned and combed over his shiny head. Large, mottled hands, fingernails broad and slightly yellow, hands that had pulled Rosie into the world (B's legs spread open!), ready or not.

She'd caught him this morning, hunched and smoking a cigarette on the patio, using a paper Dixie cup as a disposable ashtray. "Don't tell B," he'd said, as if B couldn't smell the nicotine on him. He wore thick brown glasses, and there was a perpetual scab near his forehead from all the times he kept hitting his head on the open car trunk, a bag of groceries in hand or one of B's tennis rackets — Oh God! — even when she stood near him, warning him, "Watch your head, Will, watch it," — *clunk*. She couldn't help but have empathy pains: her stepfather was old and accident-prone; but no matter what, it was impossible to respect a man who wore pink with yellow. When she'd first met him, he wore his green pants embroidered with tiny whales, sprigs of water erupting from their blowholes. Rather than change the way he dressed, B encouraged his bad taste, buying him ties decorated with pumpkins for Halloween or Christmas elves at Christmastime; and they couldn't keep their hands off each other. Rosie's bedroom window overlooked their shower window, and she could see the back of B's head bobbing up and down against the steamy glass. If they weren't having sex, they were asleep, and they were heavy sleepers, possibly from all the sex. She had no memory of affection between B and Dad, whereas Will and B were always touching.

And what about Dad, broken and defeated, living in a gated condominium in Costa Mesa, a man-made creek running down the middle of the complex, ducks quacking. Earnest, sensitive (he, like Rosie, cried at movies), in the process of healing with the help of Jesus Christ, and with the understanding of Lori, fifteen years his junior, a delicious and buxom born-again Christian. Rosie attended Maritime Church with Dad — for Dad — on Sundays, but instead of giving herself over to Jesus Christ, as Dad strongly encouraged, she'd developed a recurrent and involved fantasy: a pack of Hells Angels driving through the huge stained glass depiction of the one and only beatific and bearded J.C., his hands aloft, as if to touch the air, shattering the colored glass, shards of J.C. falling everywhere; Hells Angels wreaking havoc, the church filled with screams and drugs and the choir girls giving sexual favors, ending with her riding off — through the same gap in the window — on the back of a motorcycle with her own personal tattoo-covered savior.

Church was a participatory hypocrisy. One more place where she didn't belong, where the worst thing she could do was be herself. *What planet are you from?* And by the way Dad sometimes looked at her, it was as if he knew that sin was genetic; that she shared not only B's nose and cheekbone structure, but also B's proclivity for extramarital sexual relations. Already a sinner without meaning to be, and in any case, definitely on her way to more sin — in other words, she was doomed. But she was resigned: sinful as her life was, it would never be ordinary. For instance, she'd been flashed twice within the last month while walking near the ocean, both in stark daylight. The first time was from a distance: she gazed toward the rocks and saw a fat, squat man watching her in return, his hand flashing spasmodically at his lap. Two weeks later she took a different walk along the sand. A scrawny older man with wrinkled knees came seemingly from the ocean; he opened the Velcro fly of his wet swim trunks, revealing a patch of graying pubic hair and the curved arc of a pale-veined penis. Both times the men had scurried away like happy little crabs, and although she'd yelled expletives, she'd sensed that she'd gratified them by playing a role. These things didn't happen to so-called normal people.

"Van Gogh," Miss Deleo's voice was wistful, "painted *Starry Night* while in an insane asylum. '*La Tristesse durera toujours,*' I believe, were his last words. Does anyone know what that means?"

No answer. Long pause.

"'The sadness will last forever.'" Miss Deleo waved a cupped hand abashedly in front of her. "I'm sorry," she said. "I'll be quiet now."

Once in a while at Maritime Church, the congregation sang "Amazing Grace," and Rosie would feel *something,* clinging to it as proof: maybe, just maybe, she could please her dad; maybe, just maybe, she could become a Christian. But there had to be more than looking and acting and sounding the same as everyone else. And it was like asking her to believe in Santa Claus, after she'd witnessed her parents putting the presents under the tree. And why hadn't Dad asked her to live with him? Why hadn't he fought for her? Was there something wrong with her? When they drove out of the church parking lot, she'd stick her middle finger up, at her side by the door (where Dad couldn't see) flipping the bird one last time, a heavy mix of guilt and cynicism. Last Sunday, she'd smuggled John Updike's *Rabbit, Run* into Teen Worship, blocking out the Christian rock band, and read hungrily, camouflaging the book inside a Bible. Entering the angst-ridden world of a car salesman, it had occurred to her that she wasn't the only freak. Besides, she concluded, she'd rather be a freak than a Christian.

Miss Deleo flicked on the light switch, her fingers cupped as if holding a tiny chick. Rosie blinked, adjusting to the light, and quickly scribbled three sentences. She thought of the man with no hands: stubs, creases of skin pinched in inverted stars like the ends on a sausage, trying to get something out of his pocket, head down, crouched next to Will's idling Mercedes at the Tijuana, Mexico, border crossing.

Tijuana carried the same designer tennis outfits as the Newport Beach Country Club (Fila, Ellesse, and Adidas), but without the inflated price tags; Will had taken B and Rosie shopping on Monday (only a two-hour car drive from Newport Beach). In the back seat with the plastic bags of clothes, waiting in a line of cars to recross the border, avoiding a look out her back-seat window at the sprawl of human despair, Rosie sat, the sun sending glints of light across her arm like phantom butterflies. And then the man with no hands was tapping a stub against the glass of her window. Her eyes locked into his. Lip and chin tremble, and then she was crying—hot fat tears sliding down her cheeks. He tried to get something out of his pocket, a fruitless endeavor, moved away, merged into the sea of beggars, but there were a thousand other reasons to keep crying, *just look out the window!*—her emotions seeping out without her permission, built up from the reality of Tijuana. The same as when Grandma Dot had taken her to visit her great-aunt at Newport Crest Convalescent, and a woman with no visible chin or neck sitting in a wheelchair had grabbed at her arm and called her Frank, and then Aunt Lydia had kept saying, "When am I going to finally die? When will this finally be over?"—the corner of her mouth crusted with mashed potatoes and spittle. She'd unexpectedly broken into sobs and had to wait in the parking lot for Grandma Dot to finish the visit.

She pressed her cheek against the car window, cool on her skin. Don't look, she told herself. Tijuana all around her, even in the sounds and smells. The tears were coming but she stifled her noise. And then B's eyes caught her in the rearview mirror: she hated when B looked at her impatiently, as if her sensitivity were an ugly troll, and B wanted it gone, out of sight, so they could continue with their contented lives. "What's wrong, Rosie?"

No answer. Lip tremble.

"What's wrong?"

No answer. Chin tremble.

"La di da di da — we live and we die and that's it. Lighten up."

Rosie had her photograph taken that same day, on a burro painted black and white to simulate the appearance of a zebra, although most of the paint had faded. A sombrero, TIJUANA stitched in red thread across the brim, made her forehead itch. She leaned forward, touching the burro's strawlike fur, warm against her hand. He shook off a fly, fur rippling under her fingertips. She knew it was a male burro because of her earlier examination of his leathery, sagging testicles. She tried to convey her sympathies to the young man taking her photograph, and his look showed that he understood. He told her to say "tortilla," her cheeks stiff with an "I'm supposed to smile now" smile. A flash went off and his camera made an agitated noise. Will paid with a crisp twenty-dollar bill, saying the change was a tip. Will and B started walking down the street and she turned to go with them. The man stopped her with a hand to her elbow.

"I need your phone number," he said. "*Teléfono.* For the photograph." He looked her age, already with a wispy mustache. She didn't understand why he would need her phone number when she had that photograph (colors muted, as if covered by a glaze), but he had his look, as if they were in agreement. He handed her a scrap of paper and a pen. Hurriedly, she scribbled her name and phone number. She had the fleeting impression that she was disappointing B, a sharp jab: the lure of an action out of the ordinary. She handed the pen and paper to the man. He was pleased and her sadness lifted at the thought that she had made someone happy. She waved goodbye and ran toward Will and B. They were entering a store with cheap prescription drugs, perfumes, and clothes, and she didn't want to miss out.

They drove back to Newport Beach in silence; she was compliant and tired, spent from her earlier crying jag, watching the sunset bleed across the ocean; they drove past the warning signs for the illegal immigrants making a running break: a yellow diamond shape with the black silhouette of a family, the mother gripping the arm of her daughter (pigtails and ribbons) and pulling so hard, the girl's feet left the ground. She searched the terrain: more patrol cars. They drove past the breastlike domes of the San Onofre nuclear power plant, tops covered in bird shit, like frosting on cupcakes. At the tip of each dome, there was a red light blinking slowly — like the bell buoys — not in unison, and never completely off: barely red, and then all lit up red.

And then there was the shrill ring of a phone at two A.M. She picked up the phone in her bedroom at the same time as Will. She could hear Will's heavy breathing. She imagined his droopy boxers, his red and gray chest hairs.

"Hello," the voice said with an accent. "I need to speak with Rosie."

"Who is this?" Will asked.

"I take picture. She helps me. I cross border. I need place to stay."

She could see the burro's tail swinging at the flies, smell the dirt, hear the children pleading for her to buy Chiclets.

"Hang up, Rosie," Will said, irritated.

She hung up her phone and lay back in her bed, looking around her darkened bedroom. B had let her decorate the room, allowing her "free expression." She'd painted the walls black and taped up advertisements from magazines of scantily clad men. They stared at her with inflated chests and seductive eyes. In the dark, they looked like monsters. She thought about the strangled noise of the camera. B would be mad. Will would give her a lecture; she could already imagine it. Her heart pulsed in her temples—*thump, thump.* She hated the feel of her own blood coursing through her veins. She tried readjusting her head on the pillow. She was a chronic insomniac and this event was more fodder for a thought-infested evening. Bags under the eyes were a beauty detriment. If she didn't look good, she wouldn't belong. She wanted the bed to swallow her. She wanted to disappear. How could a stranger be calling her for help and she couldn't help him? Where would he go? How did he cross the border? Would he be okay? How could she be so stupid? How was she ever going to make it in this world? Grandma Dot had told her to "toughen up." But how was she supposed to do that? Her door opened and Will stood in the doorway. He flicked the light switch. B went back to sleep, no doubt. She would send Will to do her dirty work.

Will sat on her bed, facing her. He had on blue boxers and the tuft of copper hair near his forehead was at attention stance. She felt wide open, lonely and stupid. He smoothed hair from her face, tucked it behind her ear. "No more," he said, but he wasn't angry. He was tired, sorry, concerned. "Jesus Christ, Rosie, you can't go giving our phone number to strangers."

"Maybe he wanted to send more copies of the photo?"

"No more," Will said. There'd been only one other time, when, standing between the bathroom and the kitchen of The

Palms, she'd written her phone number on a napkin for a Mexican busboy eight years her senior, simply because he'd wanted to continue their conversation away from the clamor and bustle of the restaurant; but, after a series of aborted phone calls, Will had gone so far as to change their phone number, and she knew better than to argue with him.

"You have to stop," he said.

The bell rang and Rosie looked at what she'd written:

La di da di da. We live and we die and that's it. Fuck you and your mama.

She couldn't turn her paper in. Papers rustled, backpacks zipped, and she wrote on another piece of paper:

I don't know. There's the night sky and clouds and stars and moon, swirled together, but it's not messy. I'm sorry he was in an insane asylum. And that he said that thing about being sad forever. Didn't he cut his ear off? He must have been very confused.

Miss Deleo gave her a wet-eyed look as she turned her paper in. Outside the door, she could see the green-eyed girl, lip-locked and leg-locked with her boyfriend beside a trash can. And a soft, static, silver white rain.

John Wayne

WILL WAVES HIS HAND in what Rosie thinks looks like a peace sign, but it's his signal for bring me two more, and their waitress — cleavage bursting in a corset, lips and cheeks colored the same artificial pink — hustles to accommodate. B crosses her legs, gaze following the waitress. Rosie shifts, the skin on the backs of her thighs (she's wearing her green paisley miniskirt) rasping against the burgundy Naugahyde of the booth.

Five Crowns is Grandpa's favorite restaurant, but her grandparents canceled (Grandpa's gout is acting up again). Dinners can drag on, torturous, even without her grandparents, prime rib bleeding on plates next to Yorkshire puddings, her thoughts uncontrollable and grim. Her cousins, aunts, uncles disapprove of B (affairs are bad) and, by association, her; and if they don't disapprove, they're damn well supposed to. A whole side of her family: gone. Poof. And it takes energy, alertness, and discipline, politicking for her grandparents' affection, garnering what she can for B, memorizing jokes to amuse them, distracting them from their usual blunt judgments, Rosie spared because she might cry, and no one wants that. When Grandma Dot is affectionate with her to the exclusion of the others, kissing her on the lips with a loud "Mwa!" and holding her hand, it makes her feel powerful and guilty. And Grandma Dot is the only one who stands up to Grandpa, rolling her eyes, making dramatic expressions in Rosie's direction, as if they are privy to an underlying deception. She prefers Grandma Dot in private.

The piano man is adding exaggerated improvisations to Frank Sinatra's "My Way," hands skimming the keys, a large brandy snifter on his piano brimming with dollar bills. Near him is a waiting area with a blazing fireplace, paintings of foxes and hunters, and overstuffed chairs and couches. Darkness lends an aura of horror, candlelight from tabletop candles flickering on the white-pinkish faces of diners, jaws clenched in grind and chew.

Outside, behind B and Will, she sees palm trees, fronds shaking as if they, too, are in dread. It's dusk, the air soft and bruised. She watches the valets with their red jackets and black pants sitting in fold-out chairs, keys draped like ornaments in their small booth. She has an urge to be with the men, listen to them joke and talk. She wants to hear them laugh. Maybe they'll smoke cigarettes. "Dinners are hell," she'll tell them. And it's even more trying when there's a meeting—a first meeting— with John Wayne on the other side.

Thinking about John Wayne is like acknowledging the proverbial light at the end of the tunnel. She's curious, having watched many times late at night from her bedroom deck as he skateboarded past. The sound of his wheels on asphalt first alerted her to his presence; unable to sleep, from her bed she would listen to the pebbly noise coming closer, reaching its peak, and then receding. Being awake in a house where everyone slept made her lonely, so she started waiting at the deck. She became acquainted with his pattern of skateboarding down the alleyway, making a sharp turn at the end near the Rothbergs' garbage cans (Michelle Rothberg, an anorexic senior whose nipples poke out from her shirts, once gave her a passionate lecture on the benefits of colonics).

Sometimes, he appears to be talking to himself, swooping through the alleyway, long hair waving behind him. On Wednesdays near midnight, he gets into a man's car at the end of the alleyway — a large black Mercedes — holding his skateboard against his thighs and folding his long legs into the passenger seat.

Rosie asked her friend Chris about the Mercedes during a break in tennis practice. Chris is a year older and she has a captivating indolence. She never seems surprised. Whenever Rosie asks her something, she answers in a melancholic manner. This time, her eyes narrowed. She leaned her back against the brick of the wall behind the tennis courts and took a deep drag from her clove cigarette. Her breath came slowly, smoke temporarily clouding her eyes.

"It's a damn shame," she said.

"Why?"

"He's prostituting himself," she said, tapping ash. As if she could anticipate Rosie's questions, she continued, "I don't know how he got his nickname, he's just always been John Wayne. He's nice to look at, but he's retarded from drugs — when he talks it ruins everything; he's our age, or close, seventeen at most, and his family disowned him. His brother and sister are the Gleeson twins. The assholes pretend they don't know him."

"How can you stand it here?" Rosie asked.

After a long pause, Chris answered, in a grave tone: "Sex. Drugs. Alcohol." They were quiet, listening to the whispering palm fronds and the sporadic plunk of tennis balls.

"It's fucked up everywhere," Chris said. "Think about it: a man that dyes his hair black and pretends to be a cowboy is President."

"I guess so."

"The best thing you can do," Chris said, dropping her cigarette and grinding it with a white leather K-Swiss tennis shoe, "is not tell anyone about the Mercedes because John Wayne already has a bad reputation."

Last night—close to midnight—when he skateboarded through the alleyway, she was waiting at the deck, and she threw one of Will's golf balls, not to hit him, but to get his attention. The ball skipped in front of him, rebounded against a garage door, and landed with a rustle in a gardenia bush. He stopped, squinted up at her, and smiled.

She stared at him in the dark, the breeze cool and moist, and she could hear the soft sound of a foghorn in the distance. "Meet me tomorrow night at eight," she whispered down. "Narcissus, near the Ugly House." The Ugly House is Whitey Smith's house, from Whitey Smith Mercedes, the one modern home at the end of Narcissus at the cliff, lights usually off, made of glass and steel, reminding her of a shark with windows like teeth.

He tilted his head to one side, watched her in an abstract way.

"The one with all the windows," she said, thinking he might need clarification.

He smiled, an attractive, squinty-eyed smile.

"Good," she said, not knowing what else to say, and he skateboarded away, his wheels soothing and coarse on the asphalt, making his sharp turn at the garbage cans.

The waitress sets down two old-fashioneds—glass bottoms wrapped with cocktail napkins—and whisks away the empties. Her appearance is of a sexualized peasant, red-pleated miniskirt rustling, bonnet ties loose at her shoulders. At least they're not at The Quiet Woman, B's favorite restaurant. The logo drawing on the menus, matches, and painted on the outside wall is a peasant woman, clog-wearing feet splayed like a duck, apron over her skirt, hands at her sides, with her head cut off. No wonder she's quiet.

The waitress's pillowed breast grazes Rosie's ear as her ice water is refilled. B's on her third old-fashioned, her coral lipstick imprinted on the glass rim, as individual, ridged, and cracked as a thumbprint. She raises her cocktail, and in the dim light, the tawny colored drink matches her tan. "To the Tijuana Burro Man," she says, a recurrent toast. B has turned Rosie's mishap into an amusing family anecdote, but it happened over a year ago, and she's tired of bearing the brunt of that particular joke.

Conversations usually begin with the subject of golf or tennis and move to politics (Reaganomics equals lower taxes and smaller government equals good), in between a sprinkling of racist jokes (though not so much in Grandpa's absence), thrown in throughout critical assessments of family members; but a week and a half ago, a well-known businessman named Theo Wilson committed suicide, and the suicide and its aftermath are a frequent topic. Although she hadn't known him, the more people gossip, the more she imagines an alliance.

"I read in the newspaper this morning," B says, tennis bracelet sliding from wrist to forearm as she lifts her glass, "that he placed a towel to the side of his head so he wouldn't make a mess when he shot himself." She sips, takes her time. "He parked in front of the Newport Beach Fire Station because he wanted the firemen to find him right away." She sets her glass on the table. "He left a note, typed, single-spaced, six pages, for his wife. He even let her know how to work the sprinkler system."

"A thoughtful suicide," Will says, bemused, a hand on B's thigh. "As far as suicides go."

"Is it true that his own brother fired him?" Rosie asks, knowing it's true but wanting B to acknowledge the fact. Rosie never spent much time wondering how people came by their money or lost it before, just assuming that grownups had money and that some, like her grandparents, more than most; usually family businesses include real estate. Most people side with Theo's brother or act as if it was a sad but inevitable outcome: it seems ruthless, money and business trumping family, no matter the circumstances.

"Yes," B says, but it comes out like an acquiescent sigh. "Relax," she says, as if understanding Rosie's growing fear that her own fate might be similar. "Men kill themselves. Not women. Usually over finances." B often talks to her as if she's an adult, giving her information as a confidante, and she appreciates the inclusion, but sometimes it makes her sad, like when B disclosed that Rosie's father had been a marginal lover.

"Mrs. Moes called," B says, leaning back into the booth. "She's concerned about your attitude."

Blood rushes to Rosie's face. She has involuntarily become the focus of conversation and cannot grasp an immediate strategy for changing the course. Mrs. Moes didn't like an essay she turned in for a ninth-grade English assignment inspired by the

Pink Floyd song "Comfortably Numb," positing that people in Newport Beach are numb, further articulating her fear that she'll become numb since it has happened to a certain unnamed teacher without this teacher's awareness.

B holds a red cloth napkin to her mouth.

Will shakes his head gravely. He coughs, takes a sip of his old-fashioned, sets his glass down, and stares fixedly at her. The frame on the side of his eyeglasses is broken and he has remedied the situation with transparent tape. There's a Band-Aid near his forehead and another on a knuckle. He's always cutting himself accidentally with his Swiss Army knife or scratching himself up somehow. A few miniature plastic swords with bleeding cherries rest on his bread plate, unwanted accouterments from their cocktails. "I knew a man with Lou Gehrig's disease," he says. His eyebrows rise behind his spectacles. "Now there's a man with problems, Rosie. Not us."

Will is an encyclopedia of diseases, relaying descriptions as proof that their lives are fabulous in comparison. Last week she heard about Parkinson's disease. She has developed a deep affection for him, although she treats him badly and would never admit it. He's constantly being mistaken for her grandfather and it embarrasses her; the way he dresses is a disgrace. Tonight he wears pink and turquoise plaid pants, a red shirt, and a tie with umbrellas on it. He calls the phone "the horn"; the movies are "the moving pictures." He has an irrational hatred of Barbra Streisand (she suggested seeing *Yentl* at the movies, just to anger him). His eyes light up whenever he sees B, and he gives them money and clothes, whatever they want. And she knows she takes advantage, the cumulative effect causing him to blow up over something insignificant—like when she didn't lower the TV volume after he asked four times—making him the bad guy, though she understands there's only so much a man can take. A plate hisses as it passes their table, a glimpse of flame, along with the waft and steam from smoking meat.

"Why don't you tell Rosie what Lou Gehrig's disease is," B suggests, buttering her roll.

"Amyotrophic lateral sclerosis or ALS," he says. "*A* without, *myotrophic* muscle nourishment; *L* lateral side of the spinal cord; *S* sclerosis hardening or scarring." He pauses, letting her take it in. She knows he isn't finished. It's common for him to tear apart words, revealing their Greek and Latin prefixes, roots, and suffixes. Her vocabulary has improved as a result of his impromptu lessons.

He coughs, takes another sip, sets his glass down, and stares deeply at the wall. She imagines B's fingernails under the table, resting like chips of coral on his knee. "There's no cure," he says, gaze fixed. "None. Your body dies, but you don't. You stay alive. Your mind, your soul, whatever you want to call this thing that makes you, you and me, me. You're helpless inside the cage of your body. At the end of it, unable to move, or talk, most die from the heart collapsing, or pneumonia, too weak to cough up the phlegm." He reaches for his cocktail.

The explanation of the disease — the unjust and terminal nature — hits her with an unexpected force. Her ridiculous fears, her anxiety regarding cellulite and the centimeter-sized difference between her breasts, her increasing sexual curiosity, and her longing for meaning, all of it makes her hot with shame. Her throat closes and the room swims. The sounds of cutlery clinking on plates and chairs creaking and the plunking piano are amplified and grotesque. She hates herself, tears coming when she can least articulate her emotions. She forces the tears to a throbbing pressure at her temples, but some are rimmed in her eyelashes, her vision watery and blurred.

"Oh honey," B says, "you'll make her cry."

"I'm only pointing out," Will says, "that we have no real problems." He slices open his baked potato and steam rises from the pale insides. He lowers his face to catch the steam. "That doesn't make us bad, evil," he sets his knife down, lifts his face, "horrible people."

"Maybe just preferred people," B says distractedly, reaching for the pepper.

Rosie opens the thick wood door, glancing one last time over her shoulder at Will, who raises his credit card between his fingers without looking for their waitress. His half-devoured chocolate cake looks like a pile of dirt on its small white plate. B wipes imaginary flecks from her blouse. Rosie has told them that she's walking to her grandparents' house, and B's only admonition is that she not be home late, but she knows she can be as late as she wants: B will leave the back door open so that they won't have to get out of bed when she comes home.

The door swings closed—the valets sit near the booth playing cards, and their heads go up, in tune to the door, but go back to their cards as soon as they see that it's her. The streaks of sun have faded, leaving a misty night, moon full and orange, stuck low in the sky as if too lazy or heavy to heave further. She's early, but decides to walk to Narcissus anyway. She has a habit of walking with a hunch, but inwardly she hears B's voice, "Shoulders back, head up, accentuate your chest," and straightens her frame.

When she gets to Narcissus, John Wayne sits at the curb in front of the Ugly House, waiting with his skateboard across his lap. His feet are bare, one resting on the other. She sees that he sees her, and as she walks to him, she senses an imaginary magnet pulling her. While she stands in front of him, there's relief, as if by leaving the restaurant and B and Will, she has left her dismal and oppressive thoughts, and now the possibilities are unlimited.

His hair is longer than hers, beyond his shoulders, and it hangs in such a way that he looks angelic. He smiles, his teeth barely showing, a peaceful, sad grin, and he holds his skateboard against his thighs, wheels facing outward. Band-Aids on his kneecaps barely cover the scratches. She has an urge to clean his knees and bandage them properly. He has a long scrape at his elbow, and she imagines him falling off his skateboard onto the street. His T-shirt has a gaping hole in the armpit, and she can see his armpit hair. He keeps smiling and her body relaxes.

"Dinners are hell," she says, but rather than sounding indignant or sarcastic, her voice is timid. Dark curtains of ocean slap against the sand and rocks below, retreat, slap again. In the distance, she sees the murky expanse of ocean and sky, Catalina a darker smear on the horizon, as if finger-painted. The air smells like rotted seaweed.

He hesitates, nudges hair behind an ear. She can tell he wants to say something, but doesn't. She has a habit of falling in love when first meeting a person, becoming nervous, but with John Wayne, she senses that she can be silent or say whatever she wants.

"I watch you when I can't sleep," she says.

"You don't sleep," he says, not a question, and she chooses not to explain, believing he understands in his own way.

"Have you heard of Lou Gehrig's disease?" she asks, suspecting he hasn't, but wanting to ask anyway.

He nods, squinting in a speculative way.

"It's this horrible disease where a man's soul is alive while his body dies. Sometimes I feel like everyone is telling me to be dead inside, because then I'll be happy."

He smiles — halfway, as if unsure.

"Some people," she says, "don't worry. They look good. It never occurs to them to ask why. They're the chosen ones, the ones who live easily, laugh easily, and look carefree. Their families have big fat bank accounts and that's all that matters. They'll breed with one another to create more good-looking people with lots of money."

He scratches his arm.

"I hate them," she says, "but it's probably easier to be them." The way he looks at her makes her think he can see the constant panic lodged in her heart. "Grandma Dot — that's my grandma — she says I waste time by questioning. She says I shouldn't look too deeply, that life is really simple in the end."

He rubs his knee.

"I don't trust anyone."

He stares at her — hard — as if to make sure she sees that he's listening. He re-crosses his feet, putting the other one on top.

"I want to know," she says, "if anyone ever really knows anything, or if I have to feel my entire life like I don't know anything and just get used to not knowing. And when I get old, will I just pretend like I know? Will I just fool myself into thinking that this is a kind of knowing, not knowing, but saying I know?"

He doesn't say anything.

"Let's go to my uncle's," she says. "No one will bother us." Her uncle Stan's apartment is upstairs above the garage of her grandparents' house. His apartment is the same as when he left during the Vietnam War for Canada, never to return, because Grandma Dot won't let anyone change it. Grandma Dot stores the fake Christmas tree in her son's closet, but Rosie gathers the plastic limbs and carries them downstairs every Christmas to Grandma Dot, waiting at the foot of the stairs in her Bah Humbug sweatshirt. Meanwhile, poor worshipful B's room was changed to an office long ago.

There's a box of memorabilia beside the fake Christmas tree in Uncle Stan's closet. Inside are letters and mediocre torment-filled poems scrawled haphazardly on torn pieces of paper. The jackpot is a folder of psychological assessments. These, Rosie believes, were done on behalf of Stan's bewildered parents shortly before he fled for Canada. Perhaps they were trying to get Stan out of serving in the military on psychological grounds, so that he wouldn't leave them. She has to guess at these details since it's another topic not open for discussion. The technical language reads like a real-life novel of hopelessness. Stan's drug history is carefully documented, and Stan has taken every drug known to man, including a large amount of acid. Stan's defense of peyote on spiritual grounds seems to her to be completely valid, but the psychiatrist didn't think so: he was diagnosed as incorrigible. She wonders if Grandma Dot purposely left the box. She knows for a fact that her grandma is never careless.

John Wayne skateboards beside her: to Marguerite, down the hill to Larkspur, Iris, Heliotrope, over to Goldenrod, Fernleaf, and Dahlia, ending at Carnation. She likes the way his wheels sound on the concrete and how, when he's gliding, his toes tip over the side of the skateboard.

The stairway is behind her grandparents' kitchen, and as she walks up the steps, she sees through the kitchen window below Grandma Dot and Grandpa bent over their meals at the kitchen bar, watching the television in the living room. The apartment is angled above the garage in such a way that they can't see her, but she can keep tabs on them. She hears the soft pads of John Wayne's bare feet on the steps, following behind.

"Oh," John Wayne says when she opens the door and turns on the light with the red light bulb. He follows her inside, his voice reverent. "Wow-wee." A hammock-like chair hangs by a thick chain from the ceiling in the corner of the room. The shell of the chair is fat wicker and crimson pillows tie through the slats. On either side of a bed are two plastic reading tables in the shape of giant dice. The bedroom is soaked in an eerie red hue from the bulb.

He sets his skateboard beside one of the die-shaped tables, sits on the bed, and stares around the room. She sits next to him, fear and excitement passing through her, as if she's writing her phone number for the Tijuana Burro Man a thousand times over, and no one can stop her. His hand next to her thigh feels like it's touching her, but it isn't. She likes the way it looks against her uncle's red bedspread — his fingernails with dirt underneath them, and the pinkie filed to a triangle and longer than the rest.

"Did you see me watching you?" she asks. Supposedly, he's brain-damaged, but she wonders if he understands more.

With four fingers, he draws what appears to be a loopy S on the bedspread in the space between them, over and over, S S S.

"You're watching me," he says, and she doesn't know what to say. She tends to mistake suffering for depth, and she decides to ask a question that will help determine whether he's a really deep person.

"Do you ever cry?"

He doesn't answer, pulling at his shorts' pocket and unearthing a small plastic bag filled with marijuana.

He rolls a joint on the bedspread with papers from his T-shirt pocket; the ritual soothes him and his hands work quickly. He may not know how to talk, she thinks, but he sure knows how to roll a joint. He pulls a silver Zippo lighter from his shorts' pocket, flips the top open with a flick, and produces a steady flame. He sucks on his joint and his eyes squeeze shut as he inhales, his eyelashes peeking out, darker than his hair. His inhale is lengthy and she feels how he takes it all the way through his body, imagining the smoke coursing through him. There's pleasure in watching him smoke a joint just because he appreciates it so. She could watch him smoke joints all night.

He holds his breath for what appears an impossible length of time, and when he opens his eyes, his eyes smile and the smoke comes out in a rush. He hands the joint to her and she does her best to copy, but she's scared to hold it in so long. She doesn't want to have a coughing fit like the first time she smoked a clove cigarette by the tennis courts with Chris. After an abbreviated suck and exhale, she hands the joint back to him.

Although Grandma Dot never comes upstairs — no one ever does — she still doesn't want Grandma Dot witnessing drug use in Uncle Stan's apartment, and she gets up to shut the blinds and lock the door. At the side by the bed, she opens a window so that they can hear the bay, lets the blinds fall over the window, careful not to disrupt an assortment of hand-made yarn-fraying dream catchers propped against the wall. The small bay waves lap onto the sand, a calm sound. She goes to the closet, finds Uncle Stan's bong behind a box of clothes, sure that John Wayne will love it, majestic and intricate, tubes poking from the blue glass.

By the time she returns to the bed, he's preparing another

joint. She sees the spent joint stubbed in Uncle Stan's hand-shaped ashtray, a soft line of smoke rising from the butt. When she hands the bong to him, he smiles so beautifully, she wants to hold him in her arms and tell him she can make everything all right. He sets the bong next to his feet. The breeze rattles through the blinds. After the second joint, she stares at him, willing him to speak. When he does, his voice is soft, and he stares at his hands.

"I don't talk so much," he says.

"I don't care," she answers.

"I had an accident," he says, gazing forward. "My head got hurt."

"That's okay."

He nods and says, "I like it here. Can I stay?"

"Sure," she answers. "But you'll have to be careful. I'll give you a key." Her head floats separate from her body, and she realizes she must be high because she feels no panic at giving John Wayne permission to live in her uncle's apartment. It only seems right and true.

He drifts around the bedroom, exploring, touching, and smelling things. She watches as he strips off his T-shirt and puts a necklace over his head. It's her uncle's necklace with the sharp tooth that resembles the curved incisor of a beast, and it looks good against his skin.

"Keep it," she says, thinking it's only right since it looks so good on him. She wants to give him everything. She's feeling generous and noble.

He stares at her, but it's like he hasn't heard her or doesn't care. She's sitting on the bed and he kneels next to her legs. His chest looks like a boy's chest but it's longer. He puts a hand on either side of her hips and sets his head in her lap. She tries to work out the tangles in his hair with her fingers — blond hair streaked with sun. He smells like ocean and she imagines for an instant that he's really a merman.

He lifts his head and smiles, his eyes blue, but with white in them. She's never seen eyes like that. They remind her of clouds, making him seem incapable of bad thoughts, but also empty. She smiles back, her heart full.

He stands and unsnaps and unzips his shorts, letting them fall to his ankles, and then kicking them away with a foot. His actions appear automatic, as if he's performing a ritual. There's no life in his eyes. He isn't wearing underwear — his penis at half-mast, surrounded by light brown pubic hair. It's only the third adult penis she's seen in real life, not just photographs. Her stomach tightens, as if a dangerous animal has made an appearance. And at the same time, she's embarrassed and humiliated.

"Stop," she says, covering her eyes with a hand. "What are you doing?"

She watches through her fingers. She's hurt his feelings — his mouth turns down comically, like a clown's mouth. She pulls at his arm and gets him to sit next to her on the bed. Hunched forward, his head hangs lower. His penis is slack between his legs and she thinks it's odd that a penis can look sad. His palms are facing upwards on his thighs, as if he's waiting for something to fall into them. He brushes his left foot against his right leg, and she leans over for the bong, places it in his lap, hoping this will cheer him.

After she reminds him to put on his shorts (knowing that he would gladly get high naked), he fixes the bong instead of rolling another joint. She hears the faucet from the bathroom, and then he returns to his position next to her on the bed, holding it like a trophy. She smokes with him while the wind rattles the blinds and water gurgles in the bong.

He pulls at the glass mouth and holds the smoke, motioning with his hand for her. Pressing his mouth against hers, he blows smoke into her, his hand on her thigh, his tongue against her teeth. She closes her eyes so that she can't see his face because she knows she'll feel protective and that will ruin everything. Besides, with her eyes shut, she can just barely believe that this is the way good friends smoke pot.

Henry's House

SHE WAS NOT UNHAPPY. That was what Melody told me as she washed dishes, one year into her marriage, after the thrill of the honeymoon in Spain and Greece had worn off, and the novelty of wealth had lost some of its luster. She smiled, a false ease to her face, and handed me a glass to dry. Her eyes appeared sorry, and I knew she'd asked me to come inside and help so that we could be alone, away from her mother. This was my second summer taking literally Melody's insistence that her home was my home, no longer ringing the doorbell, simply letting myself in through an unlocked side door.

Melody had a maid that came every Tuesday and Thursday. She had a sleek stainless-steel KitchenAid dishwasher. Yet we washed and dried the old-fashioned way, as if roommates again in our cramped apartment. Etched on the outside of the glass she handed me were three delicate gold lines, and as I dried with a dishtowel, I wanted to believe that she wasn't unhappy, as she'd claimed, but I was aware of my own greed, my self-interest in her contentment, and it made me uneasy.

A sizable hallway led to her kitchen, and I heard her dogs—Jules and Jim—their nails clicking on the rose-veined marble, before I saw them. "Hello, babies," I said, though I thought of them like freakish, fragile stuffed toys, little cloud puffs with tails curling over their butts in plumed question marks. But they didn't feel delicate, damp noses pressing into my calves. I leaned over to pet Jules, whom I could distinguish from Jim by his blue collar; his fur had a woolly quality, and his body was dense beneath; his ears were shaded a darker buff, a hint of apricot color around his mouth, the remnant stain from dog food.

"Go on," Melody said, tapping Jim with a bare foot. "Get." Despite my efforts, she could tell I didn't like the dogs, and they sauntered, side by side, out the open sliding glass doors.

Their purchase, three months after Melody's wedding at the Newport Marriott, had been to stifle any maternal urges. "It's either that," Melody had explained, "or get pregnant; Henry doesn't want more kids, and God knows I don't, so there you go." We both had eleven-year-old daughters and had vowed not to have more children, knowing firsthand the difficulty of raising the girls without help from their fathers. But I couldn't understand why she'd buy dogs like that when she could have anything. Wealth, I often felt, was wasted on the wealthy, and I liked to imagine what I'd do with money, disappointed that Melody didn't share my good taste.

We'd worked together at the Newport Beach Golf and Country Club—where she'd met her husband, Henry—serving golfers iced teas, Styrofoam cups of chili, and hot dogs from a movable cart that sat along the ninth green; but now only I worked there, handling the job of two, a three-dollar raise as compensation. Melody would change that fact if she could, but instead she bought me clothes and food and paid for her and my daughter's summer camp in Catalina, which was where the girls — best friends like us — were for two weeks.

Watching Melody, it was as if she was waiting for permission to speak openly; she was unusually concentrated on the plate she washed and her body radiated need. She wore a hot pink Fendi bikini, a wavy pattern embedded in the material in silver metallic thread; her legs, arms, and stomach were lean and tan, thirty-one years old, eight years younger than me, but with a teenager's body. She wasn't wearing her seven-carat princess-cut diamond ring, and I knew that if I'd asked why, she'd say it was heavy and chafed her finger. Her eyes were weighted with emotion, blue green, the right eye darker, and in the left, two flecks of gold brushed in.

I wore what Melody called a tankini with its matching cover-up to conceal the spider-veined cellulite on my thighs. She'd bought the tan-colored Christian Dior bathing suit and cover-up at Neiman Marcus, more appropriate for my body type, which wasn't like hers, though my breasts — not too large, not too small — were in proportion to my hips and legs.

"The General is happy," she said, nodding toward the window above the sink that overlooked her pool. Sometimes she called her mother The General. Her mother, Cindy, stood on the second to last step of the shallow end, wearing a wide-brimmed straw hat and dark sunglasses; she was in some type of contented reverie, the trim of her skirted bathing suit floating, and her fingers circling figure eights, creating small rippling outlines in the water. Thick, leathery scars ran down each of her thighs from her premature hip surgeries, adding to her indomitable appearance. "Hip dysplasia," she explained to anyone who asked, "like a dog."

Cindy and I had believed that Melody would do well, that

she'd marry money eventually, and we'd encouraged her. Each of us had gained, as if Melody's marriage, her home and her pool, made up for all the bad things that had happened in our lives, for all our struggles. Weekdays Cindy arrived at Melody's wearing her dental hygienist uniform, much like a nurse's, and changed into her bathing suit in a back bedroom that was designated as hers.

The sun reflected in the pool, and I blocked out Cindy, staring instead at the deep end, a mesmerizing whitish blue ripple, magical. Part of Melody's charm was her impetuousness, how she spoke without thinking—there had been Melody's love affairs, two with women, and her experimentation with drugs. She'd been diagnosed with bipolar disorder as a teenager, although a milder form, and had been taking lithium and valproate as mood stabilizers, adding Saint John's wort and omega-3 fatty acids as herbal conduits.

I knew that Cindy worried, like I did, that Melody would destroy a good thing. "Five years," Cindy had whispered after Melody's wedding ceremony, as if we'd orchestrated a deal, staring hard at my reflection in the Newport Marriott bathroom mirror while I applied lipstick. "She needs to last five, according to the prenup. If he catches her having an affair, she gets nothing."

Melody coughed, and I turned my attention to her, saw her wipe the back of her wrist against her chin, and then continue washing her plate. I thought before speaking, wondering how to reassure Melody, wanting to find out what was going on, how she really felt. My motives were partly strategic. "It's me," I said, flagging the dishtowel in front of her. I said my full name as emphasis: "Katherine Lynn McAllister. Best friend. You don't have to pretend." When that didn't work, I used the nickname she'd given me: "You know, your best friend—Kat."

And then a change passed over her; I saw it spread through her body, a shuddering. She set the sponge and plate down. She bent over, her wet hands gripping the edge of the sink, her knuckles pink. I felt her taking deep breaths.

"His smell," she said, turning off the water and facing me. She smiled her slanted smile. I was surprised to see a twinkle in her eyes. She was talking about Henry. He dyed his hair a metallic black, but I guessed he was in his sixties. Along with his uncanny ability to make money, he was a chain smoker. She grimaced, as if imagining his smell, and her eyes stayed on mine. "It comes all the way from the inside. There's no way to get rid of it, no matter how much he brushes his teeth."

"It can't be that bad," I said.

She smiled, as though she found the subject amusing. "He can't go down on me," she said, reminding me of the lewd way she had talked when we lived together. "He tries," she said, "but he loses his breath and starts coughing." She mimicked a sputtering, hacking cough, crouched over, hands crossed at her side. "The main event isn't any better," she said, and she made convulsing motions with her hips, spasmodic, while she continued to cough.

When she was done, she looked back at me, pleased and challenging, as if daring me not to laugh at her imitation. And I laughed, even though I liked Henry and thought of him as noble for marrying Melody, because, like me, she had what people called "an unfortunate past." I couldn't help but believe that Henry had known that I needed rescuing, and in his kind way, had taken me in as well. Wouldn't it be great, I often thought, to be married to Henry, but I was almost beautiful, whereas Melody was beautiful.

"He snores," she said, wanting to maintain my attention.

She made wheezing noises; she pretended to be asleep, waking herself with a loud gargling noise. There was light in her eyes, as if she'd waited a year since her honeymoon to tell me these things.

My face was hot and there was a twirl of anger in my stomach. "He's not that bad," I said.

"Why don't you sleep with him," she said. She smiled slowly and it lingered on her face. "You'd like that," she said. "Wouldn't you?"

I stared at her, a sharp pain in my chest.

"Oh, that's right," she continued, her voice trembling a little, "you don't fuck men anymore, because of your poor broken heart."

"Please, please," I said. "You've got a good thing." I was shaky, and I wondered if my face had gone pale. Melody's lips had touched my cheek on her wedding day, when we were saying our goodbyes. When she had pulled away, her hands had stayed on my arms, and she'd given me an unswerving look. At the time I had understood, only because I knew her so well, but I had not wanted to admit what I'd seen in her eyes. I continually shook off the memory, no matter how many times the image came back, because her expression had been an acknowledgment: she'd married a man she did not love, and she'd done so in large part to please me.

I gestured at the expansive brass sink, the dishwasher, and the marble countertop, white veined delicately with rose. "Don't mess this up," I said.

She appeared shocked that we'd spoken so honestly, but rather than being concerned about my feelings, she looked around, panicked, as if her mother had come inside without us noticing. She relaxed when I nodded toward the window above the sink and we watched Cindy swimming a lazy backstroke across the pool, her straw hat and sunglasses resting on the tile near the shallow end.

Melody called me that same evening. After our obligatory apologies, we talked in a general manner for about ten minutes, before she brought up her dogs, Jules and Jim. She talked about our time together, eight years total, living in the apartment with our girls, saying that it had been peaceful.

"Stable," she said. "I felt safe." It wasn't the first time she'd told me this, and I questioned her version, since I remembered our struggles with the kids from toddlers to girls: late nights, flu and toothaches, emergency hospital visits, teaching them to comb their hair and brush their teeth, and how they'd had to share the sofa bed in the living room for a bedroom.

She reminded me of when we'd stayed up late, finding the movie *Jules and Jim* by chance on television. Even though we had to get up early the next morning, we were mesmerized, and had watched the entire movie while lying beside our sleeping daughters — their legs entwined — on the sofa bed. She made me admit that I didn't like her dogs, insisting I tell the truth, pleading, and after I did so, she was quiet for some time. I could only hear her breathing into the phone, and I thought about how when we'd lived together, I'd been responsible for her, like an older sister.

"They bred them, the French," she said, breaking the silence. "Bichon frisé. Lap dogs for the French royalty."

"Is that so?" I said, resentment stirring, remembering how I'd handled all the bills, and how I'd been forced to be the girls' disciplinarian. But then I remembered how once, when I was driving my beat-up Volvo wagon, Melody in the passenger seat and the girls in the back, Melody had mooned a Porsche full of rowdy teenagers, making the girls laugh uncontrollably. Melody would dance with the girls, make faces, and it pleased me, knowing I'd never be able to teach my daughter spontaneity.

"I'm supposed to be a lap dog," she said, breaking my thoughts. I heard her take a sip and swallow, and it occurred to me that she might be drinking again, despite Dr. Frankel's warning not to mix alcohol with her medication. I imagined her sitting on the couch, legs tucked beneath her.

"Henry's lap dog," she said in a quiet voice.

I told her that Henry was a good man, that most marriages were passionless, and that she didn't have to deal with him since he was rarely home, traveling as he did for business.

"Have you heard him drink coffee?" She made slurping noises into the phone, but this time her imitation was half-hearted.

"How sad," she said, "that I'm only happy when he's gone."

The flowery wallpaper in my apartment had faded to a disturbing brown, and as I looked around me, at my shabby couch and the frayed drapes, anger swelled inside my chest.

"He loves you," I said furiously. I wanted to tell her that she was loved as much as any woman in Newport Beach, and that she was lucky. What difference did it make—I wanted to demand—whether the words "I love you" came from his mouth or another man's? She was loved. But I was too angry to say what I felt.

"You're wrong," she said, but she spoke gently, as if understanding my anger.

"You're not supposed to drink on lithium," I said, indignant. I wanted to tell her that the last time a man had said he loved me, he'd left me for a blond younger woman when I was five months' pregnant. My herpes' outbreaks—bubbly lumps on the lips of my vagina during stressful times—reminded me of his affection, and if that didn't refresh my memory, my scheduled Pap smears every six months continued to come back level two. My vaginal canal was mildly unhealthy, probably the same gray pink color as Henry's lungs, giving me a lifelong predisposition to cervical cancer. I was reconciled to the fact that my heart had hardened. At thirty-nine, I expected never to fall in love again. But Melody already knew all this.

"He loves the idea of me," she said, her voice adamant. "I'm his property. Like his brass sinks and crystal chandeliers, even the stairway and the pool. I'm furniture, something he's purchased."

"I'm sorry," I said, a coldness spreading through my stomach, "but I don't feel bad for you."

"Do you know how he got his money?" she asked.

I admitted that I did not.

"His father sold the government firing pins for M-16 rifles during Vietnam and made a shitload of money because the war kept going on and on." When I didn't answer, she said, "I'm profiting because of Vietnam, because of guns that shot and killed people."

I was stunned, but I said, "That was his dad. Henry sells those things that help erase computer memories." I had no idea what he sold, only that large companies paid him thousands and thousands of dollars to install and maintain it.

She could tell I was bluffing because she answered, "How do you like them apples? Huh?" Then she said that her hairdresser had told her that Henry had fired his own brother six or seven years before, and that his brother had shot himself in the head soon after. "Parked in front of the fire station, with a towel at the side of his head. On the car seat next to him was that book, you know, *Seven Habits of Highly Effective People*."

"Sounds made up," I said.

"Yeah, well," she said. "It should've been called *How to Lose*. But don't bring it up with Henry. That's a no-no."

She admitted that she was having an affair with a young heroin addict we knew named Lobo (I had no idea if that was his real name), having what she called "limp sex" because of his inability to perform due to drugs. He'd worked briefly at the Newport Beach Country Club as a locker room attendant, before getting fired for insubordination. He wore moccasins and chinos with his boxers pouched out the back, and he was studying for a master of fine arts that never seemed to end. Last I'd heard, he inspected beef for McDonald's — working in a factory where thousands of pounds of beef ran down a conveyor belt, ready to be transformed into patties. Every hour or so, I imagined, he grabbed a handful in a gloved hand and ran it through a battery of tests.

"Why him?" I asked, picturing him slouched over, talking with his chin tucked in at his chest.

"I don't know," she said. "He calls. Collect. When Henry answers, he hangs up." She paused, and I heard her take another sip and swallow. "I give him money," she said. I wondered if she was drinking from a crystal glass, and I found myself hoping that she was using a napkin or a coaster so that she wouldn't mark the fine-grained mahogany of her side table. "I'm his only connection to the outside world," she said, as if still trying to understand her attraction.

There was silence, and I looked around my dim apartment and scratched my leg. I remembered how when Lobo had smiled at me, I'd sensed he was smiling at something going on inside him, rather than at me.

I thought about how Cindy's second husband had molested Melody when she was eleven until she ran away at thirteen. The molestation was often cited for her subsequent problems and promiscuity. Sometimes, I'd watch Melody staring in a melancholic awe at our girls' prepubescent bodies in their wet bathing suits — their soft nipples, slim legs, and the delicate crease of their pubis area — and I'd wonder if she was thinking about her past.

Cindy had divorced her abusive husband and there'd been an unsuccessful public trial, ending with a deadlocked jury. It was as if by going through the ordeal and coming out the other side, Cindy had become inseparable from Melody. When asked, Cindy would say that she was determined to make up for what had happened. "I might not have been the best mother," I'd heard her say more than once, "but no one can accuse me of failing as a grandmother."

"After the French Revolution," Melody said, "they could have died out, but they became street dogs. They're tough, don't you see?"

"What are you talking about?" I asked, even though I knew she was on the subject of bichons frisés again; I imagined Jules and Jim curled beside her — she was probably stroking their cottony fur.

"They're strong," she said, "even if they're beautiful. Like cotton balls, stupid little cotton balls with black eyes."

When I didn't answer, she said, "Don't tell The General about Lobo. God. She'll kill me."

Melody and I didn't come up with a plan; we never fleshed out details or talked in a pragmatic way. It was more as if an unconscious telepathy existed between us. An idea developed, unspoken, that Henry had always liked me, that I had always liked Henry, and that if I could provide a distraction, take up some of the responsibility of entertaining him, it might give

Melody much-needed autonomy; and I hoped it would enable her to end her relationship with Lobo and commit to four more years of matrimony, allowing for a worthwhile divorce settlement. Cindy was a problem. We couldn't confide in her; really, we were both afraid of her.

Henry came home for four days, and Cindy and I didn't swim in the afternoons, lest Henry become weary of our using his pool. "We need," Cindy had told Melody, "to make Henry feel like a king." When Cindy and I did come over, there was a formality to our behavior, and we were careful not to make noise when Henry napped. Cindy became less opinionated and vocal. She had told us, many times, that all men were idiots, but with Henry she acted as if he was the one exception. Although I had always been fond of Henry, like Melody, I preferred when he was away on business: his home became less ours when he was there.

We dined with him that first evening at the glass table next to the pool, the bay hazy with night, lights twinkling, and a soft breeze stirring the palm trees. Below us was Henry's pier, and at the end of the dock, a Boston Whaler motorboat was tied in its slip and knocking gently against the dock bumpers. Melody had told me that the boat had belonged to Henry's brother, and that he wouldn't let her use it.

Newport Harbor snaked around Balboa Island and Lido Island in the distance. I felt that my poverty had prepared me, especially, to appreciate the view. Jules and Jim huddled underneath the table, waiting for scraps. I found it difficult to eat, even though Melody had carefully planned the meal. I smiled in accord with their smiling faces, but I'd always been an awful actor.

Melody and Cindy minded the way Henry lit one cigarette

after another, the ashtray filling on the glass table. Second-hand smoke was a vicarious pleasure for me, having quit smoking many times myself. Cindy pretended, but her face gave her away, her lips pursing and her eyes narrowing.

"Must you," Melody said, slipping up the second night as Henry reached for his lighter. She'd just set his plate on the table, grilled swordfish with sautéed spinach, and I knew it was because she'd worked so hard on the meal: she didn't want the flavor ruined with his smoke.

"This is Henry's house," Cindy said, smiling pleasantly, answering for Henry, "and he can damn well do as he pleases." She reminded me of myself, the way she tried to mask her doubts and fears in an ironic, detached manner.

Henry was an unusually quiet man, and I liked him for his shyness. When he told a joke or spoke on any subject, it was evident that he had thought long and hard about the delivery, taking away from its success. His lips would lift into a half smile, pleased and genuinely surprised that someone had laughed.

"Did you hear about the fish that went deaf?" he asked. No, none of us had. "He had to get a herring aid."

"What did the finger say to the thumb?" he asked. We didn't know. "I'm in glove with you."

I found myself laughing more at Henry's jokes than Cindy or Melody, even though the jokes weren't that funny. My face had a tight feeling, not used to smiling and laughing so much. Cindy stared at me, but she approved, wanting Henry to feel liked.

Melody had told me that Henry's views were narrow and that he only read from the sports and business sections of the *Orange County Register*. She said that she found it difficult to talk to him, that he didn't care about the world, and for the first time I began to agree with her assessment, based not only on his jokes, but also on the conversations he initiated. But I didn't mind, believing that he was strong and effective in a different way.

I followed him the second evening after dinner, emboldened by a look Melody gave me across the table. He was walking to his study, and I planned to ask about his business, convincing myself of my interest, and wanting, in turn, to convince him. Because I wore a white Donna Karan dress that highlighted my tan, I was more attractive, and thus more confident.

"Excuse me," I said, and he turned in the hallway and stared at me. He wore shorts and flip-flops, his feet pale and wrinkled. I listened to his heavy breathing and remembered Melody saying he might die from a heart attack, leaving her a wealthy widow. "That would be so much better," she'd said, "because then no one would hate me." She was talking about his grown children from his first and second marriages. She'd never been able to stomach when people disliked her, trying in her bumbling way to change their disposition, an endearing quality because she was doomed to be disliked even more.

"What is it?" he asked, and his expression was so businesslike that I lost heart, knowing that Melody's beauty had been her selling point, and that I could not compete.

"Sorry," I said, blood rushing to my face, and I turned and walked away.

On his final evening dining home, Melody placed thin green candles on the glass table, but they wouldn't stay lit because of the ocean breeze. The view was best at night, beside the darkened pool, listening to the quiet lapping of the bay, lights flickering and boats swaying, the Pavilion studded with white lights. We were eating an arugula salad with roasted almonds when the distant sound of the phone ringing came from inside the house.

I slid my chair back, set my cloth napkin on the table. "I'll go."

As I was walking toward the sliding glass doors, I heard Cindy telling Melody that she'd used too much vinegar in the dressing.

When I answered, the operator said, "Collect call from" — a static pause, and then a male voice said, "Lobo."

"I accept," I said, but Lobo hung up.

Walking back to the table, I fingered the thick curtain that hung all the way to the ground in the living room, near the mahogany side table, appreciating the velvety smooth material. The room was kept dark because sunlight might damage the furniture. Again, I believed that my life had singled me out to value Melody's home in a way that no one else could.

We ate pappardelle pasta — fat noodles that slid off my fork — with salmon. Jules slept under the table and Jim waited for a dropped scrap, eyes alert.

"Who was it?" Henry asked, reaching for his pack of Benson & Hedges Lights.

"Wrong number," I said.

"We've been getting a lot of those," Henry said, slowly extracting and lighting a cigarette, but the way his eyes were downcast, I could tell that he was simply stating a fact. There was grease at the corner of his mouth from the pasta, and I looked away.

"Maybe you should change your phone number," Cindy said, "so that your phone bill doesn't add up."

My eyes were on a curled lemon slice, garnishing my meal, but I knew Cindy was staring at me. The atmosphere became heavy, all at once, and when I looked up from my plate, Cindy was no longer watching me, but Melody was.

We drank Vouvray from wide-bottomed wineglasses. When I chewed, took a drink, or lifted my fork, it was awkward. Conversation drifted from one subject to the next, as if we were reciting lines from a script, but everything sounded freighted with hidden meaning. Jules whimpered under the table, and when I looked beneath, his hind leg was jerking in dream. He growled, his gum black, marbled in pink.

"Leave them," Henry said, breathing heavily, a wheeze in his chest. Melody uncrossed her legs, the material of her silk wrap dress sliding open, and her hand reached under the table to soothe Jules anyhow.

"Now you'll have to wash your hands," Cindy said.

Melody didn't answer — leaned over, petting Jules — her gaze on me, complicit; although it was a cumulative reaction, something about her private look made it undeniable: she'd been looking out for me all along, and while I'd been pining for her husband and her good looks, bitterness eating my insides because of my own fate, I hadn't acknowledged that she loved me more than anyone ever had. I was ashamed, knowing that love, however and whenever it appeared, should not be taken lightly. And then I thought about our girls: closer than best friends, having been raised together. I wanted them to look out for each other and depend on each other, like sisters. I stared back at Melody, trying to convey my emotions, hiding nothing from my expression, and she smiled sadly, her eyes filling up with her smile, slightly questioning.

"You okay, Kat?" she said, no longer petting Jules, sitting back in her chair and breaking from the script. I knew that Henry and Cindy were staring at me as well.

"I'm good," I said, smiling benevolently around the table,

ignoring the sickness in my stomach. Cindy's gaze was firm on me, her eyes the same color as Melody's, with matching gold flecks — but they gave away nothing, reminding me of water; and I wanted to separate myself from her, considering we'd not had her daughter's best interest at heart: Henry would never appreciate Melody the way she deserved.

Later, when Melody and I were clearing the table for dessert, tears came sliding down my cheeks, and I told her, "I'm sorry; I'm so sorry."

"Shut up," she said, and she put her hand on my forearm and gently squeezed. "Okay, Kat." Her eyes were swimming with emotion, and I realized that she'd forgiven me long before I'd grasped what I'd done.

We continued to clear the table, and for the first time, Melody's home, her possessions, the dress she'd bought me and that I now wore, all of it was tainted and repulsive. When the doorbell rang, Melody's body tensed, and I knew that it was Lobo, and that I needed to get rid of him.

I set the teak salad bowl I was carrying next to the sink. Melody stopped me on my way out of the kitchen. "Hold on," she said, and she began flipping through her Julia Child cookbook where she kept crisp hundred-dollar bills. The doorbell rang and rang.

"Here," she said, pulling me close, sweat at her lip. "Careful," she whispered, and she tucked two hundred-dollar bills in my fist. Cindy and Henry sat at the glass table, waiting for blueberry cheesecake; Henry was smoking his cigarette, and I saw the pale flash of Cindy's face looking toward the sliding glass doors.

Jules and Jim trotted past me, their fur swiping my calves, to the front door, nails clicking against the marble. When I opened the door, Lobo was stooped there, as I remembered him, his chin pressed into his shirt, but he looked skinnier. Also, there were bruises all over the insides of his arms, congregating in an alarming pattern near the crooks of his elbows. The dogs sniffed at his ankles, but he didn't appear to notice them.

"Hello, Kat," he said. I had forgotten how he stared at my shoulder when he talked, instead of into my eyes. "Long time no see," he said.

Jules yipped, an uncontrollable outburst from the excitement and tension. His head ping-ponged from Lobo to me, and Lobo's leg moved, just a little, to shake off Jim.

"You have to leave," I said, handing him the hundred-dollar bills. He took the money quickly and smoothly, without hesitation, without acknowledgment, as if the transaction hadn't even taken place. He didn't even check to see how much it was, and a disappointed look came over his face, as though I'd inconvenienced him, but I knew he was covering for his own disgrace. Then he turned and walked out the front walkway, into the dark street.

At the end of the street, he turned to see if I was still there, and we stared at each other for a long second. He looked like a phantom, his face dark and bewildered, and as I shut the front door, I worried what he thought of me. Something about the way he'd stared at me in recognition—he knew that I'd sold Melody out, and that like him, I was ashamed.

Two significant events happened within the next year. Lobo entered a treatment facility and tried to sober up. Although he continued to relapse, he stopped pursuing Melody. When Henry was out of town for more than a week, and Lobo was in a sober period, living with his mother in Santa Ana, Melody let him come over and use the pool. I discovered for my-

self that he was a voracious reader, with a wide-ranging interest in the world, and his dark sense of humor was far more
appealing than Henry's corny jokes.

Lobo enjoyed Henry's house as much as I had, I supposed,
because when Melody tried to flirt with him, he flirted back
halfheartedly, saying he didn't want her to screw up a good
thing. Or maybe he hoped that Melody would find security
with Henry, since he knew about her past as well. Most likely,
it was a combination.

Also, more importantly, Henry decided that he didn't want
me to come over as much — or Cindy. The night he told us, the
sky was dense with fog and we could hear a foghorn in the distance. We sat in the living room near the thick curtains and
mahogany side table I had loved, but which I didn't love so
much anymore. The girls were in Melody's bedroom, painting
their toenails.

Henry sat in a formidable armchair. He bent his head for a
moment, his hands clasped before him, as if in prayer. When
he looked up, there was a surety in his eyes, which suggested
that despite seeming naïve, he knew more than we expected.

"Mondays and Wednesdays will be your days," he said, because those were the days he was gone. "Melody and I have
come to an agreement, a compromise, since I know she feels
differently about this than me."

Melody was unusually quiet, sitting on the small love seat
across from Cindy and me. She appeared afraid. Jules and Jim
sat to the left of the love seat. I had noticed that Melody had
been more submissive around Henry lately — in a doting way
— kissing him on the lips in public and smiling a false little
smile.

"But why?" Cindy asked. "Excuse me," she said, chuckling
a little, "it just seems silly. Since we're family, and all." She

looked at Melody, then at me, wanting us to back her, but we were quiet. The ends of her hip scars trailed out from her shorts.

Henry leaned back, crossing one leg over the other. Then he uncrossed his legs and leaned forward. He grimaced, turning his head so that first he looked at Melody, and then at Cindy and me sitting on the couch, as if reprimanding us.

"She's *my* wife," he said angrily.

When I saw Cindy's expression, I felt scared for her far more than for myself because she looked as if she'd been punched in the face with a fist, but was trying her best not to appear that she'd been hit. Her face convulsed, slightly, and her lips trembled. She wore a tank top, and a flush rose across her neck. "Of course," she said, her voice shaky, eyes wide open. "That's how it should be."

Melody walked me to my station wagon (my daughter was spending the night there), and even outside, away from Henry, with the stars and moon above us, I could sense the tension, as if Henry followed, lurking in a bush. She kissed me on the cheek, pressed her lips there, reminding me of when she'd kissed me after her wedding ceremony. When she pulled away, she looked around us, almost imperceptibly — to be sure Henry wasn't there, imagined or real. "I'm sorry," she whispered. "He's such an asshole."

Whenever I talked to her after that night, she acted as if she wasn't unhappy, as she had told me almost a year ago, when we'd washed dishes together, and because I wanted to believe her, and because this time she wanted me to believe her as well, I tried, but I couldn't shake the impression that she was protecting me. It was as if power had been transferred from Cindy to Henry that night; and Cindy must have thought so, too, because she sulked whenever she came over; she complained about everything, including men, even in front of Henry.

When I tried to get Melody to confide in me, she acted resigned, saying that she'd changed; she'd matured; she no longer wanted to have affairs, understanding the consequences on a deeper level. But something had been squashed inside her, even if her behavior was more acceptable, less self-destructive. Once in a while she alluded to Henry's terrible temper.

Melody and Henry began taking trips to Aspen to ski, even though Melody had always disliked skiing. I watched their home and fed Jules and Jim, but the thrill had gone, and I saw the home, pool, and view in an ambiguous light, not so easily enjoyed, always laced with a corruptive shame and guilt. Jules and Jim were lethargic and ate little when Melody was away, and I'd let them lie on the furniture, something that Henry prohibited. "I'm sorry," I'd whisper, stroking their little bodies, always firmer than I expected. "Mommy will be home soon." My daughter loved these times, not just because of the home and its luxuries, but because Melody's daughter stayed with us, since Henry wanted Melody to himself.

Maybe that was why Melody was most despondent on these trips. She left phone messages when she couldn't reach me, on my cell phone where she knew the girls wouldn't hear, and these messages were my only real hint at what might be happening inside her.

I saved one of her rambling phone messages, replaying it over and over. I had laughed when I first heard it, but each subsequent listen made my heart crack further. She was driving to town in a rented Lexus, ostensibly to pick up some tampons at a market, but I imagined her real reason was to get away from Henry, and she'd pulled the car over beside a snowy bank.

"Hey," she said, and I heard in her voice that she'd been crying. "I drove past a truck, and there were these teenagers inside it making out, completely, and I made a U-turn and drove back around. I just had to pull over and I've been sitting here, for about ten minutes, watching them, not knowing what to do with myself, and I decided to call. I don't know why." Here she coughed, and it sounded as if she was choking back a sob.

"I don't know what's wrong with me," she said, regaining her composure. "I'm going to check my medication dosage, maybe Doctor Frankel fucked it up, you know. And I've been seeing that therapist like he told me to — Anne Whateverherlastnameis, because Henry can afford it; she's okay. I like her, I guess, but so far, it's not working.

"The thing is, I understand that's not how we are as adults, not like those teenagers. We can't expect to have that anymore. I've grown up in so many ways." She was quiet for a minute, and at first I thought she'd hung up, but then her voice came back, livelier than before: "Well, what can I expect?" She paused again, as if in thought.

"I wish you could've seen them," she said. "They were so into each other, the way they couldn't keep their hands off each other, the way it is when you're in love. They finally drove away, but I'm still here." She sighed, but it wasn't a self-pitying sigh, more as if she was considering how things happen, the way we make sacrifices.

"You know what?" she said, her voice lightening, reminding me of the Melody I'd lived with and worked with; the Melody who slept with women and men, and who would let pass through her lips things that shouldn't be said aloud; the Melody I hadn't appreciated until it was too late, until I'd already done wrong by her. "Between you and me — and you can't tell anyone this, I swear to God. Henry would be so mad and really, I can't complain. He gives me everything I want. You know how it is. I say, 'I want this, I want that.' And he goes out and gets it." She paused, breathing into the phone, possibly deciding whether after her buildup what she had to say was worthwhile.

"Let me tell you," she said, and it seemed she was trying to cheer herself up or cheer me, the way she spoke confidentially, but theatrically, as if she'd pressed her mouth closer to the phone. "I don't mean to complain, but Henry's breath—" She made a noise, *hoo-weee.*

"The thing is," she continued, "he's a really, really, really awful kisser." She laughed before hanging up, and listening each time, I felt a beautiful aching sadness, because her laugh sounded wonderfully free.

John Wayne Loves
Grandma Dot

JOHN WAYNE WANDERED Newport Beach at night. An observer watching him drift through the streets might think his wanderings were random and thoughtless, but John Wayne had his own logic and pattern. He believed in things unseen. He walked slowly past certain homes, skateboard at his side, sensing possibilities, as though the homes were showing him: see, this is how it can be.

He saw the glow from inside a window, sensed the way the kids felt toward the parents, or how the parents loved each other, or even how the dog liked the way he got fed every night and rubbed on his belly. John Wayne lingered, careful not to be noticed. He didn't want to scare anyone; he just wanted to feel.

Most homes reminded him of basements or art galleries: coldness hung around them, a hint of darkness, maybe even abuse. He set his skateboard down and flew past, noticing the flickering lights of a television. His gut reaction might be wrong, but he didn't want to find out. He wanted no part. The gravelly sound of his wheels on the sidewalk calmed him.

His skateboard jumped curbs, flipped down cement steps. Darkness, shadows, moonlight, stars, the constant noise of the ocean, and no one to tell him what to do. He fell, but that was part of the adventure: scrapes and bruises, once a broken arm. A stranger drove him to the hospital. The nurse injected him and told him to count backwards from ten. He tried, but he couldn't remember what came next—ten, nine—that was it. The nurse gave him a troubled look, and he wanted to explain, "Don't worry. I had a drug overdose. I hurt my head," but his mouth wouldn't open. He went under the anesthesia, and he died for a little while. When he woke up, there was a cast on his arm and his head hurt. The dying wasn't so bad. He knew that it was a different kind of sleep, another type of waking.

After the drug overdose, his mother continued to do his laundry and set the baskets by the back door of their house, along with bags of food, but otherwise his family fired him like a bad employee. His brother and sister avoided him. His mom looked at him and sobbed. They called it tough love, but it wasn't about love: John Wayne was an embarrassment.

Although people pitied him (he could see pity in their faces), he didn't think the way he lived was such a bad way to go. He smoked marijuana, even when he took showers, his head far enough from the spray to keep it lit, and an ashtray on the toilet seat for when he washed his hair. He no longer used cocaine and heroin, and although he somehow knew that this was connected to his brain damage, it was a relief. Money was a problem insofar as he had to *do* things to get it. The men took him in their cars, but it was over fast, not so bad when it was quick, and sometimes tender. Unless they got angry and violent and pushed him down. He knew how to fight back, but he hated to hurt anyone; that's why he left home the first time. Once, he stabbed his stepfather's arm with scissors, but it was in self-defense. He had cried for a week. He let the men do what they needed just so long as he could get his money and keep floating through the streets.

Sometimes he slept at the Newport Inn, a run-down hotel on the fringe of Costa Mesa near the freeway. Henry Wilson paid his bill each month in full. John Wayne met him every Wednesday at midnight, Wilson's black Mercedes idling in the dark, the back door ajar. The hotel sign was lit up with blinking red and blue palm trees. He didn't like the loud, drunken fights and the cop cars.

Otherwise, he slept under a bridge. He dug a burrow in the dirt and covered it with cardboard. The sounds of the trucks and cars driving over the bridge was better than the screams, loud music, and sirens at the hotel, but it was cold and there was no bathroom. He used the liquor store bathroom on the other side of Pacific Coast Highway, but the owner hated him ever since he'd caught him stealing a twelve-pack of Coors. John Wayne ran across the highway, twelve-pack under his arm, and ducked under the bridge, the man yelling, "You little fucker! Try that again and I'll shoot your fucking head off!"

John Wayne went to AA and NA meetings. He sat on the raggedy couch, bummed cigarettes, and listened to the people talk. There were free doughnuts, cookies, cakes, and coffee. Once in awhile, he raised his hand, made everyone in the room laugh, announcing, "Hello, my name is John Wayne, and I'm a drug addict." That was all he ever said. The people welcomed him, patted his back, and treated him kindly, and he went for the company, safety, food, coffee, and cigarettes — not to stop using drugs.

He was sorry for his parents and his twin siblings, with their tight faces and tight hearts. They didn't know what it was like to let the ocean come inside you. He felt it course through his veins, a charging through his heart, letting him know that he was nothing but it didn't matter, it was okay to be nothing, because nothing was everywhere: wind, palm trees, even the expensive cars and clothes. How could he explain that it was okay to be nothing? His stepfather called him weak and stupid. When his stepfather yelled at him, he let the words hang over his head like butterflies.

He missed his mom. Sometimes he imagined it was her hot breath whispering in his ear, "You're so beautiful," not Henry Wilson.

John Wayne knew that Rosie watched him from her bedroom deck. His life changed when she gave him the key to Uncle Stan's apartment over the garage of her grandparents' house, where no one went upstairs, except for her.

She didn't make John Wayne do anything. Sometimes, she looked at him like she was sorry for him, but most of the time she just looked at him. People liked to look at him, and he learned not to talk, since that was when people got upset, their eyes changing from pleased to disturbed.

He took long hot showers and left the red light on. There was grace in the walls, the clothes left in the closet and dresser, and the blue bong. It was as if the clothes and bong were waiting for him. The clothes fit him and he liked the tie-dyed shirts and frayed Levi's. He wore Uncle Stan's necklace with the tooth pendant, stroking it for comfort. It was like a slender bone.

From the apartment window, he watched Rosie's grandparents engrossed in their rituals in the house below. There's

Grandpa and Grandma, he thought. Watching them made him feel safe, he didn't know why. They sat on their barstools, eating their meals, a dependability. Grandma Dot had silvery white hair. Grandpa was tanned and there was a patch of white hair on either side of his head in a U shape. The skin between the hair reminded him of a bull's-eye. Their meals were poked and prodded, they took small bites. Grandpa drank vodka martinis with speared olives while Grandma Dot drank Schlitz straight from the can. She was petite, always dressed with care, so the sight of her tipping a can to her coral lips was dramatic. She sat on the barstool with her legs crossed like an aged movie star.

Grandma Dot sensed a presence in her son's apartment above the garage. At first she believed it was poor, troubled, eccentric Rosie. She began leaving two crisp twenty-dollar bills every week (and sometimes three twenty-dollar bills) in one of Grandpa's martini glasses with Spending Money written on a piece of paper and taped to it. She left the glass at the foot of the stairs, and whoever the person was accepted the money, leaving the empty glass for her. She became convinced that it wasn't Rosie. When her Schlitz started disappearing from the garage refrigerator, she bought twelve-packs of Coors and left a note explaining that Schlitz was rather difficult to come by.

John Wayne continued to sneak into the garage and steal the Coors, and although he didn't read a note that was left there, crumpling it into a ball and chucking it in the trash, he understood that he should not touch Grandma Dot's stash.

Grandma Dot was a serious insomniac, her large booze intake also an attempt to lose consciousness. Secretly, when her mind was inebriated enough, she pretended that her son still lived upstairs, that he hadn't left her, and this allowed her to avoid the reality. She saw a red glow from the apartment every night, and the light didn't go off until she herself had abandoned the barstool for bed. She liked the attention.

John Wayne watched Grandma Dot through the kitchen window below while she played Solitaire, sitting on a barstool in the kitchen, on the counter beside her cards, her beer sweating on a napkin, her ashtray stockpiled with stubs, her pack of Merits, and her lighter. Once, late at night, she slipped fluidly off the barstool. He was ready to run down the steps and save her, so sure that she had hurt herself, but she picked herself up and sat herself right back on the barstool. Then she slowly, dramatically, drunkenly lit herself another cigarette.

He saw the hallway light through a bulbous plastic window in the ceiling of the house. It looked like a lit-up blister. He began waiting for the light to go off, and then he would go downstairs; she would leave the front door open for him.

The kitchen counter would be set up for their breakfasts with two green cloth tablemats and a bottle of fake sugar. Their grapefruit spoons lay upon green-checkered napkins, and he would rub his thumb along the sharp ridges, amused that a spoon had this jagged feature. The wooden salt and pepper shakers were between the mats. Inside the refrigerator, he found grapefruit halves, wrapped in cellophane with half cherries bleeding in their centers.

It smelled like Grandma Dot. He loved the smell: part perfume, cigarettes, and something sweet and stale, something purely Grandma Dot. His meal she left for him near a warming oven, covered with tin foil like a Christmas present. He ate at her barstool, as close to her leftover spirit as he could get, careful not to disrupt their morning setups. He became well acquainted with Grandma Dot's taco special, her meatloaf, and her pork chops. He felt privileged, and he loved the meals, as much as he imagined anyone would ever love Grandma Dot's food. There was always a cold beer in the refrigerator. He knew it was his because it was the only bottle of Coors, just one, every time, in a sea of Schlitz.

Grandma Dot's stack of cards sat beside a glass ashtray and a cheap plastic Bic lighter near the telephone. He respected these objects, passing his fingers lightly, reverentially over them. Her cigarette stubs had her bright lipstick prints, like flowers of pink and coral.

Afterwards, he left his plate and his utensils by the sink, where she washed them properly in the morning.

Once in a while, John Wayne would sleep in the small twin bed in The Daisy Room near the hallway, even closer to Grandma Dot. A light sleeper, he left the glass sliding door cracked open so that he could hear the bay. He named every room. The Green Room had wallpaper in the bathroom with green fish on it. The Daisy Room had large daisies across the wallpaper and a magnetic plastic daisy plant where the magnets held the daisies' heads.

He would leave long before the grandparents woke and go back to Uncle Stan's apartment, after making the bed, but leaving the pillow above the bedspread, a signal to Grandma Dot that not only had he eaten her meal, he had slept downstairs. He would lock the front door behind him.

One morning, waking from a deep and safe sleep, he didn't make it back to the apartment before the grandparents woke. He listened patiently to their morning ritual. Grandpa made coughing noises; the newspaper rustled. They never spoke, not even a good morning or goodbye or have a good day. There wasn't hostility; John Wayne would have left. He was done with that. It was as if talking were unnecessary.

The back door slammed. The house shuddered when the garage door opened and shuddered again when it closed. John Wayne and Grandma Dot were alone.

He sneaked back to Uncle Stan's apartment while she washed the dishes, and it was as if she took her time with the dishes, giving him the leeway. She turned off the faucet, hands sudsy with dish soap. He saw her listening for the *tip tap* of his feet.

Holloway's: Part One

WHEN I WAS SEVENTEEN years old, just out of high school, I was a waitress for a restaurant near the Newport Beach Golf and Country Club called Holloway's. The entrance had a graceful ivy-covered arch, and a small brass understated nameplate — easily missed — engraved with the restaurant name; but people in and around the country club knew where Holloway's was, and that the well-to-do dined and socialized there.

Earlier that same year, my father died from a heroin overdose. He'd been estranged from my mom and me for several years, and I thought I'd prepared myself for this outcome, but it still came as a shock. I moved out of our house soon after his funeral, even though Mom wanted me to stay. When I went to collect my clothes, I made sure to go during school hours (she was a high school chemistry teacher), but she was waiting, standing in the hallway. "We need to be together," she said. "This is too much to go through alone." Carrying hangers full of clothes, I pushed past her, shoved her a little. She started crying, loud enough for me to hear. When I did turn around, the tears were coming down her face, and when I shut the front door behind me, I felt an overwhelming sense of remorse, but I left anyway.

I got my job at Holloway's soon after. Julie Anne, owner and boss, was in her early sixties and she only hired young pretty waitresses, women with an eagerness to please. Getting the job was a coup, after an extensive process requiring three separate interviews; the final interview included a timed thirty-minute test on wines and cuisines, and three questions based on Julie Anne's "personal philosophy of service," answered in no less than a paragraph each (most of the applicants were weeded out, proving the maxim that beauty and brains typically do not coexist). The combination of exclusivity, immaturity, proximity to privilege, and instant cash contributed to the waitresses' arrogance and greed. Theirs was a self-contained little world, complete with cliques and gossip and subdivisions of friendships, and I was no different from them.

On my first morning, I "shadowed" another waitress, Jennifer, standing directly behind her, silently observing. Businessmen occupied dark oak tables covered in white tablecloths, sipping coffee, eating bowls of oatmeal, scrambled egg whites, and dry wheat toast, and shuffling newspapers. Julie Anne was a late sleeper, and because I ended up working the morning shift, I rarely saw her — besides, she worked the least of everyone. Her office was a side room, separated from the kitchen and restaurant. She shared the office with Sheila, an overweight and sullen accountant who drove a brick-red Buick with the bumper sticker "It's a child, not a choice" to the bank every other day, to deposit cash from the safe.

I was following Jennifer to a table when she stopped and said "Shit." A tall, angular man was leaving Julie Anne's office, shutting the door behind him, wearing an expensive-looking dark suit, and carrying a tan leather briefcase. His shoulders were stooped, and his hair — yellowish gray and wispy — was flapped out at the sides like bird wings. Even before I saw him up close, I could tell he was an old man who had probably once been handsome. His cheeks were sunken, giving his face a skeletal quality, and covered in grayish stubble. As he got closer, he saw us, and his face transformed into a fierce smile.

"Willy," Jennifer said, her tone harassed, "meet Harriet."

Willy put his hand out. When I put my hand forward, he swept his back, pretending to smooth his hair, which simply flapped to its original position. "Ahh," he said, "got you!" He set his briefcase on the floor; he was smiling desperately, his gums pink and receded; I caught a whiff of peppermint on his breath.

"What" — Jennifer's voice lifted, in time with her raised eyebrows, as if reprimanding a child — "were you doing in Julie Anne's office?"

Willy nudged my arm with his hand. "Business, just business." I was stunned that he included me. The corner of his mouth was red and cracked in what appeared to be a painful canker sore.

I'd already been warned by Julie Anne, told not to accept Willy's credit cards, personal checks, or to let him sign for meals (regulars had accounts). I'd been told that Willy harassed customers, sitting down to dine with "friends," making them listen to hopeless business proposals, and leaving early — an appointment, an important phone call — forcing them to pay. I'd been told about his connection to Holloway's. Julie Anne, some thirty years before, after a bitter divorce that left her as close to destitute as any woman born and raised in Newport

Beach could be, had gone to Evelyn Breen Holloway, longtime friend and heir to the impressive Vanderkemp fortune.

Thus, Holloway's was born from hard times, funded by the Vanderkemps. In honor of Evelyn's generosity, a portrait hung beside the bookshelf — Evelyn, in muted, dark colors, hands crossed at her lap, sitting stiffly in a straight-backed chair (she looked much like Julie Anne: coiffed hair, prideful expression, impressive jewelry). Five years ago, Evelyn had died from bone cancer, and William J. Holloway, Willy, as he was called, was in the process of pissing away the final dregs of Evelyn's fortune, that is, what little the Vanderkemps had left to him; a journey that he'd begun thirty-eight years before, I was bitterly informed, when he'd proposed to Evelyn, and she'd said yes, despite her family's disapproval and Willy's gambling, playboy, alcoholic ways. Julie Anne had tolerated him all these years, "for Evelyn's sake," but her charity was all used up, and even Willy's grown children were through with him.

"Listen," Jennifer said, rolling her eyes. "Don't go in the office. Okay? Just don't."

"I made one phone call," Willy said.

Jennifer shook her head grimly.

Willy turned his attention to me. "My wife" — he nodded at her portrait — "decorated this place."

I didn't know how to respond.

Willy looked past me. "Well if it isn't Henry Wilson," he called out. "What luck! Henry, I've been trying to reach you."

I heard shuffling and glanced over my shoulder: Henry had set his newspaper in a position to block himself from view.

"I don't have time for this," Jennifer said. It was like watching an old stray dog get kicked. Her voice had lost all animation.

"Hold on," Willy said, leaning over, opening his briefcase—but Jennifer was already leaving. Being new, I didn't yet know how to summarily dismiss customers, and I watched Willy shuffle through his briefcase; the inside was lined in a softer tan, pockets at the side stuffed with papers. There was Trident gum, a silver flask with some kind of engraving—possibly a family coat of arms—and one book: *The Varieties of Religious Experience* by William James.

He glanced up with a sharp smile. "Aha!" He pulled out an eight-by-ten-inch glossy photograph, held it to his chest. "Did Julie Anne say bad things about me? What'd she say?"

I kept my face neutral.

He paused, letting his fingertips touch his canker sore. "You're a cutie"—he drew my name out—"Harrrrieett. Tell me about yourself."

I told him that I'd graduated from Fountain Valley High School, that I had plans to attend El Camino Community College, about my accomplishments, my goals, blah, blah, blah—it was the same spiel I'd given Julie Anne on interview number one, but Willy seemed bored, like he didn't believe anything I was saying, and then he interrupted: "What'd she say about me? C'mon, c'mon."

When I didn't answer, he said, "Lies! All lies!"

"I'm being trained," I said.

"Let me ask a question," he said, "and I want you to think long and hard before you answer: What's the name of this restaurant?"

"Holloway's."

"That's my name!" he said, as if in shock.

He still held the photograph to his chest. The long fingers of his other hand brushed my arm. "You watch out," he said.

"She'll suck the skin right off, eat your flesh, chew you up, suck suck suck, until there's nothing left." He made a sudden movement with his hand—photograph flapping. "They're all like that, every single one." I didn't know who he meant, but I assumed he was talking about Julie Anne and the entire clientele of Holloway's.

He nodded toward Julie Anne's office. "I know the combination." His voice was low, referring to the safe. The safe required both the combination and an unlocking by key. "I wasn't making a phone call. I was looking for the key. Looked everywhere."

When I didn't answer, he said, "You got a key?" He poked his finger at my arm. "You holding out?"

There was a long pause and he continued to stare. "You think I'm kidding," he said.

"I'm being trained," I said.

"Guess who?" He handed me the photograph, and although I knew the answer, I stared at it silently, ashamed for him, my face heating up. It was a young Willy, of course, the same fierce smile, wearing an old Stanford football uniform—the leather helmet had long ears like a ski hat, his pants were laced; he was kneeling on one knee, probably in the same position he'd proposed to Evelyn, and the thin fingers of his right hand were balanced at the tip of a puffy-looking football.

I handed back his photo, avoiding his eyes, and moved away without saying goodbye.

"You don't know me," he called out.

Jennifer was placing an order that showed on a computer screen and I came up behind her.

"He's a total freak," she said, not looking at me. "Next time, ignore him." She laughed, so I laughed with her, but when I looked back, Willy was watching me, his lips in a thin frown, and he set his photograph in his briefcase without looking away.

I soon learned that our tips were collected and guarded religiously in ceramic containers beneath the cash register, labeled with each waitress's name, and decorated individually, with peace signs, hearts, and the like. We divvied out cash from our tips at the end of our shifts. There were constant complaints (warranted and ignored) about our dishonesty regarding tip totals, and tensions over percentages (2 percent dishwasher, 3 percent hostess, and 10 percent busboy, give or take, at our discretion). I made minimum wage, same as the dishwashers and busboys, but my income skyrocketed beyond theirs because of the tips.

Later, I calculated that in a year's time, I made more money than my mother. She'd been trying to get in touch with me, but I avoided her, never answered my phone. She'd leave messages, an almost inaudible, strained, earnestly stuttering "uh uh uh . . . Harriet, we need to talk," and I'd delete them, without listening to the rest. I missed her throat-clearing cough, and how she smelled in the mornings, a musty coffee smell, but I resented her; I didn't want to live a compliant life: she was always cleaning up after my dad, making excuses for him, giving him money, and after she kicked him out of the house for the thousandth time, and he really left for good, she never got over it. She used to insist on "family dinners" when Dad was around, as if to prove that we were normal, that we'd be just fine; he'd sit there, listening, trying to eat, but he always looked like he was scarcely there, like he didn't quite belong. As a kid, and even when I was old enough to know better, it seemed to me that I was somehow to blame, that if I could just say the right things, smile the right way, he might settle into his skin and be okay.

Once, when I was a freshman in high school, I heard these assholes making fun of Mom's "camel-toe" — her slacks buttoned high at her waist, accentuating her stomach, thighs, and the crevice between her legs. When I walked past their lockers, I could still hear them laughing, and I hated them, but at the same time, I willfully denied any biological connection to her. And I pretty much continued to do so, for the rest of high school: I completely avoided her. She wore sad-looking blouses, tucked tightly into her pants, and a thin leather belt with a turquoise-studded belt buckle shaped like a four-leaf clover; and I hated her for being so practical, for balancing the checkbook and paying the bills at the kitchen table, for having sallow skin, for the way her neck and chest speckled pink with emotion, for her brownish gray hair, and even for how she wore her reading glasses low on her nose.

Having been raised in a house bereft of luxuries, I was hungry for what I thought Holloway's represented. Along with a dusky green Ford Fiesta and an improved wardrobe, I was able to afford a small apartment near El Camino Community College, which I attended part time, in hopes of one day obtaining a business degree, or at least some type of practical degree that would advance my position in the world; but I secretly imagined one of Holloway's wealthy male customers whisking me away from a life of servitude and four to six years of academic drudgery, landing me in the existence that I felt I deserved. I, of course, would reimburse my husband and benefactor with children — heirs to his fortune — as well as with companionship and the simple aesthetic reward of my presence.

So I really didn't understand it when I sabotaged my chances by becoming involved with an El Salvadorian dishwasher named Marlon Dominguez, a twenty-one-year-old art student and self-described modernist painter, whom everyone called Lobo. Like the other dishwashers and kitchen workers, he wore Levi's, a thick cotton white shirt that fastened with metal snaps (Holloway's embroidered in red thread at his chest pocket), and an ugly black net over his longish dark hair. Behind the heavy swinging doors, separating the white patrons and waitresses on the restaurant side from the workers on the kitchen side, most everyone was dark-skinned. A continuous sexual tension hummed between the waitresses and the kitchen workers, fomented by race, power, and income disparity, and I was accustomed to inappropriate comments regarding my anatomy and whistles whenever I passed through the doors. But with Lobo, things got out of hand quickly.

I was working a morning shift when my busboy disappeared, forcing me to bus my table. As soon as I went through the kitchen doors, a steamy heat overcame me. I wasn't used to witnessing the amount of work that went into creating the dishes that I presented—it was like glancing behind the curtains at a play. When I set my plates at the sink, Lobo gripped my arm. He had on yellow kitchen gloves and the fingers were damp. He was tall, thin, intense, and his shoes were these crazy, greasy-looking moccasins. "Hey," he said, "hey; hey there; I haven't seen you before." My uniform consisted of black slacks, a white oxford shirt, and a slim black tie—not sexy at all, and I was insecure about it.

"I guess not," I said, which was a stupid thing to say. My hair was in a bun at the back of my head, a loose strand plastered to my cheek. I wanted to swipe at it but was too self-conscious.

"What's your name?" he asked.

"Harriet."

"Seriously?" he asked, his head going back; the other dish-washer snorted and said something in Spanish—something lewd and suggestive—but Lobo didn't laugh, his eyes on me, dark and serious. "Can I call you Harry?" he said. He didn't appear to be joking.

"No," I said, which was also a stupid thing to say. I shook my arm from his grip.

He put his yellow-gloved hands in the air, as if I were a wild horse. "Easy, Harry. Easy now."

As I walked away, I was aware that both dishwashers were staring at my backside. It felt like a heat going all the way down my legs—but it was Lobo that I really felt; the heat stayed coiled inside me, right between my hipbones, long after the heavy doors swung behind me.

Our first encounter took place a week later in the walk-in refrigerator, where I followed him as though I'd been hypno-tized. He pushed a cooler stuffed with dead fowl in front of the door so that no one could open it. Standing near the egg cartons and milk cartons, we felt each other up for close to five minutes, fierce and hostile gropings, our breath visible in puffs. Even though I tried to avoid the temptation, and I got the impression he was wary of me as well, the second meeting took place about two weeks later. It was bound to happen. We found our way inside the outdoor walk-in pantry (which had a lock that locks from the inside and eventually became our meeting place). Desperate and graceless, he bit my lip, caus-ing it to bleed, upsetting him as well. Lobo would have prob-ably preferred a bohemian girlfriend, open to discussions of art and socialism, not a business major like me, but we soon became consumed with each other—we wanted to consume each other. Just as I only wanted to smell him and feel him, I knew that he didn't want anyone else. So, in something like shock, and out of sheer practicality, I scheduled an appointment at Planned Parenthood and got my first prescription for birth control pills.

One morning, about a month into my job, Sheila came from the office, telling Jennifer to cover for me. I followed Sheila into the office and she handed me the phone. Julie Anne was calling from her home and I could hear her television in the background.

"Do you enjoy working at Holloway's?" Julie Anne asked. Sheila stood near the copy machine, pretending not to listen.

"Oh yes," I said, gripping the receiver tightly and turning my body toward the corner, so that Sheila couldn't see my face.

"Good, because we think you're an absolute delight. A gem." There was a pause. "Your mother called me, Harriet. She said she's been trying to get a hold of you."

I felt something like a hand creeping up the back of my neck at the thought of Mom anywhere near Julie Anne: her Mom Pants and her lucky clover belt, her 1970s purse, and the way she acted around rich people: superior and deferential and judgmental all at once.

Julie Anne explained that family disputes had no place in a work forum. She was a busy woman and didn't have time to be a mediator. There was an undercurrent of sympathy — she didn't blame me for my background, for having a mom like that; but Holloway's had a reputation, and just as waitresses weren't allowed to dye their hair or wear garish makeup, I needed to keep my mother from causing any scenes.

"I'll let her know," I said, in complete earnestness, "never to call you again."

"That won't be necessary," Julie Anne said. "I already told her that myself."

And for a while I was able to forget about my mom and avoid grieving for my dad, much less think about him. Good money coming in, a wallet full of cash. Watching the men's faces light up when I brought their coffee and food. My body learning all kinds of new pleasures with Lobo. Not necessarily wanting to be in love, but the words "I love you" slipping out every now and then anyway.

"Know what I think, Harry?" Lobo asked, our fifth or sixth night sleeping on the futon at my apartment. Earlier, driving away from Holloway's, I'd seen Willy in my rearview mirror — I was 99.9 percent sure it was him — staggering drunkenly across an intersection, a car honking.

"Shh," I said, "don't talk." There were two messages from my mom on my answering machine, and Lobo had already made it clear that he thought I should call her back.

"Just listen, because I really want to tell you something."

"What?" I said, turning to face him.

"You're deluding yourself. From everything you've ever told me, she's done nothing horrible. Blaming her, like she killed your dad or something, when all she did was love him." And then, perhaps as an afterthought, he said, "You don't ever talk about him."

Without wanting to, I thought of Dad carrying me to my bed after I'd fallen asleep in the back seat of Mom's Monte Carlo: where had we come from? — A long car drive, late at night; I was half asleep, my thin arms around his neck, my face pressed in the space between his shoulder and his chest. My night-light was on, and his smile hovered over me while I lay in bed, watching him. There was a sad dreaminess about his smile, in its unpredictable arrival and how it echoed the sadness in his eyes. And then he sat on my bed and stroked my hair until I couldn't keep my eyes open.

It angered me that Lobo would want me to dredge up memories, and I sat up on the futon, a sharp pain in my chest. "Fuck you," I said, without any passion. "Try dissecting your own life." There was a cottony sensation in my head, and I remembered the rushing sound I heard, like an ocean between my ears, when Mom and I came home from my swimming lesson—maybe I was five or six—at the YMCA, and Mom was still in her car, parked in our garage, looking for a stupid fountain pen that had fallen out of her purse, and I found Dad sprawled on the kitchen tile, his arm hooked under him. I stood over him, weeping, and I wanted to lie on top of him and sink into him, but I couldn't move. And when Mom finally came in from the garage, she rushed me out of the kitchen, made me sit on the sofa. After a few moments, she came back from the kitchen, put a wet towel on the back of my neck, promised me that he was not dead, that he was just sleeping. And for a long time after that, every time he left the house, or when I couldn't keep track of him, like when I'd have to go to school, or even when he'd use the bathroom and shut the door behind him, so that I couldn't see, I'd hear that same ocean sound, and I'd think, He will die. This time, he will die.

Something desperate and frightening must have showed in my face because Lobo looked at me apologetically. I leaned over and bit his shoulder, hard. "Fuck," he said, in an injured voice. My front teeth had made two matching purple welts. "That really hurts."

He gently pushed me down on the futon, set his knee on my thigh, his hands holding my shoulders. He knew I preferred our aggressions and confusions to be physical rather than verbal. I pretended to struggle; but after a moment, when I really tried to get up, he was stronger. I managed to press my knee against his chest; he shoved my knee with one hand so my thigh splayed open, the fingers of his other hand pinching my nipple. He lost his balance, landing on me with such force, that for a second I couldn't breathe, and I willingly lost myself in a black space of nothing.

I'd been at Holloway's for over three months when I was trusted with opening the restaurant, a job that Jennifer readily handed over, along with a set of keys, because of the requirement of arriving before dawn. At the end of my shift, I collected money from the register, set it in an envelope along with the receipt for my total sales, and placed it in the deposit slot of the safe. I could hear the envelope *thump* to the base, and I discovered the safe's combination taped to the back of the safe. Only Julie Anne and Sheila had keys.

Opening Holloway's ended up being my favorite part of the job. I was alone on the restaurant side, separated from the kitchen workers, and I kept the front door locked to avoid any early-bird customers. I flapped out the crisp tablecloths over the tables. I brewed coffee, the aroma filling the restaurant. I placed folded napkins and silverware, salt and pepper shakers, sugar decanters, and vases of yellow tulips at each table; all the while the sky changed — inky blue to a dark glow with sunrise to finally a clear light blue. The kitchen workers listened to Spanish radio stations, and I'd wait until the last possible moment to ask them to turn their radios off. Then I'd turn on the stereo in Julie Anne's office to the requisite opera.

One morning, unlocking and opening Julie Anne's office door to turn on the stereo, I hit the light switch and almost screamed. Willy was curled up on the floor, his suit jacket rolled into a ball as a pillow. His briefcase was leaned against the filing cabinet and his leather loafers were underneath Julie Anne's desk. Willy had been coming in less, once a month, sometimes twice, and I'd become more adept at ignoring him. He would small talk customers, displaying his usual exaggerated cheerfulness, and two or three of his longtime friends—like Mr. Deader—still paid for his meals; also a self-important pastor, fittingly named Dick: a man who always wore his clerical collar and enjoyed making me stand at the table for five minutes like a mute idiot, while he pretended to struggle over what to order.

Willy sat up, foggy-eyed, a deep crease at his cheek from the indentation of a jacket button, his yellow gray hair nested at the side of his head. There was no pretense at cheeriness, no chatter—he only stared at me, propped by his arm on the floor, defeated. The room smelled like alcohol. It was awful; I didn't know what to say. I remembered him staggering across the intersection, more poignant now than when I'd watched.

After a long and strained silence where we continued to stare at each other, he said, "Are you going to tell?" I felt more intimate than I'd ever felt with a man, even more so than with Lobo, like having sex with the lights on, but without the sex—pain, longing, unhappiness—something honest and frightening between us.

"I don't think so."

"That's a good girl," he said. His eyes stayed on me and I realized that it was his way of saying thank you.

I didn't say anything, feeling overcome. And suddenly I wanted to be a kid again, burrow my head in my dad's waist and sob—the way I used to when I had stubbed my toe or scraped my knee—smell him and feel his fingers in my hair. Bumblebee, he used to call me. My little bumblebee. I pressed my palms against my eyes, forced myself not to cry. A built-up kind of grief pushed its way back through my throat and into my stomach. I heard a soft clunk and released my hands.

Willy was having trouble standing and had knocked over a stapler from Julie Anne's desk. "Are you okay?" I asked.

"Yeah, yeah," he said, letting himself sit again, his body thumping to the floor. "Yeah, yeah, yeah, yeah." His face was turned away. I wasn't sure what to do, and I had to steel myself from crying again. And for a second, I thought he might be weeping without making any noise, but then I realized he was only thinking.

"I want you to know," he said finally, a bitter firmness to his voice, still looking away, "that no matter what Julie Anne said or any of them told you: I loved my wife."

"Okay," I said, because it seemed important to respond.

"I love her," he said, looking at me.

We were silent for a few moments—he was composing himself, putting his jacket on; but when he tried to stand again, he needed my help. "Sorry," he said, unsteady against me, getting his bearings.

He slipped on his loafers, leaning over awkwardly to get them past his heels, and then he left. I probably could've stopped him in time, let him know that he'd forgotten his briefcase. And I shouldn't have opened it, but I did. It was more scuffed up than I remembered, the corners frayed, the inside lining torn. All the papers were gone; *The Varieties of Religious Experience* was gone. A small plastic bag held a bar of soap, the size of my palm. And what surprised me most was an envelope, unsealed, containing a small child's tooth (it looked like a molar, a little dried blood, black and crusted at the top), with a note on a scrap of paper, in a child's scrawl: Dear Tooth Fairy, How old are you? Are you a boy or a girl? And an answer in careful block letters on the other side: I am neither male nor female and I am ageless. There was a yellow toothbrush, bristles damp, and a travel-sized Vidal Sassoon shampoo bottle. The flask was empty, smelling of whiskey, with its family crest now clearly visible: an eagle, talons holding a key. And that must have been how I got my idea.

Everything happened so quickly. If I'd had a day or two to think, I wouldn't have done it: I hid Willy's briefcase in the outdoor pantry, behind the stacked bags of flour, and by the time I met Lobo in the pantry for our 10:15 A.M. rendezvous, I had already taken the safe-key from Sheila's key ring, which she kept in her desk drawer, while she went to the bathroom for her usual post-espresso crap.

"You have to get this copied," I said, "by noon."

Lobo's lips were at my neck and he pushed my hand with the key in it away.

"I'm serious; but you can't ask any questions."

He took the key from me and said, with some incredulity, "Is this for the safe?" I didn't answer, and his face broke into a slow smile. "There's no way," he said. "I'm not doing it."

He got me the copy by 11:30 A.M., and the tricky part was getting it back on the key ring, but I managed by messing up my sales by ten dollars, requiring Sheila's expertise at the cash register. While she examined the register tape, forehead creased in annoyance, I slipped into her office and put the safe-key back on her key ring.

I knew Willy had his own set of keys to Holloway's, and that he would be back for his briefcase, and possibly for a place to sleep. After the restaurant closed, I parked two streets east of Holloway's. I wore sweats and walked quickly, like the jog-walkers I'd seen around the neighborhood. There was a half moon and the streets were quiet, except for the occasional sprinkler. And it smelled good: of grass and magnolia and the night itself. My urgency had to do with my anger and grief. My emotions seemed to light up all at once, reckless and destructive — almost like Willy's anger got caught up with mine.

I opened the pantry with my key and found his briefcase behind the bags of flour, where I'd left it. Willy might've already been camped out in Julie Anne's office, but as soon as I got there, I knew he hadn't arrived yet. To make sure he wouldn't miss it, I taped the safe-key to the briefcase with masking tape, and set his briefcase in the middle of the office, in the exact spot where I'd found him curled up. My blood was speeding in my veins and I kept the lights off. I imagined Willy taking the cash and jewelry from the safe, starting over somewhere else, where people didn't belittle him because he was a rich man who was now poor. I imagined him reading *The Varieties of Religious Experience,* talking to a pastor who wasn't Dick, maybe finding some kind of meaning, in part because of his struggles. And I know what the psychologists would say: that really I was still trying to save Dad. That I was grieving him, in my own distorted way. But at the time I didn't see my activity as criminal or psychologically motivated, believing that what I was doing was more justifiable than Julie Anne collecting money to buy yet another stunning piece of jewelry.

That night, instead of sleeping at my apartment, I went home. I didn't cry in my mom's arms and she didn't cry in mine, but I did tell her that I was sorry, news to which she responded with reticence and relief. And if I could've articulated it, I might have acknowledged that I'd been blaming her for what had happened, even though her endurance and practicality were born from an acceptance of her responsibilities, mainly to me: her kid. I might have told her that a shift had occurred, and that I hoped never again to mistake love for weakness or wealth for superiority. I lay in my old bedroom, unable to sleep, watching the moon and trees make shapes on my wall; and when I got up to get ready for work, Mom had placed a note for me on the kitchen table: Harriet, have a good day. Love, Mom.

When I opened the restaurant, I noticed right away, even in the dark, that the head had been raggedly cut out of Evelyn's portrait, as if with a knife, and it angered me, because I knew that Willy wanted to get caught, that part of his satisfaction was Julie Anne knowing. I opened the office, and there was no sign of him, the safe door closed; but when I looked in the wastebasket, a curled ball of masking tape was at the bottom.

I went about my morning, headless Evelyn for the first time not watching me serve. A couple of customers chuckled when they saw Evelyn, but none asked questions. The kitchen workers weren't allowed on the restaurant side, but Lobo poked his head through the swinging doors, evidently to check on me, and when he saw the portrait, he seemed genuinely alarmed. "Are you okay?" he whispered. When Sheila arrived, at first she didn't notice the portrait, but when she was preparing her espresso, I heard her gasp, and then she was moving to the phone, asking, "Why didn't you call the police?" She hunched her back away from me, clearly angry, and spoke into the phone.

The police caught Willy less than eight hours later, at the Santa Anita Race Track in Arcadia. And it was all anyone talked about at the restaurant, for a long time after, customers speaking in self-righteous tones, Dick letting it be known that he'd tried everything, but that some men were irredeemable. Julie Anne filed charges and Willy was sentenced to nine months in jail.

"I understand how Willy had a set of keys to the restaurant and to my office, because of Evelyn, of course," I heard Julie Anne tell a customer, "but what I still don't get and what the police haven't been able to figure out, even after repeated, harsh interrogations, mind you, is how he got a key to that goddamn safe."

I don't know what happened to Willy afterwards, because by the time he was released from jail, I'd been fired, along with Lobo, supposedly for our "indiscretions" in the pantry, but really because Jennifer and the other waitresses had it in for me by then. Lobo went to work at the country club as a locker room attendant, and I started living with my mom again; it broke my heart when I found out that Lobo was doing drugs, and eventually I cut all ties. Before that happened, sometimes we'd talk about Willy, Lobo amazed that we took such a risk. "All for that idiot," he'd say.

And maybe Willy's nature was self-destructive and selfish, spending the cash on racehorses instead of getting a foothold at some kind of life; maybe he was incapable of finding light and hope and redemption; maybe he was a useless fool; but I'll always remember my elation when, at the end of my shift, drama high in the air and everyone whispering hypotheses, employees waiting to be called into Julie Anne's office for our "interviews" with the police, I decided to count the tips from my ceramic container. A flap of paper billowed out, along with all the bills and coins. I recognized it from his briefcase. I am neither male nor female and I am ageless, I read. And below, he'd put his initials: WJH.

The First and Second Time

ROSIE AND HER FATHER sat at a picnic table facing a man-made pond in Tee Winkle Park. Earlier, he'd watched her tennis match at the high school and she still wore her uniform. The ducks waddled to the pond, dunked their feet, and then floated across the water's surface, creating ripples. This safe, generic park was his preferred site for Big Talks.

"Your body is a temple," he said, leaning forward with his hands pressed together, fingers creating a steeple; she thought he looked sincere. They were polite and reserved in each other's company. "And your job is to stay a virgin for that one special man you will marry." His face came up, punctuating his declaration with a steady gaze. She read the look of disappointment in his eyes, and he must've seen it in hers—they both looked away. Two Sundays ago, after a church service, he'd given her a painfully comprehensive version of this same monologue, complete with Bible passages endorsing his position, and he appeared to be making one last abbreviated attempt.

Rosie was fifteen, and her sexual experience consisted of kissing and fondling (buffered by clothing), but she was on fire with curiosity. She'd learned about sex through word of mouth and the occasional *Playboy*. As a child, she'd invented Baby, whereby she'd powdered and diapered—with a dishtowel—a fellow male playmate's "private area" and then the procedure was reciprocated. When she got her period at twelve, B had a sketchy sex talk with her because she was "officially a woman." And although she was aware of the shame and disgrace that B's sex life had wrought, she was also aware of the payoffs: "Sex can be wonderful," B had told her, "if it's with the right person." But in her observation, men had power, and it appeared that the most power women had was through their ability to obtain men.

And how could she be made for just one man? She wanted options. Grandma Dot had been married forever to Grandpa, and all that did was ensure her a life of cooking, cleaning, and serving. Grandma Dot, while ironing one of Grandpa's shirts, had even said, "Don't ever become like me."

Her father extracted a cracker package from the side pocket of his Members Only jacket. He fiddled with the wrapper, breaking a saltine and throwing the pieces on the grass near his feet. "Why does everything have to change," he said in an uncharacteristic flare of self-pity, shaking his head, "when all I want is for things to stay the same?"

A wave of tenderness swept over her: he would often tell her nostalgic stories about the fifties, and she knew that what he craved was simplicity, clear answers, what she imagined as men coming home from work wearing pressed slacks and ties, briefcases at their sides, their wives in flowered dresses with aprons, cocktails in their hands, waiting by the front doors.

Qualities that he had successfully spent his life burying were already beginning to bloom in her, namely defiance.

"It's okay," she said.

The ducks approached cautiously, waddling in a round-about way to the cracker pieces, eyeing them, making grunting noises — not quack quack — more like *unngh unngh*. In the distance, people walked dogs and rode bicycles. There was the pong sound of tennis balls from nearby courts.

She saw an old wisp of a man stooped in a wheelchair, blanket across his lap. A brown-skinned woman stood behind him with her hands at the wheelchair. They were on the other side of the pond, but she could see the man was smoking a fat cigar — puffs of hazy smoke.

"What a shame," her father said, squinting in the same direction. "He shouldn't be smoking." He looked at Rosie for confirmation, but she imagined the caretaker allowing the man this final indulgence, and her father stared down at his loafers.

She had a sinking feeling. If only she could be like Kristen Johnson. It was a recurring yearning, but a fundamental impossibility. And besides, she didn't really want to be Kristen Johnson; she just longed to please her father. The Johnsons were her father's friends. Kristen Johnson was demure with blond hair and blue eyes, near Rosie's age, and her father always compared Kristen to her — i.e., Kristen Johnson is a cheerleader. Kristen Johnson is in the church choir. Kristen Johnson is saving herself for marriage. Kristen Johnson is the leader of her Bible study group. Her father would point Kristen out in the choir. "There's Kristen. Do you see her?" "I see her," she would reply, watching Kristen's pink mouth open in song, hands crossed modestly at her front, and she would hate Kristen for being the daughter her father would never have.

Rosie had once been Daddy's little princess. Before the divorce, her father had slept in the guest room on the foldout sofa bed. Above the sofa was a crudely drawn picture of ice skaters. Her room was next to this room, and often her father would climb into her bed, on top of her beige silk comforter.

He would fall asleep easily. She never got accustomed to having her father's adult-sized body in her bed, and she would not sleep. It made her feel weird, as if she was the wife and not the daughter, but she would let him stay because she knew he was desperately lonely.

She would become hyperaware of his breathing, the way it would develop into a snore, counting the seconds between her breaths and his long breaths. She would try to time her breaths to his, but she could not.

He had hair on his arms; his lips parted when he fell asleep; a scar divided his left eyebrow; his mustache brushed against his top lip; his face relaxed. Eventually, he would stir and turn, curling into a fetal position. She would move her body if his arm or leg touched.

Always, he would wake, startled by one of his more resonant snores, or for no predictable reason. She would pretend to be asleep. She didn't want him to feel guilty about keeping her awake.

Sometimes, smelling of moist sleep, his lips would touch her cheek, his mustache brushing against her skin. He always returned to the sofa bed. She would feel relief when he left, although she would curl into the warm spot his body had created on her bed, and finally drift to sleep.

· · ·

The Clash's "Should I Stay or Should I Go?" played at low volume on the car stereo, and Rosie knew that her father wasn't changing the station because she liked the song. The first time he'd heard it, he'd said to the radio, "You should go!," and she half expected him to repeat this, because he'd made her laugh; but he was silent, their goodbye tinged with resignation and sorrow. When they arrived at her house, he got out of his Buick to come around and hug her. She knew he was anxious, hoping not to see B and Will, since Will was the man B had The Affair with and he hated them both.

"I still have to pack," she said, to distract him.

"How do you pack for a yacht?" he said, with his fake British accent. Rosie had been invited for a weekend trip to Catalina Island with her friend Isabella and Isabella's parents on their yacht, *The Golden Eagle*.

When they hugged, they were conscious of her breasts. It was difficult to hug without letting her breasts touch him. She arched her upper back so that her breasts caved inward. She noticed that he hunched his back as well.

While her father pretended her breasts did not exist, when she and her friend Chris hung out at the Peninsula or at the beach, other men offered vocal confirmation of their existence — whistles and hoots and pleas to just let them see. Recently, a marine had bought them a twelve-pack of Michelob — all they had to do was lift their tops; she'd followed Chris's lead, but hadn't ventured further the way Chris had, by pulling up her bra as well. Breasts, she believed, were powerful tools.

She stopped hugging her father first, hands dropping to her sides. His cheerfulness was usually tinged with hostility, but this time his smile was covered in grief, and she smiled back, exactly the same.

• • •

"Come on," Isabella said, when Rosie arrived. "I made chocolate chip cookies." Rosie followed her to the kitchen, where Isabella held a cookie to her own nostrils and inhaled noisily. Isabella was pretty — long brown hair, round face, moon eyes, and gentle features — but in a way not recognized by Newport standards. Her body was naturally inclined toward softness and curves, and she was at war with it. Rosie was used to Isabella denying herself the satisfaction of consumption, instead cooking and smelling forbidden food products: brownies, cakes, cookies, fudge.

Whenever Rosie came over, she rode the elevator because Isabella had an elevator in her house. There were antique vases, chandeliers, and Isabella's mom, Mrs. Leer, lurked about, noticing lint on the carpet, a lamp not in place, a painting improperly slanted. Rosie pressed a button, and they rode to the third floor. The doors opened — she pressed another button, the doors closed, and they descended.

Mrs. Leer waited at the bottom floor so that when the mirrored doors opened, she said, "That's enough," in her French accent, her foot against the door. When any type of heightened emotion engaged Mrs. Leer, she spoke French. *"Allons-y,"* she said.

Isabella apologized. She was keen on pleasing her mother, and Rosie was sorry for her: pleasing Mrs. Leer was on par with walking on the moon. Mr. Leer — a squat man who didn't talk much — walked past them toward the sliding glass doors, Rosie's suitcase tucked under his arm.

Just once, accidentally, Isabella had seen her younger half brother and half sister. Mr. Leer gave money to keep the children away. She had told Rosie about it in a hushed voice, even though they were the only ones in Isabella's bedroom: "They were waiting in a car, I saw them from my window . . . a little girl and a little boy . . . so cute. Daddy wrote a check to a woman . . ."

Isabella's willingness to toe the line came from her understanding that her legitimacy was a matter of luck; she didn't want to fuck up her good fortune and be Daddy-less; although Rosie's secret belief was that it wasn't purely luck: Mr. Leer was afraid of Mrs. Leer—he watched his wife closely, taking his cues from her.

The motor of *The Golden Eagle* rumbled and the air smelled of gasoline. Mr. Leer untied the ropes from the dock outside their house and then jumped on to the boat. Mrs. Leer had set out wooden bowls of pretzels and mixed nuts on the yacht's dining table. Mr. Leer wore a captain's hat, his hands on the spokes of a large steering wheel, guiding the boat out of the dock. Isabella sniffed a pretzel, then inserted it in her mouth and chewed. When Mrs. Leer was looking out the window, Rosie saw Isabella spit the gooey mass into a star-spangled bar napkin and throw it away.

Rosie and Isabella changed into their bathing suits in the master bedroom. They climbed steps that went to the top of the boat, Isabella wearing a blue one-piece. She had a pear-shaped body and wore a towel around her hips when ambulatory, to keep her lower half hidden. Rosie wore her new red bikini; she enjoyed the way she looked when she wore it, the bottom half tied at her hips. She liked her stomach when she sucked it in.

They lay on their towels and watched *The Golden Eagle*'s wake slicing through the ocean. Seagulls and pelicans swooped and glided with the wind; the ocean looked like brushed dark velvet. They played checkers, read magazines — pages flapping in the wind — and talked about boys. They had a heated argument over debutante balls and the charity league. Most of the tension revolved around Rosie's ambivalence about attending Isabella's upcoming debutante ball, Isabella claiming that Chris had unduly influenced Rosie. Isabella and Chris hated each other, and Rosie's friendship with Chris was a tender subject.

After two hours, Catalina came into focus: they could see individual bushes and trees. The water was aqua colored and the island was hilly and rock laden. Mr. Leer drove past Avalon Bay and anchored *The Golden Eagle* among the other yachts, near an unpopulated portion of the island. The people on the yachts knew one another; there were welcoming hand waves and hollering hellos. Most came from Newport Beach or Santa Barbara, the cities etched underneath the boats' names. One yacht was larger than the others and it was anchored near *The Golden Eagle: Big Orange.* Men wearing T-shirts, with the yacht's name across the back, polished wood and hosed the deck.

Rosie and Isabella dove into the water from the deck of *The Golden Eagle.* They jumped; they cannon-balled; they made crazy gestures — this is a crazy person running — midair. After some time had passed, Rosie noticed a man reclined on a lounge chair on the deck of *Big Orange,* one knee up, wearing blue swim trunks, and watching her with binoculars, an empty drink on the table next to him with what appeared to be a celery stalk in the glass.

He saw that she was looking at him, and he set the binoculars down so that they rested on his chest from a band around his neck. His legs swung to the side, in a sitting position. He waved, although she could see that he was not smiling.

"Who is that?" she asked.

Isabella put both her hands to her forehead, shielding her face from the sun. "Rod likes you," she said.

They were quiet, staring at Rod while he stared back.

"He's old," Isabella said, but she said it like it was a good thing. "His mom and dad let him take the yacht."

Rod continued to watch them, although Rosie knew that he was really looking at her.

"Do something," Isabella said.

Rosie stood in her bikini. She did a mock hula dance: hands gesturing, hips swinging. Isabella's hand was at her mouth, laughing.

"Watch," Rosie said. She walked to the edge of the deck, toes tipping over. She sucked in her stomach, and her hands went above her head, fingers together — an upside-down V.

She dove — a rush of air — body alert and toes pointed. She caught glimpses: blue sky, the hull of the boat. The salt water stung her eyes, but she opened them anyway, hull bobbing in the water, dreamlike. She went deeper, the water progressively cooler and darker. Her lungs hurt from holding her breath. She somersaulted, kicking her legs so that she was pointed the other direction. She swam toward the surface and the sun made wavy white lines through the water.

She liked the sensation of her head breaking through ocean and coming into air. The water looked bright and sparkly, and she took a deep, appreciative breath, her hair slicked back. She dog-paddled to stay afloat and turned in the direction of *Big Orange:* Rod was standing near the edge of the deck, as she had hoped, his binoculars right on her.

The Leers were invited to a party/barbecue on the shore, close to the beach, a location with two outdoor barbecue pits and six picnic tables. All the yacht owners and their guests were invited. It was to last all day into the late evening. People drove their small motorboats to the pier and unloaded. Other dinghies docked along the sand.

Rosie and Isabella sneaked Coronas from a cooler, hiding them in their shorts' pockets, T-shirts untucked and covering the bottles, and found a shaded place to drink, underneath a pier that no one used—white paint peeling off the wood, cracked and falling apart; not too far from the picnic tables, but far enough so that they wouldn't get caught. But they couldn't figure out how to get the bottles open. "I thought these twisted off," Rosie said.

"Oh my God," Isabella whispered.

Rod approached, two fingers hooked under the plastic of a six-pack of Budweiser. He stooped under the pier. "Thought I might find you," he said. He wore his blue swim trunks, the ends reached past his knees. A circle of dark hair ringed each nipple, a diamond of hair was at the center of his chest, and he had a slight paunch. He folded his legs to sit with them on the ocean-hardened sand. Attached to his swim trunks was a key ring with a bottle opener. *"La cerveza más fina,"* he said, opening the Corona bottles and passing them over. Rosie thought he was handsome: a man, not a teenager. His forehead, cheeks, and nose were sunburned, and because he'd been wearing sunglasses, the paler skin around his eyes gave him a startled look. He ignored Isabella, but she didn't mind. "What's your name?" he asked.

She told him.

"Rosie, Rosie, Rosie," he said. She lit up with the sound of her name in his voice. He asked questions—Where do you live? What classes do you like? How old are you? And she answered as cleverly as possible: I don't like school and I'd quit if

I could. How old do you think I am? She showed him her sunburn and he peeled skin from her shoulder.

Twenty minutes later, Rod walked with them to the picnic tables from the pier because Isabella didn't want her parents to worry about her. Everything was arranged buffet-style on two picnic tables underneath an awning: plastic bowls of potato chips and tortilla chips; a stainless-steel bowl filled with strawberries and another with pineapple slices; plastic trays with cupcakes and cookies. The barbecues were large and made of stone, and the men took their grilling duties seriously. Folding chairs stuck out from the sand at the beach. Somebody's golden retriever fetched a tennis ball from the water: back and forth, back and forth, tail wagging. The tide was low, small waves lapping the sand.

When Rosie had to go to the bathroom, Rod said he would take her. "That's what happens when you drink beer, young lady," he said in a mock stern tone. She ran ahead, kicking water at him, and he laughed. "You're so cute," he said. Her face warmed even though she wasn't facing him. The bathrooms were a concrete affair, steel toilet rims, flies circling, and no mirrors. He waited outside. As they walked back, he held her hand briefly and she was awed.

Mr. Leer sat with the others, eating a hot dog. He wore a ridiculous straw hat with a wide brim and it made Rosie fond of him. Isabella was next to her father, glowing with belonging. Rosie would have felt left out, but she didn't mind because of Rod. He sat next to her, his arm touching hers, and she felt like her throat was being tickled.

The sun was sinking, shadows and coolness, and the sand on the beach looked silvery gray. People pulled on windbreakers and sweatshirts. It smelled like campfire, ocean, and burnt hamburger. Rod poured Heineken into a plastic cup for her, and no one asked what she was drinking. Conversations revolved around real estate, golf, and yacht maintenance, and Isabella played cards with her father. Mrs. Leer drank red wine from a plastic cup, making hand gestures when she spoke. "We plan on visiting Europe this summer for a month or two, with a week in Venice," she said. "No one should stay long in Venice."

Rod hid his face with his arm, rolling his eyes so that only Rosie could see. He pulled on a blue hooded sweatshirt that ruffled his hair, as if someone had slapped it to one side. He asked if she wanted to see his boat. She nodded, heart thumping, glancing at Isabella, who was completely occupied with her card game; she knew Isabella wouldn't mind.

And then she glanced at Mrs. Leer sitting at the other side of the picnic table. Rod leaned in and whispered, "Trust me: I've gone to these parties for years. They're just going to get more fucked up, no one cares. They'll forget where you went." The sun was gone, sky dark with purples, oranges, and reds.

Mrs. Leer had a slight flush from her wine, setting her hand on Rosie's forearm. "How exciting," she said, eyes sparkling, when Rosie told her she was going to see Rod's yacht.

"Careful," Rod said, taking Rosie's hand to help her aboard his dinghy. He pulled on the starter, his back to her, arm yanking three times, until the engine sputtered to life. The motor hummed as they made their way from the barbecue, winding around the anchored boats. He asked her to hold the flashlight, even though there was a full moon and the dinghy had a light at the front. She lay on the bow with the flashlight tucked in her arm, a small beam of light bouncing on the water. It was dark and beautiful, the stars blinking. She felt like her insides were on the outside, like the world was wide open.

He killed the motor and they floated, away from the yachts, where the current was a little rougher. He opened a wood panel. Underneath a life preserver was a small bottle. *"Un tequila reserva especial,"* he said, with a bad accent, twisting the cap off. *"Muy especial."* He took a long pull from the bottle, and when he moved it away, his mouth was twisted, and he shook his head as he swallowed.

He handed her the bottle and she took a sip. It tasted like fire and her insides melted. He leaned over and kissed her, his fingers sliding down her forearm to take the bottle. She was lost in the kiss, eyes closed, body swirling, his tongue moving around her mouth, blurring with her mouth. He tasted like salt and tequila, and she felt wetness on her bathing suit bottoms. He pulled away and watched her.

"You're alone . . . " he said, staring at her broodingly. She wasn't sure what he meant but was eager to understand; and kissing him she'd felt a connection—a thousand times more than she did with Isabella, Isabella's parents, and even her own father and B.

". . . Like me," he said, looking away and taking another pull from the tequila.

They took turns sipping from the bottle, passing it back and forth. The boat rocked—the current sucked and slapped against the wood—and faint voices from the party carried across the water. There was a soft breeze and the tequila hummed inside her.

"I don't know who I am," he said. There was a pause and she watched his face, wondering if he was done, but it turned out he was only mulling things over. He told her that he was a trained paramedic and that he had loved his job, but that his parents were making him go back to law school, now that he was older. He told her stories about dead bodies: how they can still move after death because their synapses continue to fire away. She thought he was authentic because he spoke of death. He said that he once had to lift a lady who had jumped off a building; he held her underneath her armpits, since they were hauling her dead body. Her head fell back and a long audible gasp of air came out of her mouth.

"I was so scared, I dropped her on the ground," he said.

When he talked about being a paramedic, his voice was animated, but when he talked about himself, his tone was derisive and condescending, especially when he spoke of law school and his family's business. She thought perhaps this was characteristic of worldly adults.

"Once, before I got kicked out of law school," he said, shifting on the wood plank seat, "I hated it so much that I got drunk and lay down in the middle of an intersection near the parking lot, just to see if the cars would stop."

"That's crazy," she said, and she laughed even though she wasn't sure why.

"When people get run over by cars," he said, ignoring her, "it almost always knocks their bodies clean out of their shoes, no matter how tightly their laces are tied. You can find their shoes at the accident site while their bodies have been dragged or thrown. Sometimes, the shoes are tipped to the side, but there they are."

Rosie was conscious that she smiled for him, laughed when appropriate, and frowned often. But she didn't mind, because she was drunk, a wonderful sensation, as if she would never be troubled by anything again.

"And rip currents," he said. "I've seen drowned bodies." Her father had warned her about rip currents, ocean a lighter color, calmer; she knew not to swim against one, but rather to swim parallel to the shoreline or float until the current moved away.

When they finished the tequila, he tipped his hand over the side of the boat and filled the bottle with seawater, put the cap back on, and then dropped the bottle. It sank into the dark water, softly. He started the motor and drove back, to where they wove between the yachts.

He tied the motorboat to the side of *Big Orange* and they climbed a ladder to get onboard. She leaned against him because she was losing her balance, and he held her hand while he showed her the kitchen, the dining area, the bedrooms, the living room, ending at the master bedroom. His finger went to his lips, warning her to be quiet, but his eyes laughed. The men she'd seen wearing *Big Orange* T-shirts slept on a different section of the boat, reserved for staff. The boat rocked, and she wondered if she would be sick. He took his sandals off and she noticed patches of hair on his toes. She took her tennis shoes off without unlacing them, spilling a little sand; she wasn't wearing socks—her feet cool against the wood floor. She told herself that no matter what, she must try to remain upright.

"Rosie," he said huskily and he slid his hand under her shirt and bathing suit top. He leaned into her, her back against the wall. His body was dark and strong, his breathing heavy. The wall seemed to be moving, and then she was pulled to the floor, the back of her head hitting the ground, the ceiling vibrating in a jolt of light. He tugged down her shorts and her bathing suit bottoms. When he spread her legs, instantly she knew that he was going to have sex with her, and she was terrified; but she couldn't control it, like a child being slammed down by a wave. A heat moved inside her, a ripping sensation, and she wanted to explain that this wasn't what she wanted, even if she had wanted to see what came next. "Please," she said, "no, oh God, oh please." In time with his knee knocking against the wood, her head thumped against the wall.

When it was over, she went to the bathroom where she put herself through the motions of urinating—a horrible stinging, a small amount of blood coiling in the toilet bowl; she gently wiped toilet paper against the moist numbness (not looking at the toilet paper)—afterwards washing her face and hands. She thought briefly of her father and B, but she felt as separate and distant from her parents as she'd ever imagined. She listened momentarily to the beating of blood in her eardrums, but avoided her face in the mirror. When she walked back to the bedroom, she bumped into the wall. She had the sensation that her body was made of vapor, that Rod could put his hand right through her.

They climbed back on the motorboat to make their way to shore. The lights from the party were twinkling in the distance. She tilted her head back and the sky spun: stars whirled and the full moon swayed. Her throat was slippery, and she knew that if the sky did not stop sliding, she would be sick.

She leaned against the side of the boat, vomiting beer, tequila, potato salad, half of a cheeseburger. Afterwards, nothing left in her stomach, she used a life preserver for a pillow, and an oar pressed against her back. Her entire body was damp with sweat, and she wiped the back of her hand against her mouth. When she saw that he was watching her, she looked away, dunking her hand in the ocean to wash it. She watched the water break around her wrist and a light from the boat flickered across the current. Weariness sank into her, filled her with a deadening weight, and she heard herself making a whimpering noise.

When the boat bumped softly against the dock, he killed the motor, held on to a rope, and jumped ashore, the boat dipping with the loss of his weight. The front end swung around before he was able to secure it. There was a space between the dock and the water looked black. The motorboat wobbled; the dock swayed; there was an instant — as she jumped — when she thought she could make it, but then she was in the water. She was scared and she gasped, but she didn't scream, even though she thought of eels and sharks.

He held his hand out, and she grabbed hold of his forearm. He pulled her to the dock and she felt the pinch of a splinter in her knee. They looked at each other and she said something about being cold, but her words were garbled and sounded like they were coming from far away. The water was dripping off her and she was shivering.

The coldness sobered her like hard slaps, along with the vomiting, so that she felt it when he pulled her in the bushes near the old pier and took off her clothes. Between the leaves, in and out of focus, she saw the red fire pits from the party, so she closed her eyes. When she listened closely, she heard laughter. He moved on top of her, his breath on her neck. Because she was wet, the dirt stuck to her legs and back. She bit the tip of her tongue, tasted blood; a rock scraped against her back.

His body clenched and he fell on top of her with all his weight as if he'd been shot dead. At first, she thought he might have fallen asleep, but then she realized he was only catching his breath. She squirmed underneath him, feeling disgrace and disappointment, the cold reality of humiliation. This was sex?

"Sorry," he said, and moved to give her room. She wiped

the dirt from her legs with her shirt, and he handed her his sweatshirt. It was long, reaching her knees. She couldn't comprehend what was happening. For a second, she couldn't even remember where she was and had to wait for the word "Catalina" to come to her. And then the word wouldn't leave: Catalina, Catalina, Catalina.

He drove her in the dinghy back to *The Golden Eagle* and she could sense him climbing onboard after her. She took a shower in the trickling hot water from the showerhead, hoping that he would leave. There was a cut on her back from the rock, and she tried to reach it with the small oval of soap. And while she showered, she let herself evaporate into a nonreality, a tolerable disbelief. She changed into sweatpants and a T-shirt in the bathroom flooded with steam. She brushed her teeth three times, the back of her head tender from where she'd hit it on the floor, tiny scratches on her arms from the thornbush leaves. When she opened the door, she saw that he was still there, and that he'd put her wet clothes in a plastic bag. She had the sensation of not being able to keep her eyes open while reading. He gave her a questioning look when she handed him his sweatshirt.

"Let's get you to sleep," he said.

She was lying in bed with her eyes closed and could feel him staring down at her. Finally, she heard his footsteps moving across the floor. His motorboat started and she listened as the motor faded. She wanted sleep to temporarily black out her existence.

She stayed in bed the next morning. Isabella couldn't get her to do anything. She was a wet blanket, a party pooper—no fun. Mrs. Leer came into the bedroom.

"You need to get up," she said. "You can't sleep all day. We're going water-skiing."

When she did get up, she refused to wear her red bikini. Instead, she wore her jeans. The insides of her thighs were bruised.

That night, Rosie and Isabella ate dinner at the dining table on the boat with Isabella's parents. Mrs. Leer had made Tater Tots and scrambled eggs with cheddar cheese, Isabella's favorite meal. There wasn't much talk, and the silverware clanked against the plates. The cut on Rosie's tongue was swollen, making it difficult to chew. Isabella drenched her food in ketchup and Mrs. Leer gave her daughter a disdainful look.

Rosie didn't want to watch Isabella try to please her mother anymore. She was angry with Isabella and didn't know why. Isabella sensed it and left her alone. The four of them were going to play Spades — the girls against Mr. and Mrs. Leer — but the sound of Mr. Leer shuffling the cards made Rosie sleepy. Mrs. Leer complained that they would be left with an odd number, but Rosie excused herself and went to bed anyway.

Isabella was asleep next to Rosie, snoring softly, her body warm. The boat made creaking noises; the ocean lapped. Rosie's hands were outside the blanket and she stared around her. She'd gone to bed early, only to wake up — alert — with everyone asleep. She moved her tongue to the side of her mouth, touched the cut against her teeth. The ocean made wavy shadows on the walls. The moon was still very full; the night had a lit-up darkness.

She heard the hum of a motorboat, and that was when she

knew: Rod didn't get enough the first and second time and he wanted more. She sat up in bed, her motion waking Isabella.

"What is it?" Isabella asked, rising to a sitting position. She rubbed at her eyes and yawned.

There was a thump against the boat and steps above them coming closer.

"Dad," Isabella called. "Dad. There's someone on the boat."

They heard Mr. Leer getting out of bed, cursing.

Then they heard voices:

"What are you doing, Rod?" Mr. Leer: angry, exasperated, inconvenienced.

"I'm here for Rosie." He was drunk, slurring his words.

"Rod. She's fourteen." She was fifteen, the same age as his daughter.

"I don't care."

"You're going to have to leave, Rod. This looks bad."

Mrs. Leer's voice joined — "What's going on?"

"Nothing, sweetheart. Go back to bed."

"I'm here for Rosie."

"Oh, Rod. You're drunk." Mrs. Leer's voice was sympathetic.

Rod began crying — they could hear him. Isabella's eyes widened.

"Jesus," Mr. Leer said.

There was a shuffling sound. She knew that Rod was trying to get past Mr. Leer, but Mr. Leer was blocking him. They heard more shuffling. Someone fell.

More weeping, childlike.

"Rosie," Rod said. "Rosie."

Isabella's eyes searched her face. She could hear Rod moving.

There was a hand pressed on the window between the curtains, like a pink sea urchin. Then she saw Rod's face, but it was quick, a flash of one eye, frantic. She didn't think he saw her.

She could see him rising, his leg between the parting of the curtains. He kicked the side of the boat softly. Thump.

She heard stumbling footsteps. He was getting back into his motorboat—she could feel it. The engine sputtered, the sound of the motorboat faded.

Rosie went to Maritime Church with her father two Sundays later. She sat in the pew and watched the Perry Como–like pastor. The church offered a brand of Christianity where monetary success was considered a good thing, brought on by Jesus' favor. During the service, she had the urge to shout, Okay, Jesus died for my sins! Can we move on to something else? And she knew this was very wrong. She saw Kristen Johnson standing in the front row of the choir, her hair pulled back in a ponytail.

When Rosie was a child, her father would hold her hand and squeeze a certain number of times, and she would squeeze back the same number. She would concentrate because sometimes he would squeeze up to twenty times and she wanted to get the number right. No one else knew, and it would make her think he was paying attention to her, that they had a connection, and that she was special.

She remembered this as she let him hold her hand. His hand was moist and they rose. He began singing with the others, the words on a screen for everyone to follow, his eyes brimming with tears of faith or joy or whatever it was that he felt, whatever it was that she was unable to grasp. To her, he looked naïve.

All I need is You
All I need is You Lord Jesus
Is You Lord Jesus

She sang out of an inherent desire to please her father, to make their estrangement bearable, but her body was hot with shame, holding on to secrets, aware that more would follow. Her father looked at her — he was proud, misty-eyed — mistaking her emotion as inspired by the church service. But she was mourning their relationship, aware that she was lost to him, that even as he stood there holding her hand and watching her, she was strangely invisible.

Many times after, she imagined accidental meetings with Rod — in restaurants, at the beach — their shared looks of shame, because she would confront him about what had happened; he was the only one who knew. But she had a feeling that she would never see him again. He had left her with a surreptitious desire, a longing for danger, a readiness and need.

She would comprehend that she had been defrauded of dignity, and her anger would rise, but she would direct it at herself. She would feel the futility of any attempt to articulate her sadness or to salvage her innocence — most of all the impossibility of finding her place in the world; and these times scared her the most, leading as they did, to periods of inconsolable loneliness and grief.

Winter Formal:
A Night of Magic

ROSIE SAT AGAINST the chainlink fence, legs crossed, hands pressing down her tennis skirt, hiding her tennis underwear with the blue trim. She was watching Christine Polmer play Heather McNamara. The yellow tennis ball — as it flew across the net — made an oblong, moving shadow.

The women on the next court also watched Christine Polmer play Heather McNamara, in between points of their own comparably dull tennis match, because that's what happened when Chris played tennis. Parents and spectators sat in the stands, rapt with attention, now and then audibly sighing. It was a beautiful thing. Chris's forehand was a graceful stroke, like the flap of a wing.

Chris waited for Heather to serve, right hand gripped around the handle of her racket, left hand lightly holding the strings of the head, swaying slightly. She looked confident and bored. The serve, when it came, was surprisingly strong, but Chris sliced a backhand to the corner. Heather ran, her face showing signs of strain, and barely lobbed the ball back. Chris drove the ball to the opposite corner, and Heather lurched, swinging her racket and missing. She set her racket on the court, bent forward, hands on her knees. Rosie imagined she was catching her breath. Chris liked to cruise past Rosie after such winning shots, adding her personal commentary.

"I got a leather jacket from some man in the navy. Patches and fake fur on the collar. I'll show you." Chris's voice was a hardened monotone, as if she'd just smoked a pack of cigarettes, not matching her appearance: white perfectly shaped teeth, golden legs lean with muscle.

Of course she got a leather jacket from some man in the navy. Men followed Chris. They gave her gifts. She was seventeen years old, and she could already credit herself with two teenage stalkers. She had blond hair that looked like there was light glowing in each strand. Her eyes were a cool blue. She was tall and skinny. And she lured men with her languid walk, and then ignored them, moving on as they continued to stare, taking her beauty and slapping it in their faces: You like to look at me? Fuck you.

Chris walked slowly to her position, a tennis ball creating a lump in her skirt where it was tucked in her tennis underwear. She bounced the ball three times — she did so every serve — leaned forward, and peered across the net. She tossed the ball up and in one defined, smooth stroke, drove it across the net. Heather hit an unwieldy forehand, and the ball landed outside the white line.

Rosie saw Chris hesitate, and then Chris gave the point away. Chris's father, Walt, sat in the stands with the other parents, but it was as if he was sitting behind Rosie, breathing down her neck. He couldn't contain himself, standing and yelling,

"That ball was out! Goddamn it, Chris! Call it!" He wore silver tinted sunglasses.

Rosie knew Chris would ignore him, but she saw her wince. When Walt got angry, he cussed and yelled, but the other parents tolerated him because he was Chris's personal tennis coach. He'd been threatening to send her to reformatory school. "It's in one of those small states — Rhode Island or Delaware," Chris had said. And he'd already sent her to a military-style tennis camp over the summer, where she'd claimed that a counselor had "stuck a curling iron up a girl's twat."

When Chris walked past Rosie — dead eyes, smart-ass comments, tennis racket dangling, radiating with rebellion — Rosie was pleased to be her friend. Yet she couldn't help but worry that it was only a matter of time before it all ended: badly, quickly. It was because Chris talked about death, telling her the different ways she thought of killing herself: "I'll slit my wrists in the bathtub. The warm water will make it flow. Not cut across, but along the veins."

"I wonder what it feels like to drown? I could hold on to Mom's hand weights and sink in our pool."

She typed eerie notes for Rosie in their typing class, on flimsy tan paper:

Have you ever had an experience or thought you've been somewhere before because you've dreamed the place, and you know it's going to be the same when you're dead? Let's leave today. Let's take a razor and cut our arms and then suck the blood.

Chris signed her notes — *Friends Forever* — as if to avoid doubt and ensure her loyalty. Chris's rebellion was bottomless, rooted in a lost and sad dreaminess. "Anyone home?" Rosie would say, waving a hand in front of Chris's face. And still, Chris would stare off.

Chris liked to tell her, "You're different. You feel things. You're going to do something with your life. Not just marry some dumb-ass executive and go to the country club. Not just have a couple of babies and play tennis."

Chris was winning; she always won. She was the number-one singles player on the varsity tennis team. Her next serve was gentle and slow, as if trying to help her opponent. Heather hit a deep backhand and ran forward on the court. In an effortless gesture, Chris lobbed the ball over Heather's head to the backcourt. Heather ran fast and hard, but she netted the ball, her arms spread for balance.

Rosie began to wish for the end of the match, and Chris brushed back a loose strand of hair and frowned in her direction, as if to say, Let's get this done. Three requisite bounces of the ball, serious stare across the net. She tossed the ball in a serve and swung down on it. Heather sped toward the ball, swung and missed.

Another serve, another ace. On Chris's fourth serve, Heather managed to lob the ball back, bringing a collective *aaaahhh* from the audience. Chris's racket head waited between her shoulder blades, her elbow pointed at the ball. There was a thwack. Heather's legs were spread wide and slightly bent, racket listless by her side, and she watched with the others as the ball bounced inside the white line and slammed into the fence.

Applause erupted from the spectators, and Rosie heard Walt whistling, but Chris was bored by the praise. She walked slowly past Rosie, head down, expressionless.

"Take that," she said flatly.

• • •

Rosie and Chris sat on Chris's bed making plans for the winter formal dance. This year's theme was "A Night of Magic." Chris would supply her with a date, one of her leftovers. Older and handsome was how she described him.

Rosie's grandparents were fly-fishing in Montana, the spare key to their house hanging on a hook in the garage, an invitation. Chris had decided that they would make an appearance at the dance, take the obligatory photographs as proof for parents, and then spend the entirety of the evening at Rosie's grandparents' house, away from the restrictive gaze of adults.

Chris's mom poked her head through Chris's bedroom door, blond hair swinging — "Can I get you girls something to eat?" Doris drove a canary yellow Jaguar. She belonged in a canary yellow Jaguar, Rosie thought. Doris was an older, lit-up version of Chris, if Chris weren't suicidal and promiscuous. She had an optimistic smile that Rosie never trusted. Doris and Walt were born-again Christians, and she knew that they prayed before meals, holding hands around the table, even if they were at restaurants.

"Leave," Chris answered. Then, as if she pitied her mom, she softened her response, saying patiently, "No, Mom. Please leave." Rosie saw a flash of red from Doris's manicured fingers as she shut the door.

They could hear the mumble and canned laughter of the television from the living room. Caitlen, Chris's twelve-year-old sister, was watching a sitcom. Caitlen was the opposite of Chris — compliant, eager to please. Her chances of becoming a professional tennis player were good.

Chris sighed heavily, her mother's interruption darkening her mood. She reached underneath her bed and pulled out a shoebox, setting the lid on the bedspread. Inside the box were a blue and white package of Ex-Lax, various pill bottles, the white packaging from a container of diuretics, three tattered matchbooks — each advertising a different bar, folded squares of paper, a green plastic pill container with the days of the week, a small bottle of Lemon Zest air freshener, and a ceramic lizard. The lizard's mouth was the receptacle for lighting and smoking the pot, which Chris retrieved from a drawer beneath her underwear, in a Ziploc sandwich bag.

"John Wayne," Chris said, prepping her lizard, initiating a game she'd invented: speculating about sex with different men, whether random (Tom Hanks, their high school janitor), repulsive (Ronald Reagan, school principal Mr. Johnson), or desirable (the actor from *Kiss of the Spider Woman*). "Not that bullshit macho John Wayne," she added, "our John Wayne."

Rosie knew that Chris thought of herself as her personal sex-mentor, and she'd told Chris in a vague way about Rod; but she'd buried the memory of what had happened: the only proof that she hadn't invented the loss of her virginity was the large X she'd marked across the page in her journal, with the date September 21, 1988.

"No good," Rosie said.

"Like having sex with a five-year-old," Chris agreed.

"Like incest or something," Rosie said.

"Yeah, well," said Chris. She sucked the lizard's tail, and then passed the lizard to Rosie. Rosie sucked. "I'm all fucked up," Chris began in a choked voice from holding in the smoke. She let the smoke stream out, picking up the Lemon Zest air freshener, and simultaneously squirting and waving her hand in the mist. "I read about it in *Cosmo*. I have sex because I think that sex will bring me love. Really, there's a hole inside me. It can never be filled. I'm destined to be lonely forever."

"Shut up," Rosie said, and they laughed.

• • •

After much tactical negotiation, Walt had agreed to allow Chris to get ready for the dance at Rosie's grandparents' house (although he didn't know that her grandparents were out of town). Their dates were freshman varsity tennis players from USC, and Walt was pleased: as long as Chris was back by curfew. It was dusk, and rain, blown by the wind, tapped on the sliding glass doors, streaming down the windowpanes.

Chris had giant rollers in her hair. "The trick," she said, sitting on a barstool and peering at her face in a lit-up mirror where Grandma Dot usually kept her beer and ashtray, "is to use men the same way they use you." She squinted at Rosie. "That way you don't get hurt."

"Sure," Rosie said. She wore a red satin gown with a V-back, smooth against her skin, but she felt like a splotch of color, nothing more, compared with Chris. Chris took out the bobby pins and rollers, and the rollers rocked on the bar before settling. Her hair bounced with release, and her dress shimmered, silver and strapless.

Rosie glanced out the sliding glass windows toward the deck, the view soft and blurred through the rain. She thought the lounge chairs looked like skeletons. In the distance was a streak of dark, as if painted with a brush, and she knew that it was raining even harder there.

"Did Walt make you practice last weekend?" she asked, looking back at Chris.

Chris smiled sadly, as if the question were inconsequential. "I have this recurring nightmare," she said. "The first time I dreamed it was when I was five: the tennis balls kept shooting at me, like from a machine gun. I'd duck, but the balls kept hitting me." She applied her lipstick, pursed her lips, and blotted with one of Grandma Dot's Kleenexes. She set the crumpled tissue next to her rollers, the scarlet mark reminding Rosie of Grandma Dot's lipstick prints.

"Why don't you fix us a drink?" Chris asked.

"You sound like an adult," Rosie said.

"I feel old," Chris said. "Really old."

The Smirnoff vodka bottle in the bar had been marked with a faint line: Grandpa was paranoid about his vodka, and she knew better than to touch it. Instead, she opened a Schlitz and one bottle of Coors from the refrigerator. Since when had Grandma Dot started drinking Coors?

A loud knocking came from the front door, and Chris stood from the barstool. "They're early," she said, and she hopped barefoot on the kitchen tile over to Rosie. They held hands and stared at each other, excitement increasing, until Chris said, "Ready?" She nodded, although she wanted to tell Chris that she didn't seem really old now.

Chris set her feet carefully in her high heels and made her way to the front door. The men entered with paper bags, unloading in the kitchen: twelve-packs of Coronas, a bottle of Jose Cuervo tequila, and plastic corsage boxes with white carnations inside. Chris settled her body against the taller of the men, Tate, and Rosie discerned the other, Sean, to be her date. Tate was better looking: eyes sad and hostile and a downturned mouth; Sean was smaller, more tightly put together, with darker hair. Their manner with each other had an edge of confidence, as if their bond was entirely rewarding, and the surrounding world didn't measure up.

The night progressed rapidly into shots of tequila, beer, and the blurring of everything into a whirl of motion, colors, and laughter. The rain stroked the windowpanes, and the ocean seemed to rock the house, back and forth, as if supporting them. They played quarters on the marble coffee table, bouncing the quarter into one of Grandpa's martini glasses. Rosie and Chris weren't as skilled, they lost their eye-hand coordination quickly, the quarters clinking against the rim, spinning, and then landing on the table or the carpet.

Tate and Sean went out on the deck in the misty rain and puffed greedily on cigarettes, consulted with each other, flicking ashes in the bay, now and then glancing at them through the sliding glass windows. Their orchid boutonnieres looked like wadded tissues. "God," Chris said, laughing, and Rosie knew that she was telling her that she was drunk. "Yeah," she said, and they stared at each other, happily. The men reentered, the glass door sliding open and closed with a gust of cold air.

Rosie was woozy, noticing the static coming from her grandparents' stereo. She rose to change the station, and she was aware that she walked unsteadily. When she returned to the couch, Chris and Tate were leaned into each other, kissing. She sat next to Sean, and he put a hand on her knee. He kissed her, his other hand sliding down her back. The warmth of his lips dampened her earlobe.

As he pulled her to a stand, she knew something was going to happen between them, and her throat tightened. He opened the door in the hallway, leading her by the arm to The Daisy Room. (John Wayne had told her that he'd named the rooms, and she'd come to think of them the same way.) She looked back at Chris, who smiled lazily, her body flopped out on the couch, one leg crooked underneath the other in a position that looked uncomfortable. Tate was leaned forward, reaching for his pack of Marlboro Reds.

On the wallpaper in The Daisy Room, she could make out clusters of dark flowers, reminding her of children holding hands. She looked at Sean, and his eyes glittered at her. He had a scar across his eyebrow, a pale slope dividing the hairs. It made her uncomfortable since her father had a similar scar and she couldn't help but think about him. She didn't like her father popping into her mind as Sean urged her to give him a blowjob.

She did her best, it was only her second time, but he wanted her to go fast and deep. He was not patient, and he grabbed the back of her head and forced her down on him until she thought she might gag, tears welling. When it was over, and she'd swallowed, as Chris had instructed ("Just get it down quickly; it's not so bad, and it's good for your skin and hair"), she lay in the bed and watched the dark familiar shadows waving from the walls.

Sean lay silent for a few moments until his breathing normalized. His weight left the bed; she heard him zipping his pants. He left: the door shut. She slept; she didn't sleep; she wasn't sure. And then she missed Chris. Where was Chris?

She walked down the hallway, past the kitchen and the living room. All the lights were off, except for the kitchen's sleepy-yellow light. She thought about telling Chris what had happened with Sean, but decided she'd tell her later, when she'd arranged events to be less humiliating.

The door to The Fish Room was open, and she saw the silhouette of Tate and Sean in the dark: Sean was moving up and down on the bed — steady, rhythmically. Tate stood beside the bed, a hand on his friend's back, as if to push him or guide him. They were calm, concentrating, and did not notice her.

She saw a flash of Chris's hair — her head against a pillow, face turned away; she couldn't see Chris's body, only the rise and fall of Sean's back. Her stomach dropped, and she felt a panicked relief that it wasn't her in the bed with the men. But seeing Chris humiliated her in a helpless way, less easily dismissed.

When she left the doorway, her hand was on the wall for support, and she was shocked, knowing that it was still happening, even without her watching. She felt blood drain from her face, and when she set her hand out, it shook.

The phone was next to Grandma Dot's can of pens and pencils, and Grandma Dot had taped a list of phone numbers to it. Uncle Stan's was second on the list, even though he was long gone. She dialed, hoping to reach John Wayne, phone ringing upstairs in the apartment, an echo to the beep from the receiver—ten, eleven, twelve times. When she looked toward the bay, her body jerked involuntarily. John Wayne stood on the deck, his palms spread on the sliding glass door like wet leaves.

She slid the door open, and wisps of rain licked her skin, blown inside from the dark. The sky and bay seemed connected: she couldn't distinguish one from the other, only darkness. He came inside, wearing her uncle's bell-bottom jeans, cuffs wet and turned under his bare feet. He stared at her, and she got the impression that he already knew.

"Get them out," she said, gesturing toward The Fish Room. His eyes narrowed, as if considering, and he looked from her face to the room and back again. He walked toward the dark doorway, and when he turned on the light, it bounced out the door and hung in the entryway. She heard John Wayne's voice, although she couldn't make out what he was saying, and then Sean said, "Fuck this shit."

The men walked out of The Fish Room—calm, just like before—and her chest tightened at the sight of them. Tate took one of the paper bags and loaded it with leftover Coronas, leaving the empties. They spoke in hushed voices, and then Sean moved close to Tate, whispered something, and Tate glanced over his shoulder at her and laughed.

She closed her eyes and leaned against the sliding glass door, glass cool on her back, a dull nausea settling in her chest, and when she opened her eyes, Tate and Sean were leaving by the front door. She could still taste Sean in her mouth, and she had the urge to brush her teeth.

Rosie and Chris climbed up the hill from her grandparents' house to Chris's house, high heels long gone, mud clinging to their damp dresses, cool against their legs. They wore sweatshirts over their dresses. The succulent ice plants that covered the hill crushed under their feet, unleashing more wet, and the leaves glistened from the earlier rain. Chris's home was at the top of the hill, a block down. Her curfew was one A.M., but it was past two A.M. last time Rosie looked, the neon numbers glowing from Grandma Dot's alarm clock. She was spending the night at Chris's house.

Chris was scared, she was sure of it. Chris had vomited twice while she'd held her hair, her chest heaving afterwards, and she'd come back to the world enough to be afraid. Her mascara had dripped down her face, smeared across her cheeks.

A dog barked. Rosie turned back to look at her grandparents' house, and behind it, the bay. It had stopped raining, everything slick and wet; the moon's reflection bounced on the water, faded and soft, and dark clouds moved across the sky, as if they, too, were rushed. John Wayne sat cross-legged on the roof, watching them. She waved her hand, but he didn't respond, even though she was sure he saw her.

They sprayed the mud from their legs and feet, using a coiled hose at the side of Chris's house. The house was dark, and Chris took this as a good sign: "Maybe Walt is asleep. Maybe he isn't waiting."

Chris opened the front door with a key from under the mat. She shut the door quietly, and flicked on a light by the couch. Two sleeping bags were arranged next to the fireplace in the living room. "They must want us to sleep down here," she whispered. "I'll get you something to wear." She tiptoed upstairs, turning on the stairway to look back at Rosie, her face a blur. She was gone, and Rosie stared around the house. The furniture seemed to be watching—couch, chairs, kitchen table, curtains—alive, breathing.

Chris returned, handing her one of two long T-shirts with "Chuck Boyle's Tennis Academy—Everyone Is a Winner" written across the back. They used the bathroom, splashing cold water on their faces, brushing their teeth, wiping away the night. They changed quickly, silently, wadding their muddy dresses into balls, and leaving them under the sink, next to the trash can. They arranged themselves in the sleeping bags. The house ticked and creaked; the refrigerator hummed and was suddenly quiet. Rosie could hear Chris's breathing—Chris was not asleep because her breaths were alert.

And then Rosie fell asleep, the sway of alcohol overcoming her: dreams and images hovering. She heard a loud smack and woke to find Walt standing over Chris. A tangle of nightmare and reality, she gagged back the acidic taste of alcohol and swallowed. Chris was pleading: *"Please don't. Please don't."* And Walt was yelling over her words, his face jumbled and tight, the whites of his eyes and teeth flashing.

"Stop," Rosie heard herself say, and her hand went to her

mouth. She tried to look back at Walt and not cower, but she cringed, believing he might go after her as well. She'd never seen someone that angry.

His arm went back. "I — told — you" — and he slapped Chris again — "not to be late!" Chris's head swung to the side, and she stopped herself from going down with a hand to the floor.

"Goddamn whores," he said, lifting Chris beneath her armpits and shoving so that she landed on her sleeping bag. He looked helpless then, bleary and sad, and he turned and walked back up the stairs, muttering under his breath.

Chris was crying and Rosie tried to comfort her, her own heart racing, as if she'd been running. She put a hand on Chris's back and decided to leave it there. Chris's pillow stifled her crying, but it was the kind of crying that can't be helped.

Finally, Chris spoke into the pillow, muffled: "You can't tell anyone. Promise me."

"I promise."

"Promise?"

"Yes. I promise."

Chris rose and turned on the lamp beside the sofa. "I'm going to tell you something else," she said, wiping her face with her T-shirt. Without looking at Rosie, she went to the kitchen. She returned with a package of frozen peas pressed against the side of her face. She sat on her sleeping bag, and Rosie rested her back against the couch.

"You're good at secrets," Chris said.

Rosie nodded, even though it wasn't a question and she knew Chris was going to tell her no matter what.

"He used to touch me," Chris said.

A whirl of nausea sprang inside Rosie. She was sure she didn't want to hear this.

Chris set the frozen peas on the sleeping bag. Her long

T-shirt hung at her thighs, and her fingernail polish was chipped. Her eyes were serious, fixed on Rosie. She bent her knees and stretched the T-shirt over her legs like a tent, tennis racket elongating. "He doesn't think I remember," she said.

"God," Rosie said, looking away, toward the window. It had begun raining again, the glass wet and misty.

"You can't tell anyone," Chris said.

Rosie looked back at her, saw a birthmark on the inside of her ankle: the size of a nickel and shaped like Africa; her tennis socks normally hid it, her feet paler than her legs.

"I want to kill him," Rosie said, iciness around her chest and stomach.

"Don't worry," Chris said, pressing the peas against her face, watching her closely. "I just wanted you to know. I don't want you to feel sorry for me."

They didn't speak for some time, their thoughts filling the room. The visual of Tate instructing Sean came to her. Beneath was a darker fear that had to do with her connection: what she'd witnessed and her silence. She thought briefly of telling B about Walt, but the idea was hopeless, and she abandoned it.

"It only happened once or twice," Chris said finally, and Rosie knew that she was lying, but that she had to believe her anyway.

"He never had sex with me. He just touched me and he liked to look. He didn't with Caitlen."

Chris's face was blotchy, but her eyes were steady. "I didn't tell you because I wanted you to make it better. I just wanted you to know. But you can't tell anyone. Ever."

The next morning, Caitlen ate her cereal while Rosie and Chris rolled their sleeping bags. Rosie saw Caitlen lifting the spoon to her mouth, milk dripping; she heard the slight *crunch crunch* of Caitlen chewing. Doris was in the kitchen scrambling eggs, the smell drifting through the house.

"Caitlen hates eggs," Chris said.

Caitlen finished her cereal, carrying the bowl to the sink. She turned on the television in the living room to cartoons.

"Breakfast," Doris called.

Rosie and Chris sat across the kitchen table from Walt and Doris. Doris fidgeted with her napkin, squeezing it in her hands. Chris wouldn't look at her parents, the side of her face streaked — three fingers — raised and red. Not knowing what else to do, Rosie took her knife and started buttering her toast.

"Show some respect, young lady," Walt said. "We haven't said grace."

Tears worked their way to the surface, but she forced them back, thinking that Chris would prefer it. I hate him, I hate him, I hate him, she thought. A helpless shame similar to when Tate and Sean had left the bedroom — calm, talking and laughing.

Chris's head was down, but she rolled her eyes for Rosie's benefit and passed a secret smile, leaving Rosie both elated and scared. A silence gathered, and when Walt finally did speak, it was as if he'd been planning exactly what to say.

"You do realize," he said, staring at Chris, "you're going to the school we talked about. One last strike" — his hands made a small motion, as if hitting an imaginary baseball — "you're out."

She got the letter two months after Chris left. B set the envelope on her pillow, with her own note beside it, scrawled on notepad paper from one of Will's prescription drug companies:

I hope this helps, Rosie. I really do. We love you, even if we're not the best at showing it. Please know that. Always.

She opened the letter and read it right away. She folded it and put it back in its envelope, carrying the letter with her in her pocket, now and then touching the soft edge of the envelope with her fingertips.

Rosie and John Wayne walked to the beach two nights later; she'd told him that she wanted to say a final goodbye to Chris in her own way. He arranged wood and cardboard in a fire pit. His hair was in a braid, held together loosely with string. Tucked behind his ear was a joint. He used his Zippo to light a thin stick, and he lit the fire with trash he found from the beach. The waves hit the sand, released, steady, one after another; the motion calmed her. He stuck a board into the fire, fanned it, and wisps sparked loose. There was no one on the beach, except for a couple tucked under a blanket near the lifeguard stand, but they were busy, that was obvious. Though she had the letter memorized, she read it one last time by the light of the fire. John Wayne didn't ask her what it said, or tell her to read it out loud. He looked at the fire, but she felt like he was reading the letter with her.

Dear Rosie,
  They want to sell you small dreams. That's the problem. Don't let them do that to you. I'm not dying anymore. I met someone at school. We're hippies. I guess that's what you'd call it. On weekends we drive places you'd never believe existed. The states are tucked close together. You can drive an hour and be somewhere else. He has a truck with a camper shell. It's brown and old.

I've decided to become a Catholic. Candles everywhere, incense burning, and the sad old ladies get down on their knees to pray.

I'm learning to play the saxophone. No more tennis. I swear it. At least for now. Not even in my dreams.

Friends Forever,
Chris

She threw the letter into the fire, flames rising. She recalled the disgust she'd been unable to express at Walt's kitchen table, her helplessness. There was anger in her sadness, as if a decision had been hardening inside her, not to be submissive, not to cower again. She was aware that danger and mystery stretched around her, deep and vast as the ocean, and that she had moved closer to it, watchful and respectful. And she was lonely for Chris, glad and envious of her escape, while at the same time toughened by the secrets she'd been asked to keep. She watched the wood cave in on itself — giving way — and the letter made a soft blue flame.

The Locket

B DIDN'T LIKE to be called Barbara, so only in the brazen emotion and solitude of masturbation did Anne allow herself to say it. Barbara, Barbara — the final syllable an exhalation, Bar ba rahhh. Anne's voice was a whisper, but it excited and frightened her, as if she were admitting something. She wore a large cotton T-shirt and she adjusted her back because it was bunched beneath her spine. Fingers massaging her clitoris, hand just inside her vagina, bent knees splayed open, making a dented tent of the sheets. Her eyes were closed; she shut them during any kind of sex, even masturbation, mostly because pleasure was better in darkness, allowing a heightened concentration and privacy. She imagined the curve of B's breast in a bra, seen through the loop of a loose sleeve; the feel of her body when she brushed past; a look she had, both arrogant and vulnerable. Images and sensations, the way B's tongue might feel or how her hand would uncover her. Wetness, a blur of skin, fingers moving faster, faster, dizziness and heat, her cheeks flushing.

Her body clenched in on itself, falling into black. One, two, three, four, five, six, seven, until her orgasm ended. She placed a pillow between her legs, as if it were a person, and turned on her side, allowing herself to sink into numbness. The slightly unbalanced aftermath.

She opened her eyes, vulnerable, as if she'd unwrapped, released, and shared a part of herself with B. The thin curtains above her desk window moved faintly with the breeze, giving the impression of a disapproving stranger in the room, stirring the light material. She rose and shut the window. Back in her bed, pillow cradled between her legs, she whispered the name again—Barbara.

Certain the curtains weren't moving, she shut her eyes, savoring her loneliness, her private world of desire. Her wishes were best held down, far away, where no one could judge or reject them. She liked the cleanness and simplicity of controlling her yearning, the object of her fantasy unaware but strangely involved. Her desires were most concentrated when she went to sleep at night and when she woke in the morning.

Lesbianism sounds like a disease, B had told Anne yesterday after their tennis match. Anne remembered the sentence when she woke, as she did every morning at six-fifteen, her body an alarm clock. The words came as if they'd been hovering over her while she slept, waiting, more powerful than when B had spoken. As often happened, Anne went over conversations, realizing in retrospect where she'd sounded foolish or where she'd been articulate. Usually she did her remembering while showering, brushing her teeth, drinking coffee; but this morning she lay in bed, the sunlight muted through the thin, transparent curtains of the window above her desk.

"Did you know," B had asked, putting the last tennis ball in the can, "when you were just a girl that you liked girls?" They'd been playing singles for over three years, the pro at Newport Beach Tennis Club having matched them, and their conversations came easily. B wore her blue tennis skirt, and although her legs were tan and muscular, she was feminine. A heart-shaped vaccination print was on her right arm, near her shoulder. B was so pretty that even in the beginning, before Anne had fallen in love, she would enjoy herself more than usual by just being around her.

Anne often asked herself, How could this have happened? She was forty-two years old, two years younger than B. When had she crossed the threshold from friendship to love? It was most likely within the murky space of B's husband's first heart attack and the second one, six months later, that took him away. Their tennis matches had become longer and sweatier since the funeral, B typically saying, "One more set," after they'd played two sets. Watching B grieve had finalized it: B was vulnerable, spoke more freely, and along with the intimate late-night phone calls, there'd been all the times she'd held B while she cried. She'd been helping her with the basics: paying bills, grocery shopping, dealing with lawyers. Often she went over and washed dishes because if she didn't, the dishes would collect in the sink—food remnants hardening on plates and dark tea stains rimming the insides of mugs—until B threw them away.

"Yes; I knew at an early age," Anne had said, sitting on the bench, setting her racket next to B's on the ground. Anne took care of herself; her stomach was hard and her calf muscles defined. She wasn't bad-looking; she thought she was average. Her hair was pulled back in a ponytail at the nape of her neck, and she wore contact lenses instead of glasses. She was a foot taller than B. She imagined her expression as eager, like a child wanting to please. She didn't mind being average: it must be difficult to be pretty and noticed all the time. She preferred doing the noticing and appreciating.

It wasn't the first time they'd discussed sexual orientation, and she could sense B's amusement. She often felt that they'd revealed more of themselves than what was actually said — she knew that B thought of her outside their conversations as well. She had laughed at B's feigned distress, but even then, it had bothered her that her sexuality was a topic of entertainment; and she wondered: if B weren't a widow, if she weren't in love with her, would she have let her make light of it? In the privacy of her imagination, she had deeper, more honest discussions with B.

"Or cannibalism," B had said, sitting on the bench and smiling directly at Anne, her leg brushing against Anne's, a thin J-shaped scar on her kneecap from a surgery. "Lesbianism," hands on her thighs, "cannibalism, practically the same." They both laughed. When they were done laughing, B smiled, and her face looked affectionate and flirtatious.

And then Anne had said that sexuality was a fluid thing, labels and definitions were pointless. She had the sensation that B inhaled ideas, then breathed them right back out. In retrospect, she realized that B was asserting her power, similar to a man reminding a woman that she was on a lower rung with a facial expression or a derogatory comment. But it had another more insidious effect: it kept their intimacy at bay.

Anne stretched her arms above her head and a knuckle hit the headboard. She lowered her arms. The memory of the conversation made her ashamed. At the time, she'd been lighthearted and amused, as if she didn't mind being compared to a cannibal. Rarely, she thought, were her feelings and actions synchronized.

She had a habit of making herself sound more stupid, and thus more easygoing, than she was. She caught herself mostly during conversations with B — to make B like her, to get her to laugh — and she understood that she came off sounding like a happier version of herself. Who she was, what she talked about, her surroundings, her lifestyle, did not fit with who and what she knew herself to be: introspective, sensitive. She was practiced at safely, calmly, and responsibly being a different, more agreeable Anne.

She got up, took a shower, and got dressed. As a well-known psychologist in Newport Beach, Anne was talented at hiding her emotions. Another thing she hid: after years of studying psychology — Freud and Jung — and years of working with her patients, she'd come to the conclusion that people's problems and aberrant behaviors occurred for core reasons. Hers had always been transparent — loneliness and shame. But patients wanted the reasons to be more complicated, and she complied. When her patients' lives improved, the catalyst was usually mysterious, a combination of circumstances, her participation a small contributing factor. Although her reputation grew — her patients were dedicated and often grateful — she had ceased taking credit internally long ago. Sometimes the reward was that she'd listened without displaying boredom. She believed that to learn to live was to learn to accept limitations, and perhaps the most difficult to accept was that daily experience was neither dramatic nor passionate.

Yet in her relationship with B, she was losing control, and she felt both passion and drama. What kind of Anne would she be — what would be left of her — when she lost all control? When there was nothing more to lose? She was meeting B that afternoon to go to the movies. B liked seeing French films, where the characters were bold and lived accordingly, and sometimes that made Anne hopeful, but she speculated that B preferred to watch it rather than live it.

After the movie, Anne planned on giving B a necklace her great-aunt had left to her: an antique-gold watch nestled inside a locket, which hung on a beautiful double chain. B had admired the pendant once while visiting Anne's condominium, turning it over in her hands, and saying, "My God, Anne. It's just gorgeous." The watch face was about the size of a half-dollar, and the pearly white background looked like swirling clouds. The gold front had a pinprick-style etching of intertwined roses. On the back was engraved TO THINE OWN SELF BE TRUE. The risk frightened her, but she planned on saying it was a token of her love and respect, to tell how much their friendship meant.

And they were good friends; she knew as much and probably more about B than anyone: how B left one last sip in her Diet Coke cans, a half-inch of liquid, because she didn't like to finish them (Anne found the cans throughout the house and poured out the remains before throwing them away); and how her feet stuck to the floor of the bathroom after B had been "getting ready," because of the fog of hair spray.

And they were as emotionally close as she'd been with past lovers. She knew that B worried that she lacked some fundamental maternal instinct, that she'd failed her daughter; and that B's parents controlled her by withholding love, so that she constantly sought it. And she was sure that she was the only one who knew that B's husband's last words before his heart attack, sitting on his bed in his thick terry bathrobe monogrammed with his initials, hands on his knees, had been, "I don't think I'll bathe tonight."

• • •

The impetus for falling in love with B — a certain type, really — came from college, and her first sexual experience, an act that had caused a deep and permanent need. She'd been a freshman at the University of Southern California, a middle-class girl from Tustin. The other women on the tennis team had come from wealthy families, and she saw the things that wealth allowed: selfishness, a carefree attitude, and a basic ineptitude concerning practicalities. She didn't envy them or hate them but was drawn to the way they moved in their environment: an aura that was intangible, associated with growing up with their needs and wants met, and a confidence that the future held the same.

Anne fell in love with a beautiful sophomore and an arrangement was made: Anne helped the woman with her math and science homework and was graced with the woman's company; and if Anne expedited the process by doing the homework, she was rewarded with the woman's attention. One night, they'd been drinking vodka and 7UP, and the woman said, "I'm using you; tell me something you want." Anne said it was okay, she didn't mind; but later, they were on the floor, lights off, and the woman put her hand inside Anne, first one finger, and then it was more fingers, back and forth, soft, then hard, whispering, "You like that, don't you? You like that?" Anne moaned and cried, her eyes closed, and the tears came down her cheeks. Her body was all sensation and she had the terrible realization that she would do anything for this woman, anything at all. She'd never let herself go like that; but afterwards, the woman pretended that the experience had never happened and she ignored Anne. Anne spiraled into a lonely depression, and sometimes she would see the woman walking around campus, holding hands with her boyfriend.

From then on, Anne made sure not to reach those emotional depths, only developing relationships with women that were reciprocal: she'd had three long-term partnerships since college, each respectful and solid, in between long periods of being alone. Her last partner had been more like a sister than a lover. They'd broken it off after six years, amicably, when her partner had decided that she wanted a child (Anne had decided long ago that she did not). She still dog sat for her ex when her ex traveled.

Anne often warned patients about negative patterns: she'd recently advised a female patient in her thirties with a history of falling for abusive and neglectful men: "Desire can come from a repression of sexuality, even if that repression is in your best interest. It's very lonely not having desire returned, and yet, against our better judgment, love can form from this dynamic."

Anne rang the doorbell of B's house and waited. B had been coming to her for advice concerning her unhappy and sexually promiscuous teenage daughter, Rosie, for as many years as she'd known her. People were always trying to get free therapy, yet with B she didn't mind. But she didn't like being near Rosie. In front of Rosie, her motives appeared base and exposed — she liked to think of herself as more noble — so she was glad when B answered the front door.

A FOR SALE sign was pushed in the grass of the front lawn, and B waved at it dismissively. "Come in," she said, turning and walking into the living room. "I'm almost ready."

Since her husband's death, B had been a flurry of irrational decisions and inconsistencies, moving in a haze of grief, trying to sell her house, even though she and Rosie obviously needed a home base, and the house was her best investment. B wore a white sundress with faint lilac-colored embroidery, and Anne could see creamy white streaks on the backs of her legs where she hadn't rubbed lotion all the way into her skin. "Rosie was supposed to come by," B said. She paused and faced Anne. "She's never home."

Anne was numb, as though suspended in time, watching the seconds move beyond her. In her cardigan pocket, her fingers touched the crushed-velvet box that held her watch-in-a-locket pendant. She didn't like being in a living room full of reminders of B's deceased husband—like Rosie's presence, it stirred guilt: glass brandy snifters, his collection of *Who's Who* leather-bound books, scrimshaw artifacts, musical boxes, antique clocks, and porcelain figurines of doctors.

"I hope you don't mind," B said, bending to rub the lotion into her legs, "if we stop first at a storage facility."

"Are you sure?" Anne asked. She didn't understand why they would go to a storage facility before the house was sold. Lately, B's actions tended toward the illogical, and Anne didn't know how to remedy the situation. She blamed B's friends and family for deserting her, as if B deserved her husband's death since he'd been twenty-three years her senior, and she'd broken up his thirty-plus-year marriage. She'd been his wife for only five years. His son from his first marriage, a lawyer who specialized in financial transactions, was contesting the will, his hatred for B finally having a socially acceptable outlet.

"Yes, yes," B said, looking around for her purse. "I want to make sure it's the *right* storage facility."

UKeepSafe was located at the end of a cul-de-sac on a street of drab buildings. As they pulled up in B's Mercedes, Anne saw an Asian woman wearing glasses watching from the window of an office. The woman pushed on a device like a garage door opener and an iron gate began to clank open, but Anne had to get out of the car and pull at the gate when it stopped halfway through.

The storage sheds were beige with one bright orange stripe across the doors. At each shed, Anne lifted the door, turned on a light, and B stood at the entrance, in a type of stupefied awe, glancing around nervously, pointing out variations. "Why is the light switch on the wall when at the last one it was a cord that hung from the ceiling?" She was out of place in her lilac embroidered sundress, and her incompetence made Anne feel a weary responsibility.

They were walking to the last shed, number thirty-two, when a fight broke out right next to them at number twenty-seven. Anne's instinct was to protect B, and she pulled her by the elbow to a safer position near a U-Haul truck. Anne turned to face the fighting couple, ten feet away. The woman held a rifle pointed at the man's chest. Barefoot, she moved from side to side, swinging the rifle. He yelled something incoherent, it came out like a bark.

Anne had never seen a gun before. She felt as if someone was pricking her in the stomach, a spiky fear. She couldn't see a way to cross beyond the fighting couple without being directly in their path. The woman waved the rifle, but the man continued to call her bitch and cunt. B moved closer to Anne and their arms touched. B's hand reached for hers, then hesitated and withdrew.

But then it came back and held, tight and damp. She turned and looked at B, saw her eyes, nose, and lips, and B acknowledged her by moving even closer. Anne tightened her bicep so that her arm would feel stronger. She looked back to the couple, and it was as if her head were covered in gauze: everything looked muted, except the rifle, which she saw as clear as if she were holding it, even as it bounced around. At the same time, she was satisfied with the way B needed her, and she was aware that the feeling might not last.

As soon as the police sirens could be heard, B's hand let go, and her arm moved so that they weren't touching. B had a way of making her feel as if what had passed between them was in her imagination, and for a terrifying instant she wondered whether she had made up B holding her hand. The man and woman calmed down, the adrenaline of the scene drained, and the woman placed the rifle on the ground even before the police cars parked. They left in separate police cars, moving slowly past Anne and B. The rifle woman stared from the back seat directly into Anne's eyes. She had long dishwater blond hair, and there was no telling how old she was, her face aged from hard living. Her eyes seemed to say: this wasn't supposed to happen to me. Anne wanted to tell her, I know what you mean.

B didn't want to go to the French film after all. She had a headache and was shaken by what had happened at the storage facility. She didn't want to go anywhere, not to dinner, not to Anne's condominium; she was ready to call it a day. But they decided to pull the Mercedes over at the curb along the crest of a cliff and watch the sun sink into the ocean from Big Corona Beach.

The joggers and dog walkers who walked past the Mercedes pulled their sweatshirts on, hair whipping in their faces from the wind. "Maybe we'll see the green light," B said, her eyes concentrated on the dot of sun that melted, orange glow wobbling, as it sank. The green light was a flash, a speck of shimmering, at the last dip of the sun into the ocean-horizon; it was like the bluish green sulfur spark of a match when struck, and it lasted about as long. Anne had only seen it once.

A walkway sloped down to the beach, to the brown rocks and sand. The sand was darkest where the waves had hit, creating a wavy, delineating line all the way across the beach. They were quiet, and in their silence B also seemed aware of an impending change between them.

Anne looked at the expanse of sea, gusts of whitecaps blown along the ocean like powder. Near the shore was the unmistakable sleek black hump of a seal swimming, going under, disappearing, and coming up farther away. She wanted to point it out, but the seal went under, and she couldn't find it again.

"Well," B said, the edge of sun slipping past the rim of dark blue, "no green light—not this time."

As they were about to enter B's house through the back door, Anne said, "I have something for you." She crossed her arms over her chest, instantly vulnerable. The timing was bad, but she'd promised herself not to let one more evening pass without recognition of what had developed between them, and the handholding at the storage facility had furthered her resolve.

"Come in," B said, but her voice was wary. She left the back door open and moved through the TV room into the kitchen.

An island in the kitchen with a stove, and above it, a hanging rack of pots and pans, separated her from B, who was already kneeling, sifting through a cabinet drawer. She could just see the tip of B's head and hear the clinking of pans. And then B came up, frying pan in hand, hair disheveled.

Anne pulled the crushed-velvet box from her pocket. She saw the way B's shoulders sagged when she saw the box, and her spirit sank. "This is for you," she said anyway.

B made a long noise, it sounded like *oh no no no no no no no no* and shook her head. She set the frying pan on the island, and the way she placed it was unusually careful and gentle. She came around so that the island didn't obstruct her, a few feet away, staring at the box, but making no effort to take it.

Anne opened the box and scooped the necklace so that the locket hung from the chain in her fingers. Her eyes were on B, and she saw that B pitied her. All at once, she knew that B was conscious of how she felt and had been aware for some time, that she'd let herself be used by B, and that it was over. There were layers to friendship, to love, to attraction, but she'd crossed a line.

"Take it," Anne said.

B moved forward and embraced her. Anne almost lost her balance, holding the box against B's back and the pendant in her other hand. They leaned against the island, the hug stiff and awkward. She knew that B was acknowledging that B had shaped a possibility between them when there'd never truly been one.

B said, "You can't do that. You can't. You can't," and then she was quiet.

B sometimes called her five, six, seven times a day, so it was noticeable when the phone stopped ringing. They had different friends, so it was easy not to run into each other. She only had to make sure to go to the tennis club on Tuesdays and Thursdays instead of Mondays and Wednesdays, and she didn't ask about B, even if she wanted to. The absence of their relationship created a space within her routine, and she went through her days with a numb expectation of taking care of responsibilities. She had had the vague notion that B couldn't survive without her, and most unsettling was the way life went on regardless; her newfound realization that B would be just fine without her. She began to understand that she'd been under a spell, succumbing to the conviction that B was a victim of a specific kind of world; she'd behaved even more irrationally than B, as if for a time span she'd been wearing what she termed MSB glasses: Must Save B. She'd been capable of perceiving why she might fall in love with B, but she'd been unable to do anything to stop it from happening.

But it wasn't until a month later when she saw Rosie at Pavilions Grocery with a young man that she realized the extent of what she'd lost. The ache came sharp and clear. She didn't want to be seen, yet she wanted to observe, so she pretended to read the label on a box of Raisin Bran, although she was fairly certain that Rosie was aware: an almost imperceptible acknowledgment in the space between where Rosie and the young man stood in the cashier line and where she stood at the end of the cereal aisle. A twelve-pack of Coors rolled down the conveyor, and she wondered how they could get away with purchasing alcohol when both looked so unabashedly underage. The young man wore no shoes and had long hair. Rosie looked like B in profile — she had the same nose and chin, but she didn't have the same grace and assurance. She wore cut-off blue jeans and a shabby gray shirt. Anne felt bad for the teenager: it must be rough to lose a stepfather and then to have your mother behave increasingly recklessly. A sudden wave of guilt swept through her: all the times B had come to her for advice, she'd been biased and ineffectual.

Then Rosie turned to face her, and she saw that the locket hung between her breasts, the gold pendant watch face unmistakable. Her guilt swiftly distorted into a jagged hurt that went through her body, as if B were standing in the cereal aisle, denying what had happened between them. She had let B keep the locket because she loved her — and from pride; and B had accepted it, whether from graciousness or expediency or a combination. She wondered whether Rosie was purposefully letting her see, whether she was trying to hurt her, but she could read nothing in her expression, as if she were looking for someone behind Anne; and then she turned and whispered to the young man.

He looked over his shoulder, directly at Anne, his face sympathetic. She steadied her hand against a metal rack of cereal. It was only a second before he looked away, but in his glance she saw that he was aware that someone she loved had used her, and it made the truth indisputable. She remembered B watching the sunset, hoping for the green light, and against her willpower, the love she felt for B filled her chest afresh, mixing with the hurt, making it worse. She had lost herself to B in the way she was afraid would happen, and the self that remained was lonely and craving an implausible love. Her longing was sincere and deep, but it only intensified the ache.

Her pain brought her to B, she could smell her and see her, and for the first time she fully comprehended what B had gained, beyond Anne running her errands and washing her dishes. There was power in someone wanting you, unable to have you. For B, it didn't matter if the person was a woman or a man; it helped her navigate grief, find her bearings.

Ironically, she felt as close to B as she ever had—compassionate—imagining what had happened clearly: Rosie, home for the first time in days, lifting the necklace off the kitchen's island, handing it to B, asking, "What's this?"

"Nothing," B says, her expression a combination of vulnerability and arrogance. "Anne gave it to me." She waves her hand dismissively. "Keep it," she says, and now she looks disdainful, but it's a practiced, defensive look; and because Anne knows B so well, she recognizes the masking of pain. "I sure as hell don't want it."

Joe/Christina

THE BOURBON STREET VILLAS apartment complex was at the end of the cul-de-sac on Bourbon Street, fourteen blocks from Orange Coast Community College in Costa Mesa. Above the Bourbon Street Villas, beyond the wall of shrubbery and palm trees, was the freeway. From the villas, the traffic sounded like the ocean. The apartments were dung-colored and each one came with a parking slot with matching decaled large black numerals. There was a steady chlorine smell from the over-sanitized pool and Jacuzzi. The pool was the nucleus, and next to it was a room with a washer and dryer, pool table, and lighted soda machine. Sixteen apartments bordered the pool, a turquoise eye, in a horseshoe pattern. Rosie's was number two. The man with the long legs lived in number one. His apartment had a small gate-enclosed patio, and hanging next to his bright pink birdfeeder was a set of wind chimes with dangling silver shards that glinted in the sun and tinkled in the breeze.

Rosie had seen his legs that first day when she was moving into number two—ripped blue jeans with grease stains. He was under his truck, parked in slot number one. B was helping her move, the heavy futon giving them the most trouble, and B *ahem*ed. The man ignored them. They managed, but B mouthed *How rude*. When they were done moving the big pieces, B sat on a kitchen chair and drank a Diet Coke, the large diamond on her ring glinting, and Rosie was anxious for her to leave.

Rosie's stepfather had died three months earlier from a heart attack. B wanted Rosie out of her hair, and she wanted away: grieving was a private matter, and she wanted to leave B to it. Orange Coast Community College and the Bourbon Street Villas were a layover, until she decided what to do with her life. Eventually, she needed to catapult herself from her humiliating, impulsive, and rebellious predisposition into the law-abiding, ladylike, marriageable person her family wanted her to be. But at this point, she doubted if it was possible, and really, she'd never wanted that anyway.

Across from the Bourbon Street Villas in a strip mall next to a TOGO'S Sandwiches was a Red Onion restaurant and dance club. She liked to drink and dance at the Red Onion, especially on Thursday nights, Ladies Night. The bouncer, Teddy, let her in even though she was underage, because, as he explained, "You're damn cute." Businessmen in stiff suits and loosened ties bought her margaritas and tequila shots, sometimes letting it slip that she reminded them of their daughters, and she twirled on the dance floor with the colored lights, going from one partner to the next. She kissed the men in the darkened booths, the fathers of the daughters like her, and their tongues were eager.

She met Janice there. Janice lived in number six and drank at the Red Onion because she could walk there, thus avoiding another DUI. Her father had been the mayor of Villa Park. Janice bragged about throwing up her booze so that she could drink more, yet she kept her apartment spotless and had a manic way with order, evidenced by her insurance job, where she was granted menial organizational tasks.

"I don't have any woman friends," Janice warned her, that first night at the Red Onion. "Women hate me because they know I'll fuck their boyfriends and husbands." Later, Rosie wanted to bum a Djarum clove cigarette, and she opened the back door near the bathrooms, looking for Janice. She found her and one of the businessmen prone on the cement leading to the steps of the alley. It was dark but she recognized the man's mustache: he was the one that reminded her of Tom Selleck. He'd been steadily buying them drinks. His pants were at his thighs, the buckle of his belt clanked against the cement, and his white shirt covered his backside, striped tie turned so that it rested on his back. She saw the side of Janice's face, her mouth and eyes closed beatifically, her head bobbing slightly. She shut the door quietly.

Two days after the move, Rosie sat on a chaise by the pool, sipping a beer from a plastic cup, with White Mike and Black Mike, longtime residents of numbers ten and fourteen respectively. They could see a woman through an open doorway, folding her laundry, Lee Press Ons dramatic and red jutting from her fingers. She stuck out like a wild, exotic orchid, at least six-foot-eight in heels. She hung flannel shirts and folded slacks, and there was an air of loneliness so strong that Rosie looked away.

"Who is that?" she asked.

Black Mike took a sip from his beer. He had an afro and a mustache, and he kept a red-pronged pick comb in his back pocket. "That's Christina," he said. "Your neighbor. Otherwise known as Joe." He looked off in the distance. She looked back to Christina, recognizing the Adam's apple, the long, skinny legs, teetering precariously on spike heels. Black Mike's tone was respectful. "Just leave her be," he said, still looking beyond. "She just wants people to see her, that's all."

"But why?"

"How should I know? She doesn't ever hurt anyone. The landlord has threatened to kick her out twice, but she doesn't deserve that. Just leave her be." Black Mike worked at Disneyland as a janitor and he had a side business selling marijuana. They liked each other, but she was careful: Black Mike had a jealous girlfriend. White Mike was twelve years old and he lived with his mother, but she was never home. White Mike kept his hair long and wore T-shirts with surfing logos. Black Mike was like a dad to him, and he wouldn't let White Mike drink a beer, no matter how much he begged.

Later that afternoon, the sky was a chalky orange from a fire in the mountains. She was driving to Albertsons supermarket when she saw Christina for the second time, walking down the sidewalk, pushing a shopping cart with three paper bags of groceries; the shopping cart's front left wheel was spasmodic, and she was struggling because she wore the black spike heels.

Rosie slowed, pulled over, and rolled down her window. Christina teetered past a bus stop, and the hostile eyes of an old couple sitting on the bench followed her.

"Do you need a ride?" Rosie called out.

"No," Christina answered. "I like to walk." Her voice was deep and throaty. Cars whistled past; a truck thundered by, and her car shook from the aftermath. A horn honked and someone yelled, "Faggot!"

"Are you sure?"

Christina nodded, her foundation darker than her neck. She wore a stick-straight blond wig with a red headband. Her light blue eye shadow was swooped beyond her lids, and her eyes looked excited, fake eyelashes like black-gloved jazz hands. Rosie had never encountered a real-life transvestite before. She imagined it would make for great conversation, and it fit well with an image she'd been cultivating—friend of transvestites, that crazy free spirit—but the honest-to-God truth was that Joe/Christina scared her.

Two days later, she rang Joe's doorbell. Joe's eyes were brown and hollow, and there were purple crescents underneath, as if he hadn't slept. "What is it?" he asked. The room had the hazy look of cigarette smoke, and behind him, she saw an ashtray on his coffee table, filled with butts. He looked grease-stained, all elbows, knees, and Adam's apple, a longer, skinnier Neil Young, and she thought, I've been a miner for a heart of gold. He stared at her, impatient. He was nicer as Christina than he was as Joe.

"There's a kitten," she said. "I can hear it, stuck in a truck."

Joe reluctantly followed her to a rusted Ford Bronco, abandoned beside a fence. The kitten mewed plaintively. Joe lay down on his back under the engine, his legs visible, and within minutes, there was a shrill cry as he grabbed the kitten's tail. He emerged with the scrawny, dirty kitten, like a baby cupped in his hand.

They named the kitten Bronco, and Bronco lived between numbers one and two.

"You sure you don't want to wear nylons with that?" Christina called out. "You can borrow mine." The wind chimes jingled as Rosie walked by the patio, wearing a miniskirt and heels, on her way to the Red Onion. They'd been neighbors for over two months, and she was used to Christina critiquing her appearance when she passed the patio.

She looked down at her bare legs. "No thanks," she said. Besides nylons being uncomfortable, she thought of them touching Joe's crotch.

"Won't you come in for a little bit? I'm real lonely." Usually, Rosie declined, but Christina looked miserable, and Rosie unhooked the latch on the gate to the patio. There was a small barbecue that she hadn't noticed before. Christina wore a flowing Stevie Nicks gypsy number, and her wig was long brown curls. She followed Christina through the open sliding glass door, and Christina shut the screen behind them, but it was stuck, and she had to push at it before it closed.

The lampshade was covered with a sheer red scarf, giving the light a muffled pink-bordello feel. Bronco was sleeping under the coffee table, his tail tucked beside his body. A portable heater sat in the corner, the size of a shoebox, its coiled prongs lit up orange. The couch was low to the ground and it sank even lower with her weight. She rubbed between Bronco's ears and his purr became louder. Christina came from the kitchen with two wide martini glasses, and Rosie wondered if they were pre-made, waiting for this moment.

Christina set the martini glasses on the low coffee table and sat next to her so that their legs touched; Rosie shifted away. Christina's long bent legs reminded her of a cricket's. She sipped from her glass, grateful because the drink was strong.

"You don't respect yourself," Christina said sadly, lifting her glass by the stem; her fingers were large and calloused, and her fingernails had shooting stars on them. She knew Christina was referring to Lance: he'd been spending the night. She'd met him in her Religions and Ethics class. He was from Florida (although he had an odd Australian-like accent), he wore vests, and he dealt cocaine. Handsome, like Robert Redford, he talked about living all over the world. She suspected he was a liar, but she liked him because she'd seen him crying when the professor showed the film about the Holocaust. In the dark classroom, he'd looked over at her, wiping at his tears with his sleeve. That was the first night she'd slept with him. He'd been more interested in the cocaine, insisting she try a line. They sat on the carpet, naked, and he chattered like a teenage girl. He kept saying, "Didn't I tell you? Isn't it great?" She felt like she was suspended, and every time he touched her skin, it crawled, as if she might burst open. She preferred the deadness — the steadiness — of alcohol, but she agreed with him, just to make him happy.

There were two women in her Religions and Ethics class, Avery and Leah, best friends and roommates, one short the other tall, who hated her although she'd done nothing to them. Leah said that she was Lance's girlfriend, and that Rosie had better stay away from him. Lance told her that Leah was his connection; he got his Valiums from her, nothing more. Avery and Leah frequently glared at her in the campus parking lot and yelled that they were going to kick her ass.

Lance would come through her sliding glass door at night, and she would let him stay. Once, he pissed and crapped in her bed, and he sobbed like a baby. She stripped him and washed the sheets and clothes in the early morning while he slept naked. She dressed him. He didn't remember any of it, and he left soon after waking, hung over and unhappy, no goodbye. She wasn't sure why she let Lance use her, but she didn't want to discuss it with Christina, so she left for the Red Onion.

She woke the next morning on her floor, a fuzzy, unrecognizable blanket covering her, a pillow near her head, and vomit tangled in her hair. She probed her tongue around the inside of her mouth, hoping to generate saliva, but the tissue continued to have the consistency of sandpaper. She touched her cheek, hot and with the imprint of the carpet. She couldn't remember anything beyond dancing at the Red Onion, spinning, free, the colored lights snowing on her, the music loud and tasteless, a rotation of men.

She rose slowly, her head throbbing. There was a note on the kitchen table, stationery bordered with multicolored hearts:

Rosie,

You left your keys in the door and your purse on the ground. You didn't even make it inside. I found you by the pool!!! That is very bad and I worry for you. I took the keys out and they are in your purse. Don't worry. I will take care of you.

Love,
Christina

Bronco was crouched in the litter box below the cutlery drawer, back legs kicking, sand airborne. There was an odor of fresh cat feces. She opened the front door, and Bronco sprinted through.

John Wayne visited Rosie later that morning. He'd hitched a ride from Newport Beach to her apartment, and he sat on her futon, waiting, his skateboard next to him, while she took a shower, attempting to wash off her hangover. She looked forward to hanging around the apartment and doing nothing, not even talking much; maybe ordering a fat submarine sandwich from TOGO'S loaded with meats and pickles and cheeses and lettuce, and eating it with her friend, since she hadn't eaten anything in a long time, and the food would probably make her feel better. She was coming out of her bathroom, dressed in jeans and a T-shirt, a towel wrapped like a turban around her hair, when she heard a knocking on her front door. Even before John Wayne opened the door, she knew that it was Christina, by her signature knocking song: dum da da dum dum — dum dum.

"Oh," Christina said, sizing up John Wayne, "aren't you cute." Without acknowledging Rosie, she moved inside, made her way to the kitchen. "Butter," she said, opening the refrigerator and leaning into it. She spoke into the refrigerator: "I'm making shortbread cookies." She wore a white leather mini-skirt with a matching short jacket, fishnet stockings, and white heels. Her backside looked bony. "Should've known," she said, turning to face them. "No butter, only beer."

The sudden presence of Christina both confused and alarmed Rosie; she wasn't embarrassed for John Wayne to meet Christina, like she might've been had it been someone else meeting Christina, especially someone from her family (her dad!); but she was worried that Christina might associate him with the other men that came through her door, or think he was stupid; and she felt as she often did after a blackout, plunged without warning into a panic at the reality of her life, her inability to escape. And for a moment she experienced an intense longing to be someone else, to be a better person, but this emotion morphed into resignation because she knew that it was useless: she'd tried before.

John Wayne had been watching a television show about drug trafficking, and the television was still on. He was barefoot, as usual, wearing shorts and a long-sleeved Shark Island T-shirt, and there were dark bruises at his kneecaps. His long hair looked like it hadn't been washed in quite some time, and she decided that after Christina left, she would make John Wayne shampoo and deep-condition his hair, and she would comb out the tangles.

"Does he talk?" Christina asked Rosie. Then, turning her attention to him, she said, "Do you talk?"

John Wayne shrugged, a gesture vague enough to allow Christina to read whatever she wanted into it.

"Hmm," Christina said.

Rosie felt protective of John Wayne — even more so since his boating accident — and of their relationship. She hoped that Christina would leave. Christina sensed it, walking to the door, big manicured hand at her hip. Before she left, she turned and said, "He's the first one I like."

Within that same month, four notes:

Rosie,
   I knocked last night. No answer. I haven't seen you in a couple of days. You were making a sad moaning noise, but when I knocked, you were very quiet. I just wanted to know if you were all right.

                                        Love,
                                        Christina

Rosie,
   There was a man hanging around outside your apartment. I stared at him until he left. He didn't look so nice. Be careful!!!
   I would like it if you can come over tomorrow night. Spend some time with me. Maybe take some pictures and

have some fun. I am really lonely plus I would really like to
see you in nylons and all dressed up.

Love,
Christina

P.S. If you want to, tonight you can come in and give me a
big good night KISS.

Rosie,

I found your keys in the door for the third time!!! That is
very dangerous! Your purse was in a bush and you were by
the pool again! I cleaned up the yuck you made on the bathroom floor. (You almost made the toilet!)

Love,
Christina

Rosie,

Please be careful! He told me he got out of jail only last
week! And you let him stay with you?

I was hoping that you would have been around Satur-
day. It was my birthday and I didn't even get a hug or a kiss
from you for my birthday. Maybe tonight you'll have time
to come over and give me that present. Christina would like
that (42 and sexy).

Love,
Christina

Rosie worried at the mildly salacious suggestions in the notes;
but that feeling was nothing compared with the dismay
she experienced at the undeniable proof of her behavior
during blackouts, presented in Joe / Christina's loopy handwrit-
ing.

• • •

Two days after the last note, White Mike stole her car in the late morning; she'd left the keys on the kitchen counter, and he said he just wanted to watch cartoons, but he was gone in a flash. She called Black Mike and Janice and they came over. Black Mike leaned on the kitchen counter, and Janice sat on the couch, her legs tucked under her. Janice was no good at comforting: she was a fair weather friend and didn't pretend otherwise.

"Don't call the cops," Black Mike said. "He'll be back soon. He's had a hard time of it. They'll send him back to juvie if you call the cops."

She was crying: she knew she was crying for other things, but she couldn't help it. She thought of the sirens from the ambulance. The paramedics had rolled her stepfather onto the stretcher. They had put a lime-colored sheet over him. She remembered B, crouched in the center of her bed, sobbing — a gasping cry — with the bedspread wrapped around her. She had comforted B but it was awkward.

"Maybe you could call your boyfriend," Black Mike said.

She thought about the men, counting in her head: she would get AIDS and embarrass her family. She thought about her bathroom: she threw up when she drank, and her bathroom smelled acidic, no matter how much she cleaned.

The door opened and White Mike walked in sheepishly, setting her keys on the kitchen counter, in the same spot he'd taken them from. He stood next to Black Mike. "I'm sorry," he said, looking down at his feet.

"Get out," she said, without conviction.

"Listen," Black Mike said, "it's going to be okay. You just wait. You're just scared." Black Mike's hand was at White Mike's back, a dark starfish, and he guided him out of the apartment. Janice dropped her cigarette in a plastic cup of left-over vodka and orange juice. She left the front door open behind her.

Later that afternoon, after Religions and Ethics class, Avery and Leah followed her to the Bourbon Street Villas. Lance hadn't shown up at class, but she'd seen him in the commons area, smoking and talking with friends. When she'd walked past — wearing her sunglasses, her eyes swollen — he'd ignored her. She didn't notice Avery and Leah until she was parking her Honda Accord in slot number two.

Leah drove a white Mitsubishi truck, Avery in the passenger seat with her arm out the window. Rosie looked away, pretending she hadn't noticed. Leah pulled into slot number four, but there was a screeching sound as she pulled out again, after reading the warning sign: TENANTS ONLY. VIOLATORS WILL BE TOWED.

Rosie walked past Christina's wind chimes, a hummingbird at the feeder, suspended like a tiny helicopter, and behind it, the shadow of Christina moving through her kitchen. Rosie closed her front door and turned on her television as a distraction. The show was Sally Jessy Raphael and the subject: My Daughter Is a Teenage Lush. A mother shouted at her daughter, and Sally Jessy Raphael looked bemused.

"You're a slut!" the mother yelled.

Thuds came from her front door and she turned off the television. Through the peephole, she saw the dark blue of Leah's shirt.

"Open up," Leah said.

"We just want to talk," Avery added.

She unhooked the chain on her door, deciding to believe

Avery, but before she turned the doorknob, the door swung open.

"Are you afraid?" Leah asked. They moved inside and she backed up. Leah scared her the most since she was tall and naturally mean.

Leah turned to shut the door, but Christina stood in the doorway, wearing a pantsuit with a safari pattern and a red scarf tied dramatically around her neck. Rosie recognized it as the scarf from the lampshade.

Although she was Christina, the way she stood at the doorway, legs wide, face angry, she looked more like Joe. "What's going on?" she said, voice gruff and businesslike.

"They're from school. They just want to talk."

"Mind if I stay?" Christina walked into the apartment and sat on the couch, crossing one leg over the other. She wore sandals with turquoise rocks embedded in the leather straps.

Leah laughed but sounded nervous.

"Well," Christina said, her arms spreading along the back of the couch.

Leah tried to look disgusted, shaking her head. "Let's go," she said, tugging Avery's arm. "Lance is my boyfriend," she added sadly, not looking at Rosie. She walked to the front door, Avery following. After the door closed, Rosie looked over to Christina, who raised her eyebrows disapprovingly.

Christina got her birthday kiss that night. She'd bought her own belated birthday cake at Albertsons supermarket, and Rosie presented it to her, lights off, candles twinkling: *Happy Birthday Christina* in dark blue frosting. Christina wore a shoulder-length thick black wig with red highlights, one that Rosie hadn't seen before, and when Rosie complimented her, she said, "It's my Tina Turner wig." She wore red silk pajama pants and a matching long-sleeved button down top. Her wedge-heeled slippers were open-toed so that Rosie could see that she'd painted her toenails a matching magenta red.

They sat at Christina's small kitchen table, wearing cone-shaped party hats. Christina had tucked the rubber band at the back of her head behind her wig, hat propped forward on her forehead, reminding Rosie of a unicorn. When she asked Christina about her family, Christina said, "I don't want to talk about it," and for a flash, in her hostile tone, she was Joe. Christina took off her party hat, setting it on the table, and Rosie did the same. Through the kitchen window beyond the wind chimes, the moon was smeared inside a cloud. When Bronco jumped on the table, Christina didn't shoo him, and she rubbed his head as he licked frosting from her plate. "That's my sweetie," she said, and Bronco regarded her with a blue stained mouth.

Christina kissed her. They sat on the couch. It was a long kiss, the stubble from Christina's face rough on her skin; she kept her eyes closed. In her mind, Joe/Christina flipped back and forth from the deep-voiced, black-haired, chain-smoking, misanthropic, brooding, mechanic male to the multiply be-wigged, sensitive, heavily made-up, heartbreakingly lonely, exhibitionist, and talkative female. Later, she would think about her own rebellion: some of it was good and necessary; most of it was awful and relentless. Her actions and motivations were mixed so that she couldn't tell the difference. She didn't want to die, and what scared her most was that she was crossing lines, taking herself further down, coming closer and closer to fucking up for good.

Christina's hands were on Rosie's knees and Christina leaned into the kiss. Her tongue was large and Rosie wanted it to end. When Christina finished, she leaned back, elbows crooked, hands behind her head. Her head went back, eyes closed, and her Adam's apple swelled.

Rosie thought of all the times Christina could have taken advantage of her: The blackouts when Christina put her to sleep; the times she took her keys out of the door; how she stared the men away. Christina was the first gentleman she'd kissed. It was the least she could do, but when Christina got out her Polaroid camera, she drew the line at a photo shoot.

They settled for one photograph, sitting together on the couch. Christina applied a fresh coat of lipstick and handed her the lipstick tube. Christina put her arm out, camera in hand, and they tilted their heads together. There was a bright flash. The camera spat out the photo and Christina wagged it between her long fingernails. She set it on the coffee table, and they watched their faces emerge from the square of greenish brown chemicals. Their eyes were at half-mast, reacting to the flash so that they both looked drunk. Although they were smiling, they looked sad, each in her unique way. Their lipstick colors matched, and there was a fleck of magenta on Rosie's front tooth.

The Morning After

JOHN WAYNE STRETCHES his legs in the leather passenger seat. The black Mercedes is parked high atop the hill of Newport Cemetery, at the end of Marguerite. Sparkling and clear, the way it can only appear after a hard rain, the view extends beyond the graves to the flower streets and homes, and farther still, toward ocean and sky. From the rearview mirror, he sees his skateboard in the back seat, and he wants to hear its wheels against the street, but he knows that Henry Wilson will take an hour at least.

Wilson doesn't drive him to the Newport Inn anymore, although he pays for a room. Wilson doesn't want to fuck him or touch him. He still gives him money, but ever since the boating accident, less than a year ago, Wilson only makes him sit in the Mercedes. He knows Wilson thinks it's his fault for letting him use the boat.

That afternoon, as he untied Wilson's sixteen-foot Boston Whaler and started the engine, sun danced on the water. Wilson had let him use the boat only once before. He saw clouds, a hint of gray weighting their bases, and a pelican flying low, its wings skimming the bay. On the other side of the bay was Grandma Dot's house — he imagined her at her barstool, playing Solitaire, setting the cards down slowly, indifferently, a cigarette burning in her glass ashtray. Every now and then, he sleeps in Uncle Stan's room, but ever since Grandpa caught him coming down the stairs and installed an electronic alarm system, he's careful, although he knows they never turn it on.

John Wayne backed the boat from its slip, and there was a plunk — at first he thought a fish had jumped near him. Another one came, a flashing white and splash. He turned to see Wilson at his deck, sun casting a glow over him, his arms swinging a golf club back in an arc. His club paused for a smooth second and clacked as he made contact. Wilson's hand went up to shade his eyes, and even from a distance, there was an admission of unhappiness in his grin.

John Wayne drove beyond the flying golf balls, and when he neared the jetty, he increased his speed. Wisps of water hit his arm. Beyond the jetty, the hull of the boat rose on the swells and thumped down with a noise like a crack, as if the boat would split. He went faster, hair thrashing behind him, gut smacking with the hull, rattling his bones, clattering his teeth. His tooth pendant swung on the chain behind him and tapped steadily between his shoulder blades. The red kill switch danced loose, hit his thigh, and he let his fingers graze the steering wheel, as if he were flying without direction. The wheel jerked to the right, spinning quickly against his fingertips with a humming noise.

The boat made a sharp turn and he was tossed; his ankle hit the side of the boat; he saw sky, the edge of a cloud, and ocean. And then he opened his eyes underwater but couldn't see. The sound of the motor vibrated loudly, coming closer. When his head came out of the water, the blades of the motor spun as if in slow motion, and he pushed with his right hand, a blade slicing his palm. But the boat circled—the steering wheel had stuck hard to the right, and it came again. He curled his body protectively and pressed with his left foot, blade cutting through the sole of his foot, and then his left hand. His blood blended with the sea making the water around him purplish. Dog paddling, trying to extend beyond the motor, he took one last hit with his right foot. The motor vibrated in his chest, but he was beyond its reach, floating, fading in and out of consciousness.

When he was pulled from the water by his underarms and set against the solid floor of another boat, he thought he was still in the ocean, weaving with the current like seaweed. He couldn't understand what the voices said, and then he imagined himself napping in the hazy sunlight on the bench by the Newport Marriott water fountain, while people moved busily around him.

The same nurse that took care of him when he broke his arm skateboarding took care of him now. She tried to explain what the doctors had done. Pins and needles in his hands and feet. He would need physical therapy, of course, a few minutes more and he would've bled to death; there'd been a blood transfusion; he would have S-shaped scars on his palms and the soles of his feet, the motion of a propeller blade lined in his skin forever.

An anonymous donor had paid his hospital bill in full, she said. There was no need to worry about that. He saw tenderness and sorrow in her eyes and he smiled. His soul extended beyond his body, and he gave from it as smoothly as a wave cresting and reaching, knowing that it always came back.

Wilson sits in the driver's seat, adjusting the car stereo. His fingertips are yellow from smoking. His shirt is a creamy cotton material, the top button undone, and the hollow beneath his Adam's apple is a coarser tan than the rest of his neck. Sharp creases run down the front of his slacks, and he wears leather loafers without socks. He looks up from his car stereo. "What a view, what a view," he says, sliding his hands along the material of his slacks. He usually talks about his divorce, his adult children, his fiancée, his computer software business, and sometimes his younger brother, Theo, who committed suicide; but when he talks about Theo, he changes the subject abruptly. "Put your seat down," he says, lowering his own seat. "I want you to hear this with your head back."

John Wayne lowers his seat and adjusts his head on the headrest. The tinted sunroof is closed, fingerprints and thumbprints smeared across the glass. The music is swooping and filled with melancholy. His spirit moves in the chaos of his conjurings. He remembers walking on the wet sand at night, feet sinking, his dark footprints pooling with seawater, dissolving. He imagines fingerprints across his soul, from letting others handle him—the reaching and touching.

"Goddamn it," Wilson says, reacting to the sunroof as well, pressing a button to open it. "Those Mexicans left fingerprints when I got my car washed this morning."

Dusky gold and red cover the sky as John Wayne gets dropped off near the Ugly House. He holds his skateboard against his thighs and listens to the sleek car's engine until it's gone, and then he hears the sound of ocean carrying across the night. And beyond, the rustling fronds of palm trees, and if he concentrates even more, the wind itself.

The drug dealer lives on Balboa Island; by the dimming sun, Rosie guesses it's around four or five in the afternoon. She's been partying with Janice Faslender since ten that morning. Janice Faslender, daughter of the mayor. When her father was mayor, Janice passed out shirts with lettering across the front: I PARTIED WITH THE MAYOR'S DAUGHTER. Rosie didn't know her then, but she likes the story, and thinks of that Janice as more heroic than the Janice who lives in her apartment complex near Orange Coast College, who doesn't care about anything other than getting loaded, whom men make fun of, right in front of her, but then linger because she's that easy, and they know it's only a matter of waiting.

She remembers pieces of the day: the windows of Janice's Toyota Corolla were down, sky sparkling and bright from the previous night's rainfall, and Janice's hair whipped in her face, a strand stuck in her mouth. Janice opened a bottle of Coors on a bottle opener she'd attached to her dashboard, one hand on the steering wheel; she drove, tipping the bottleneck to her lips. After finishing, she set her arm outside her window — bottleneck loosely in fingertips — and lightly tossed it. Something about the nonchalance struck Rosie as sexy. They heard it shatter. Rosie finished her bottle and briefly considered smashing it on the road, but settled for placing it on the car floor, where it rolled back and forth with the momentum of the car, knocking against her feet.

While peeing in an alleyway, Janice's fingernails snagged on her nylons, creating a run like a zipper, an inch wide from crotch to toe. Squatting next to Janice, Rosie's stream made a soft thudding sound, smelling of alcohol, sending up a slight vapor. Next to her, clouds reflected in a leftover rain puddle, a sensation like being upside down, making her feel even more intoxicated — the sky in the ground.

A picket fence surrounded the drug dealer's small front yard, with a medium-sized trampoline taking up his dead brown lawn. Two young women jumped without enthusiasm on the trampoline. One wore a white bikini and her small breasts bobbed with her jumps.

The drug dealer sat next to Janice on a ratty couch and they passed the pipe back and forth. Rosie sat across from them in a rocking chair, but she kept her feet on the ground to keep from rocking. Janice sucked on the pipe with a raspy intake, held her breath, and then let it out. After each hit, she wanted another. Her face looked pale and the shadows under her eyes were brown. Shirtless, the drug dealer's chest was hairy; his head hair was dark and curly, like his chest hair. Afghans covered the couches and generic waterfall paintings hung from the walls, as if an old grandma lived in the house. Each time the dealer lit the pipe, the lighter made a *chack-chack* sound. He tried passing the pipe over the coffee table to her. He flipped the lighter in his other hand, as if it were a coin.

"All right, all right, all right," he said.

A man came through the back door, and the drug dealer said, "Lobo, the timber wolf — my man." The man sat on the couch, forcing Janice to squeeze closer to the drug dealer.

Rosie stood from the rocking chair, and although they didn't say anything, she felt everyone's eyes on her back as she walked to the front door. She noticed that she was sweating while she walked — her whole body was wet.

She's at least a half-mile from the drug dealer's house, still walking. A fresh bruise on her forearm catches her attention, what Janice would call a mystery bruise, in honor of its un-knowable origin, acquired some time during their drinking. The sun is shaped like a bowl, sinking at the horizon. Janice has a name for the hangover-remorse she'll have tomorrow: The Morning After Sadness.

She thinks about John Wayne. Her high school graduation ceremony was the day of his boating accident, and while she stood in line in her cap and gown waiting to cross the stage and shake hands with her vice principal—drunk from the warm bottle of Smirnoff she kept stored in her locker—she sensed something terribly wrong and began to weep.

Iris, Jasmine, Larkspur, her fingertips pass over flowers and bushes. She doesn't want the same future as Janice, and she misses the anticipatory feeling she had as a girl when she thought of her life as full of promise. Because the sun has dis-appeared and the sky is changing colors, she thinks of Grandma Dot, pausing from her Solitaire and lifting a cigarette from her glass ashtray, not smoking it, but gazing out the sliding glass doors to the same red and gold view.

Rosie hears the *clack clack* of a skateboard coming closer. A shadow passes, a flash of blond hair. She's a block from home, near the Ugly House; a row of palm trees strung with lights gives the street a faint glow. Her legs are tired from walking, but the long distance has sobered her, and she's grateful for a home, since it hasn't sold yet, and for B. She steps from the sidewalk to the grass, and she knows that it's John Wayne. It pleases her: like they're twin ghosts haunting Narcissus.

He comes by again, passing her, and he jumps the curb, one hand holding the skateboard's edge, the other hand out from his body like he's riding a bull, his shirt wrapped around him and tied by the long sleeves at his hips. He lands abruptly, flinging the skateboard in the air with his foot. He reaches to catch it, misses. It clangs to the street. His hair is tucked behind his ears and parted haphazardly in a zigzag near the center of his head. The tooth pendant hangs in a white comma below the dark hollow of his clavicle. His chest is hairless, but there's a golden trail of hair descending from his navel down into his low-slung jeans. He reaches into his pocket, extracts a joint rolled tight and long, and sets it between his lips while he searches his back pocket for his Zippo. The lid makes a click noise as he taps it open and produces a blue flame. He lights the joint and sucks deeply.

With his breath held in, he hands her the joint. "Long day," she says, declining, thinking about Janice and the women jumping on the trampoline: she doesn't want to be drunk or high anymore, she only wants sleep. Smoke leaves his mouth, slowly, sinuously, and it smells sweet and grassy, like wet trees.

Joint between his lips, he reaches for her hand, his scar a fold of skin against her skin. He stares at her and she can't tell what he's thinking. She realizes she's smiling, a surging of delight at the open-ended scope, at the impossibility of knowing. He lets her hand go, takes the joint from his lips, and exhales. Smoke floats behind his head, makes vague shapes, and disappears.

He smiles back at her, squinty-eyed. He stubs the joint carefully against the sidewalk, the end going from red to black, leaving a dark marking like an S against the cement. He tucks the remaining joint behind his ear like a pencil, sets his skateboard down, and flies away, wheels making their gravelly noise against the sidewalk, no goodbye, shirt flapping behind his hips.

The skateboard jumps a rise in the sidewalk, wheels suddenly silent, rising over the curb. His knees bend and he hunches so that he and his skateboard are impossible to tell apart. For a second, it looks like he's soaring, his shirt fluttering behind him like a cape. She knows he knows she's watching and this makes her smile again.

He lands gracefully, wheels clacking to the street, his arms lifting and falling, and he makes his skateboard move in a wavy line, his body leaning to the left and then the right. He shifts, aims his skateboard's direction in a straight line. His bare foot pushes him forward, one-two-three-swoop-one-two-three-swoop.

He turns the corner, vanishes.

ACKNOWLEDGMENTS

I wish to express my gratitude to Michael Carlisle, for his boundless enthusiasm and his commitment to an unknown literary writer; to Ethan Bassoff, the most incredible agent's assistant to ever walk this earth; and to Anjali Singh, for her generous efforts to make these stories better, and for giving them a home.

I wish to thank my colleagues and professors at UC Riverside, in particular Joshua Hardina, Andrew Winer, Susan Straight, Michael Jayme, Chris Abani, and Dwight Yates. And a very special thanks to Dana Johnson, for being an acute reader, a great writer, and a true friend.

Thank you, as well, to David Partridge and Jim Galbraith, for serving a waitress, by acknowledging her as a writer: they gave me a space to work, in their offices and conference rooms, away from the countless interruptions of libraries and coffeehouses.

And my deepest gratitude and affection goes to my friends and to my family, who encouraged and supported and believed in my work through my years of waiting tables, through the raising of my sons, through the endless rejections, and through it all: Courtney Gregg, Holly Stauffer, Natasha Prime, Ry, Cole, Chris, and many many more. You carried me through.